GW00585018

THE FATE OF STARS

THE FATE OF STARS

S D Simper

The Fate of Stars

Cover art by Jade Merien

Cover design and interior by Jerah Moss

Map by Mariah Simper

ISBN (Paperback): 978-1-952349-08-9

Visit the author at www.sdsimper.com

Facebook: sdsimper
Twitter: @sdsimper
Instagram: sdsimper

For Ruth

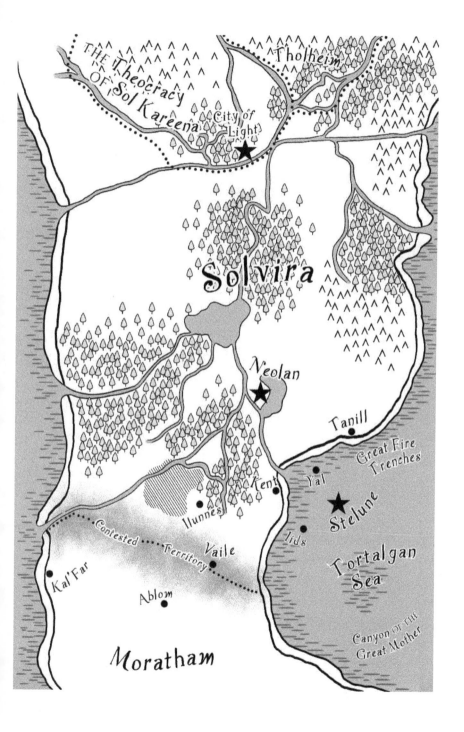

One thousand years before the Old Gods return,
the Moon Goddess reigns supreme.

And by her side...
the Stars shine glorious and bright.

Chapter I 🐚

In the undersea city of Stelune, a mermaid tried to wish her mother farewell.

"I'll be fine," Tallora insisted, placing a quick kiss on her mother's cheek. "What can the storm do? Drown me?"

Her mother caught her hands, worry etched into her features. "There're no stars out tonight, my Tallora. What if you're swept away? You won't find your way home. The king's guards even spoke of a ship on the horizon—what if you're seen?"

"Then I'll wave or sing a song like the sirens they think we are." Tallora laughed, though a glimmer of regret panged in her heart at her mother's obvious worry. "Not that I can sing."

"Perhaps, but Goddess Staella will understand if the weather is too dangerous."

"Mother—" Tallora cut herself off, guilt filling her at those apprehensive eyes. Instead, she wrapped her arms around her mother's torso and held her tight, her pearlescent skin familiar and warm. "I have to do this. I made a mistake, and this is my penance."

Her mother kissed her hair and silently nodded.

"I'll return in an hour. No need to worry." With those final words, Tallora swam out of their little shared home.

The city of Stelune was a beacon of light, her beloved home, but the dark sky held its own wonders. As she swam higher, the waters grew turbulent, but not wilder than she could master with her powerful tail. She clutched the string of beaded sea stars and pearls around her neck, the sigils of her goddess reassuring her of her safety.

Water sprayed as she breached the surface, both from the waves and the pelting rain. Lightning tore across the sky, illuminating a distant ship struggling against the storm. Black clouds hung low, blocking any

1

view of the stars, but they were ever-present all the same.

Last night, the dark moon had reigned, no light cast from its silver mass. It had been a clear sky, the night the stars shone brightest, a perfect time for worshippers of the Goddess of Stars to pray and bask in her love and light. Priestesses-in-training were required to attend, lest they lose their vestments, and Tallora was nearing the end.

But she had been absent.

As she lay upon the tossing sea's surface, she thought fondly of the beautiful girl she'd met—not that she ever cared to see her again. She hadn't meant to get so carried away, but she'd always been weak for charming smiles and full lips and had spent the night admiring them.

And so, after begging the high priestess for a second chance . . . or a tenth . . . she had been told to perform her prayers tonight instead.

Tallora's body rose and fell with the turbulent waves, and though she would have preferred to perform her small ritual on a peaceful night, she laid on her back and steadied her breath. With each influx of air, the waves became a lull in her mind, and Tallora finally whispered the first words of her prayer: *"Blessed Stars who bring us light—"*

Thunder rumbled across the sky, the bellowing roar assaulting her concentration. When Tallora opened her eyes, she floated in the shadow of the approaching ship. Blinding light struck the mast; fire burst from the wood, despite the wind and rain.

Tallora's sensitive eyes saw stars and spots. In her panicked daze, she dove beneath the water. Her powerful tail kept her steady despite the tumultuous waves—

A human plunged into the sea.

A trail of bubbles followed the rapid descent. Tallora barely dodged, then watched fear and shock flash across the mortal's face. This was a woman, Tallora realized, a lengthy braid of hair floating beside

2

her, trousers covering the slight curve of her hips. The human's body suddenly stiffened, and she did what all mortals did when plunged beneath the waves at night—swim the wrong way.

Humans were feared, yet this woman was helpless, having fallen into Tallora's domain. She dove, wondering if there was any salvation she could bring. Perhaps this had been her purpose this night—not to pray, but to deliver the mercy her goddess always preached of.

When Tallora grabbed her, the woman fought, shaking in her grasp. She spared a moment to smooth the woman's hair, touch her face, emphatically scream: *I have you, you're safe . . .*

In the dark waters, the woman's eyes followed the necklace of sea stars floating among Tallora's locks of hair. Realization flashed through her features. She clutched Tallora, and Tallora swam.

The woman gasped for breath once the water broke, only to be splattered by ripping waves and a spray of foam. She coughed over Tallora's shoulder, her gloved hands rough against her slick skin. Tallora swam toward the ship, and the woman at her shoulder yelled, *"Lower a rope!"*

Amidst the spray and the thunderous rumbling of the sky, her voice was a drop in a bucket. Tallora held her tight, her own mind frantically weighing options, when from the woman's hand burst a flash of silver light. Startled, she nearly released her, but the light combusted into flame, shooting up into the air as a vibrant beacon.

Within seconds, a knotted rope fell into the water, its damp fibers clinging to the ancient wood of the ship. Was this woman some kind of sorcerer? The concept of silver fire rang somewhere in her memory, but Tallora's focus rested in the moment. She swam to the rope, even helped the woman grasp it—

Who wrapped the rope around Tallora's core, expertly tying it into a knot. Tallora heaved when she was forcibly dragged into the air. As she struggled, a strong hand gripped her hair—

And slammed her head against the side of the ship.

Stars flew across Tallora's vision. She hung limply, rope digging into her stomach as darkness threatened to steal her sight. With all her waning will power, she fought to stay awake, but next she knew she toppled against the deck.

Her body smacked against the damp wood. The woman's hold released; Tallora whimpered and curled into a ball, clinging to her sleek, scaled tail.

Footsteps sounded amidst the rain. Tallora's hair splayed across the deck, the stark white locks greyed in the dank atmosphere. Her head ached, but when a gloved hand clutched the string of stars and pearls around her neck and yanked, it broke apart.

Suddenly alert, she dared to look up and saw an array of sea-faring men, drenched and exhausted from the storm, and her captor inspecting the religious sigils. The fire on the mast still smoked.

"We thought we'd lost you, princess," said one— an old man who wore not the breeches of the men daring the storm but opulent robes of purple and gold. He spoke Solviran Common, and Tallora understood him well enough—their languages hailed from the common root of Celestière.

The woman scoffed, standing tall amidst the winds, silhouetted by a distant flash of lightning. "Magister, the gods wouldn't dare." Her braided hair clung to her face in matted, salt-drenched loops, like dried seaweed. Tallora had heard of uplander princesses, known in stories for their legendary beauty and ostentatious tastes in clothes and jewels. Instead, the woman wore boots and a tunic dirtied from the salty spray, no finery on her person, her skin tanned and cracked from the sun.

The princess tucked the broken necklace into her trouser pocket and knelt, her gaze matching Tallora's. "You are an unexpected bit of luck, mermaid," she continued, her eyes calculating as they studied every curve and scale of Tallora's body. She stiffened, curling tighter into her protective ball. "My name is Dauriel Solviraes, eldest daughter of Empress Vahla. You are now property of the Solviran Empire."

Fear washed over Tallora, colder than the icy spray of the sea. It stiffened her tongue; when Princess Dauriel signaled for her men to take Tallora below deck, she could not manage a scream as she batted away their hands. Her tail knocked one back, but she could not fight them all. A rough hand grabbed her hair and dragged her forward—she clawed at him with her nails, but a man twice her girth nearly crushed her against his bare, weather-beaten chest. She trembled and covered herself, exposed among her clothed captors. Light appeared as he stepped through a doorframe, the dark clouds replaced by glowing receptacles lining a narrow wooden hallway.

She was taken to a small room—a storage closet, filled with supplies Tallora had never seen before. When she was unceremoniously dropped, she released a slight cry, biting back tears at the throbbing pain in her head and back. Already, her skin itched from dryness, and she wondered if she would waste away, crusted and starved.

The magister had followed, studying her from the doorway as the large man stepped aside. "Do you speak?" he asked.

She merely stared, struck dumb by fear. The magister released a disappointed, *"Hmm,"* then held his arms aloft. From the very walls, damp and moist, water emerged, collecting in an ever-expanding ball floating above Tallora's head. When it matched her in size and a little bit more, the magister beckoned to his burly companion. "Put her in. This will serve her well enough."

Tallora braced herself as work-worn hands lifted her once more, shutting her eyes until wetness enveloped her entire form. When the man placed her within the globe of water, she remained suspended—a bubbled prison undulating like the waves themselves. "It'll only be a few days in here," the magister said, his voice palpably bored despite the storm. "You'll see the sun again."

That did nothing to soothe her. Beyond, the seas still heaved, thunder bellowing across the sky. The door shut, leaving her alone and drenched in darkness.

Tallora had little to do but sob. She thought of her home, of her mother all alone in the world without her. She craved the seafoam, the stone castles of Stelune, decorated with a rainbow array of coral and life. She thought of Yaleris, the dragon within the Canyon of the Great Mother, whose scales glittered in opalescent shades of blue and white, who protected her people from evil and wondered if he could save her.

But he was not a god to pray to. Instead, Tallora prayed to her beloved Staella, Goddess of Stars, who painted the sky in illuminate art, used by her people to navigate the open waters, and known for her mercy and her gentle heart. *"Mother Staella,"* she recited, unable to summon the heart to sing, *"deliver me. Take my burdens; set me free . . ."*

The passage of time was felt only in the growing, gnawing hunger in Tallora's stomach.

When light expanded from the door, Tallora cowered, hiding her head behind her arms, her back facing the interloper. The light burned her eyes, and a familiar, feminine voice said, "If you ignore me, you'll starve."

The seconds grew long, tension settling. Tallora covered her eyes, letting them slowly adjust to the light and the princess' silhouette in the doorframe. Though she'd tried a thousand times, she pressed once more against the swelling walls of her prison, but never touched air—the water merely shifted around her. "What do you want from me?" she managed to whimper.

Even as she spoke the question, countless horror-filled options flooded her mind: to be eaten, to be displayed, to be held as a pet until the end of her days.

"Your name, actually," Princess Dauriel replied.

There was magic in names. Names could bind. Tallora merely stared, tongue stiff.

"No?"

Tallora shook her head, daring to stare into her captor's silhouette.

"Lost your tongue? Fine."

The door shut, and Tallora sobbed in her dreary cage.

Her hunger grew. She had nowhere to relieve herself save her magical pen, and her stomach and bowels ached in her stubborn refusal to swim in her own shit.

Tallora thought often of her mother, surely out of her mind from grief and worry. Once, her mother had said to move through hardship one day at a time, lest you lose your mind from grief. Tallora wasn't sure how to apply that counsel when she couldn't tell day from night.

Light filtered through the door once more, and this time Tallora did not flinch, instead forcing her composure to steady.

Princess Dauriel entered, holding two buckets. When she placed them down, she said, "Good evening." From her hand, Tallora saw a spark, then a burst of silver flame. She touched some sort of receptacle with her fingers, which quickly caught fire—first silver, then fading to orange. Dauriel's eyes reflected the vibrant colors, the fiery tones mingling with what Tallora realized was a striking silver.

Whatever their soft color, they held cruelty unmatched. "I brought supper." She gave Tallora an expectant stare, eyebrow raising in the ensuing silence. "Nothing? No greeting? No gratitude?"

Tallora's mouth filled with obscenities, but she swallowed them back. This woman was irked to be ignored, and so she merely crossed her arms and sneered.

Dauriel lifted the two buckets. "I don't quite know what merfolk eat," she continued, and Tallora glared at the cruel twist of her lip. "I brought options, one alive and one dead." She held up one. "Blue Flounder, caught this morning by an off-duty sailor with a penchant for fishing. He said you might like it—it's raw but prepared, wrapped in seaweed and given a hint of Zauleen spice."

Tallora's mouth watered, but she held to her pride and said nothing at all.

"This one's alive," Dauriel continued, holding up the second. "Onian Octopi—"

Tallora's skin crawled at the mere name.

". . . starved a day or two but just a beauty, don't you think?"

The poisonous octopi promised boils to last for days, and if ingested would cause a miserable death spent puking blood and your own ravaged entrails.

"Which would you prefer?" Dauriel kept her mischief, either a fool or as evil a person as Tallora had ever met. "I wouldn't want you to starve—I suppose I could dump both inside your pen if you refuse to tell me."

Tallora fought to control her breathing, instinctively floating to the edge of her prison when Dauriel hoisted up the bucket with the Onian Octopi. She had tried time and time again to breach the barrier, but though her cage pulsed like the waves, it held a wall stronger than stone.

Dauriel held the bucket against the cage and tilted it, the water within steadily spilling inside. The multi-limbed monstrosity flopped and pulled itself closer—

"No!" Tallora cried, shaking at her own weakness.

The bucket fell back; Dauriel placed it onto the floor. "There's your lovely voice," Tallora heard, victory in every hateful word. "Blue Flounder?"

Tallora cursed her tears as she twisted away from her heartless captor. Clenching her fists, she bit back the urge to sob. "Why are you doing this?"

"I'll do all manner of things if it gets me what I want," Dauriel said, holding up the bucket. "I'll take your name in exchange for a meal."

Her stomach weakened her will, but she was not defeated yet. "Go to hell."

"Starve, then." The light snuffed out.

Tallora breathed, the creaking wood of the ship all she had to soothe her troubled mind. *"Mother Staella,"* she whispered, lest her captor hear. *"M-Mother Staella . . ."*

The relevance of Silver Fire struck her like a blow to her stomach.

She was a fool to forget that while she called Staella 'mother,' for Dauriel and her lineage, it was more literal. Staella was the wife of a feared and ruthless deity—of Neoma, the Moon Goddess, progenitor of the very line of sorcerers Dauriel descended from, and whose callused justice had led the people of Solvira to topple countless kingdoms and dominate the continent. Tallora knew little of history, but the whole world feared Solvira. The world trembled before their tyrants' power—the mysterious Silver Fire, wielded by Neoma herself and passed on to her descendants.

She shut her eyes, crippled in her tiny bubble, heart sinking from no plan and no hope.

Chapter II 🐚

Despite her best efforts, Tallora did sleep. She prayed and wept and slept.

For the third time, light from beyond cast into the room. The princess did not come alone—with her followed the magister and at least two men, though they waited in the hallway. "We've made port in Tanill," she said, as though this might mean anything to Tallora. She gestured with a tilt of her head, power conveyed through a mere flick of her eyebrow. "Adrael."

The magister—Adrael—held out a hand. Tallora's prison slowly lowered to the floor. Upon touching the deck, it burst, water draining through invisible holes in the wood. Tallora stared up, surely a pitiful sight. With little ceremony, one of the men scooped her up, taking no caution to avoid groping her nude form. Tallora trembled, exposed and embarrassed as he set her into a worn metal cage, large enough to hold a shark.

Tallora flopped within, cringing at the sensation of rust against her scales and skin. She tried to pull herself up, balancing upon her scaled tail, but when her head breached the open top, the princess' hand shoved her down—in time for them to swing it shut and lock it. "Take her out," Dauriel said, and two men hoisted her new prison up.

Tallora's stomach churned, both from starvation and their unsteady gait. As they climbed the stairs, she blocked her eyes from the offending sunlight, the heat abrasive on her sleek skin.

With care, she blinked, realizing she no longer saw the open sea but a human town.

Upon the ship's deck, the entire crew had come to gawk at her. Humans found merfolk to be an exotic sort of attractive, or so she'd heard. Unhindered by sweeping rains and winds, they leered at her like some animal in a pen, and Tallora curled her chest against her mighty tail—brilliant pink in the light, and utterly useless out of the water.

The sunlight cast her opalescent skin in glimmering hues of pink and blue and purple across a pale palette. She hid behind the shade of her white hair as tears streamed down her face. Beneath the sea, the water carried them away; here on land, they dried upon her face, leaving her raw and vulnerable.

The sound of their steps changed, the hollow clomping of their feet replaced with sturdy, creaking wood. She dared to glance up, noting the seafaring village, hating its bustling inhabitants. Humans held upperworld shades, from sand to earth to cliffs, and Tallora thought them ugly, like vermin, each of them bearing the face of her captor. Princess Dauriel stood beside her glass prison, imposing in her steps, a true empress in the making.

For the first time, she saw Dauriel in the light and wondered if she were ugly only to Tallora or particularly plain for a human. She held herself like she owned the world, yet there was little femininity in her broad jaw and sharp cheeks. Perhaps on the open sea, she simply gave no care to beauty.

Nevertheless, Tallora wished a curse upon the wretched woman, for Tortalga's Ocean to eat her whole. Sadly, when they stepped off the dock and onto dry land, the princess remained.

She withdrew some sort of pendant from her leather pocket and tapped it with a gloved finger. It illuminated her face, though Tallora could not see what image it held. "Mother, we've returned," Dauriel said to the pendant. "And with a gift."

Tallora heard a voice from the pendant but not well enough to decipher. Dauriel set it back into her pocket. "Any minute now. Brace yourselves."

In Tallora's heart, she knew some impasse would soon be crossed, that what happened next would seal her fate—whatever horrendous fate that was. Swallowing her pride, she stuck her arm through the metal bars and gently tugged the princess' tunic.

Dauriel immediately swatted her, perhaps out of instinct given her noticeable shock. "I'll have you left out in the sun to dry next time you touch me without permission."

Tallora's tears had not staunched since she'd been dropped in her new prison. "Princess Dauriel," she said, her first words in days, "I'm begging you—"

"Good luck with that tactic," Dauriel interrupted, quirking her eyebrow.

Tallora swallowed a sob. "Please. I don't know your quest, but I've done nothing to hurt you and yours. I don't know what justice you subscribe to—"

Sudden sickness lurched her stomach. All at once, the world vanished, replaced by a sea of stars. Weightless, Tallora attempted to reach beyond her prison, wondering if it were all in her mind as a nameless force ripped her across the planes.

She suddenly dropped, her cage all that prevented her from rolling along a cold, stone floor. Nauseated, she might have vomited if her stomach had something to process. Instead, she retched. Hardly proper, but what use was groveling now?

"Dauriel, Solvira celebrates your return."

The world had changed. Tallora dared to look about and saw sweeping walls of finery and great windows showing the sky and mountains far beyond. Dauriel stood beside her, as well as Magister Adrael. Before her was a gilded chair upon a pedestal, and approaching was a woman with Dauriel's soft eyes and a dress decorated with delicate gold chains and studded with more gems than Tallora had ever seen in her life. While the princess had been tanned by the sun, this woman's skin bore shades of porcelain.

"Thank you, Mother. I'm happy to be home."

Tallora knew her name from her studies—this was Empress Vahla of Solvira. The empress stared directly at her, intrigue passing through her breathtaking features. "By the Triage," she whispered, hardly breathing it.

12

Behind the wickedness in Dauriel's grin, Tallora swore she saw relief. "A gift for you. A mermaid from the Tortalgan Sea. But this was found on her person." The princess pulled Tallora's beloved necklace from her trouser pocket. "She's a Priestess of Staella. I think you'll find a use for her."

Tallora's face paled, her limbs numbing in tandem.

Vahla looked to Dauriel, the unspoken words between them indecipherable, then took the offered necklace. When her gaze returned, the empress placed a hand over her mouth. "Have you ever seen anything so beautiful? Call the council—they must see this."

Elsewhere, Tallora heard people scatter, unsure if they were of human or angelic descent—the latter of whom were deemed 'Celestials.' The empress, she knew, held angelic blood, thus setting her apart from humanity with unearthly beauty and an inborn talent for magic. Descended of Neoma and thus her daughter, Ilune, The Great Necromancer, who it was said handpicked a man to impregnate her—only to slay him in the afterglow of their lovemaking.

A brutal beginning for a tyrannical empire.

Tallora cowered as the empress studied her. "Does it speak?"

"When it chooses. I've yet to know its name."

The empress smiled, practiced charm in her visage. A true monarch, and Tallora hated her. "What is your name, Mermaid?"

Tallora merely pressed herself deeper into her cage.

The empress' kind façade slipped by degrees. "My name is Vahla Solviraes, Empress of Solvira, the greatest country upon this mortal realm. I hold the power to drop you from the highest tower of the Glass Palace and let vermin pick at your corpse. I'll ask again—what is your name?"

Death was a predictable path, the chance to rest in the arms of her chosen deity. She said nothing, merely stared at the stern monarch.

13

"Perhaps not killed—merely flayed." She returned her attention to Dauriel. "Starve it until it's compliant. Rel can keep it at the brink of death until it bends—"

Beyond, Tallora heard a door echo across the high walls. "Empress, we hear you have something worth seeing?"

Tallora turned to the new voice, one bearing the guttural tones of the De'Sindai tongue—the descendants of demonic and mortal blood. Three figures approached, each of different sizes and builds, and the one who led them held a giant's size but a demonic form—hooved and horned, with deep blue skin. Striking, with her glowing eyes and silver tattoos, she led the rest.

Two human men followed, one in robes to rival the empress, and the other bearing dark clothing and a hood, yet the hands peeking from the engulfing sleeves and the hint of his countenance suggested this might be the oldest person Tallora had ever seen.

"General," the empress said, practically biting the word, "I would never purposefully waste your time."

"Only accidentally," the De'Sindai replied, and Tallora saw then the extent of her vast musculature— her height made her imposing enough, given she towered above the rest, but her bulk made her massive. "This is a mermaid. I have seen mermaids."

"And a lovely creature it is." The richly dressed man practically fawned over her, causing Tallora to cringe. "My darling, what a fantastic gift, truly worthy of your title." He kissed the empress on her cheek— somehow, Tallora found this strange, given his groveling tone. He, too, had eyes as silver as the moon's light—perhaps this was a Solviraes trait.

"Where is Greyva?" Vahla said, her focus shifting to the ancient man.

He replied with far more power than his feeble pose suggested. "The High Priestess prays to her

Goddess, esteemed empress. Neoma summoned her, for what we do not know."

Neoma? The goddess herself? Whatever Tallora's fears for her life, she realized it hardly touched the surface—she lay surrounded by beings of true power and influence.

The empress looked merely perturbed. "High Priest Rel, this creature's disrespect has set it and myself at odds. Prepare a prayer to Ilune—perhaps a bit of necromancy will sustain it until I've been appeased."

The threat in the words caused Tallora's breath to fail. Lightheaded and starved, her will steadily depleted. She could still speak, she could say her name, perhaps grovel an apology—

"Empress, give her time. What use is a tortured woman to your collection? None would look upon her and be impressed—only think you cruel."

Tallora dared to stare at her savior, the blue De'Sindai who spoke with absolute disregard to the Empress of Solvira. "You would humanize this creature?" Empress Vahla said.

"I would."

Tallora suppressed a nervous smile at the blatant disregard shown to the esteemed empress. Could she possibly have found an ally here? Beyond, she watched Dauriel fight the same amusement. Immediately, Tallora swallowed it.

Vahla looked murderous; her husband looked merely nervous. "My love, my heart, my *dearest* empress, perhaps we should turn our attention to creating an enclosure for her—for the creature, yes? Lest she dry out in the air."

The empress had turned quite red, an unflattering color with her sea-green dress. "Take it out," she spat, then her husband led her away, proclaiming apologies with every step.

Magister Adrael said, "Perhaps to the menagerie? We can set up a temporary enclosure until we've designed something grand."

"I'll supervise." Tallora hated Dauriel's voice and wished for a stone dagger to cut it out. "Whatever it takes for Mother to be appeased."

Priest Rel went away. So, too, did the general, but Tallora reached out to touch her, desperate to cling to her only ally. "Wait," she whispered, grasping the callused, blue hand, but it echoed all about. Everyone turned, each as surprised as the next. Save for the general—she remained utterly aloof. Tallora stared only at her. "Thank you."

The general looked unimpressed. Tallora's heart sank. "For what?"

Beyond, Dauriel stared at their interaction with absolute bafflement. Tallora ignored her. "For saving me from a terrible death."

"Death would have been more merciful than the empress' justice." The general pulled her hand back. "You are welcome."

She continued away, her steps more pronounced than the rest. "Khastra, wait," Dauriel said rushing to meet the general. She whispered, too quiet for Tallora's ears.

"I will not ask her name," General Khastra said, making no effort to curb her volume. "This is your doing and thus your problem." In an affectionate gesture, she patted the princess' arm, but perhaps harder than necessary given Dauriel's flinch. "I will see you tonight for training."

Khastra walked away. Tallora's hope went with her.

Dauriel returned, in tandem with scuffling servants. "To the menagerie," she ordered, and Tallora prepared her stomach as she was hoisted up.

Tallora lay centered among a sea of exotic beings—animals with fur, with scales, some who roared and bared fearsome teeth and some from across the sea. A giant spider stared behind bars, its ominous web sweeping to the ceiling, and a smaller, insect-like creature clicked from a separate, shady enclosure, surrounded by strange green crystals. Nothing humanoid, save herself. They paced in cages, magnificent beasts enslaved to these royals' whims, the greenery lush but tainted with cruelty. The sky sat open, no roof to trap them, allowing birds to enter, but not the ones kept within to leave.

Tallora stared out from her cage, watching as Magister Adrael created the same sort of water globe as he had below the ship—but enormous now, large enough for her to stretch her limbs and tail.

The servants had scattered, leaving only Adrael and Dauriel. The princess heaved a great sigh when Adrael lowered his hands. "It will do." She turned her attention to Tallora. "I'll have to lift you. Fight me, and I'll let you flounder in the dirt."

The cage lid creaked as it tilted open. Tallora cringed at Dauriel's touch, though the princess held her with care. Her hands, no longer gloved, held the roughness of work, not the softness of royalty. Tallora wondered at that, but more so at the glimpse of tattooed ink upon her wrists.

Still, Dauriel did as she said—she pushed Tallora through the watery barrier and released, then withdrew her hands and shook them off, her cotton sleeves and skin drenched. "Adrael, leave us. I wish to speak to her alone."

Adrael merely nodded and left them.

Tallora trembled, filled with a sudden, overwhelming rage. "You would grant me the dignity of a gender, now?"

"I'd happily grant you the dignity of a name, if you would share it."

Lip trembling, Tallora glared, struggling to control her breathing. Anger pulsed with every beat of her heart as reality descended—she would die here.

"No? Perhaps you'll change your mind after a few more days of starvation—"

"You absolute *bitch!*" Furious tears welled in Tallora's eyes, but by Staella's Grace she *would not cry.* "How sick are you, to entertain yourself with my suffering?"

Dauriel's silver eyes turned to steel. "Take care how you speak to me—"

"Or what? You'll starve me more? You don't want me dead; you want me compliant."

"I can make your life hell."

"And that would be different than this?" Tallora gestured about her orb of water, to the caged creatures beyond. "I am a person. I have a soul. I am a worshipper of the very goddess you're descended from, yet you treat me like an animal—" The word broke her. Tallora gasped, all her will spent fighting her betraying tears. She drove her nails into her palms, desperate to hide her weakness.

Dauriel watched, her captivating gaze utterly stoic, stinging Tallora's pride. "I'm certain Staella herself will come down to save you, assuming she cares. Now, your name?"

"Make my life hell," Tallora spat. "It's where you'll go, upon your death."

"And Staella will let you weep upon her breast? A pity for you that our goddesses are aligned. Perhaps we'll live out eternity together." Dauriel stepped back, hands held up in a grand gesture. "Make yourself comfortable. My mother will surely bring my brother here to see you as well. He's the heir apparent, so you'd best make nice. He'll decide your fate upon her death."

She left Tallora alone. Tallora barely withheld a scream, longing to shout obscenities at her hated conqueror. Instead, she swam around her new prison, body reeling from hunger, from her absolute refusal to relieve herself, lack of sleep ... Perhaps she'd die of infection. She'd add that to her prayers.

She looked up at the sky—the Sun Goddess' grace shone upon her prison, but by nightfall, a different illumination would invigorate her soul. Perhaps to see her own goddess' light would give credence to her prayers.

Or perhaps her goddess did not care. She feared her own loss of faith.

Tallora pushed upon her cage, finding it as strong as the last.

At sunset, the royal family came—Empress Vahla, her husband, the hated Dauriel, and a young boy, no older than five.

Not what Tallora expected in an heir. The Solviraes held no care to male or female heirs—why, then, would Dauriel not inherit the key to her prison?

Curious, Tallora swam to the edge of her confines, the child's gaze pure. "Momma, why is she naked?"

"Darling, beasts do not wear clothing. It isn't expected of it."

With some demure, Tallora wrapped her arms around her breasts, recalling how exposed she truly was. "Below the sea, there's no need for clothing—too much of a nuisance if your cloak were to be snagged on coral or tangled with fish. We only decorate ourselves for special occasions."

The empress looked faint, her expression awed and furious all at once. "And so it does speak."

The boy smiled, oblivious to his mother's aggrieve. "What's your name?"

Thinking quickly, Tallora grinned and held a finger to her lips. "My name is as secret as the mysteries of the Goddess Neoma herself." She spared a glance for Dauriel, her own malicious intent hopefully conveyed despite the perpetual urge to pass out. "If I speak it aloud, the moon's light will strike me dead." She returned her attention to the small boy, noting his wide-eyed wonder. "But won't you tell me yours?"

"Eniah."

"A lovely name for a prince." With every word she spoke, the boy grew more enthralled by her presence. Perhaps she was the most exotic thing he'd seen in his young life, but whatever the cause, he ate straight from her hand. She realized, with absolute glee, that perhaps her true ally came in a small package. "Eniah, I hope you and I shall be friends."

"Yes, please—"

"A pity—darling, it's your bedtime," the empress said as she grasped his arm. Ire stirred beneath her tempestuous smile. "Perhaps we'll all come to visit her tomorrow, hmm? We'll bring her breakfast." The empress turned her fury onto Tallora, who elected simply to smile and wave, still hiding behind her arms. "Assuming she behaves."

"But, Momma, where will she sleep?" Eniah asked, and Tallora might've been endeared to his childish mind were she not so bitter.

Empress Vahla spouted some nonsense about 'mermaid magic,' all while the empress' consort groveled to appease his wife, his incessant whining echoing through the menagerie until the door slammed behind them. Dauriel remained, arms crossed, stance tall and regal. She had cleaned herself of the salty spray of the sea, her hair impeccably braided, her clothing a rich ensemble of black leather and cloth, trousers loose but her doublet well-fitted. Her powerful aura spoke of an assurance running deeper than even her title and inheritance—this woman knew herself, she knew her worth, perhaps built it from sand and thus earned every piece of it.

Tallora glared, unwilling to bend.

"You're charming, when you try to be."

"Oh, fuck off." Tallora swam to the top of her bubble, showing only her back to the princess.

But Dauriel, unfortunately, elected to not fuck off. "My mother has placed you under my care and protection. I caught you, and now it's my responsibility to tame you."

Truthful or not, Tallora knew it was bait. She knew it, and she took it anyway. "Tame me? The wild beast with her naked body and refusal to worship you? It won't be easy, I assure you."

"Khastra said I should try being nice. You attract more flies with honey, or some shit. She's right."

"Basic decency? What a novel idea. Is that what this is? You kidnapped me for some sick game?"

"I'm not that petty," Dauriel replied, and it took every ounce of Tallora's self-control to not scream. "It's not about you. It's about what you represent to the world. And if all goes according to plan, the world will be better for it."

"What kind of cryptic nonsense is that?" But when Dauriel said nothing, Tallora returned her gaze to the sky, refusing to grant the princess her attention. "Leave me alone."

"Listen—"

"You want to be nice? Perhaps try listening to what I say. Leave me *alone!*"

Tallora screamed it to the sky, swallowing the rest of her furious words. When she heard nothing, she looked back. The princess had gone.

She waited, giving the sky her full attention, watching as the first smattering of stars appeared amidst the waning sunlight. "Goddess Staella," she whispered, anger seeping away, "you're a patron of mercy. Of kindness. Of love."

With the setting sun came the rise of the waxing moon, its glow bright enough to outshine the smaller, celestial bodies surrounding it. Was this the fate of stars, to be subsumed by the moon's light? Tallora wondered, not for the first time, if this were the true relationship of the deities—a gentle goddess

21

overshadowed by a powerful, tyrannical figure, whose people nearly ruled the world. Neoma was not wicked, or so she had been taught. She was justice incarnate, but to a system different than Tallora's.

As it was, Neoma's people had stolen Tallora and kept her imprisoned. She couldn't fathom the justice in that. "Goddess Staella," she continued, pleading now as more stars broke through the lingering sunlight and the encompassing moon, "I know not what to ask for. But grant me aid, I beg of you."

Tallora's world fell silent, the animals in their cages settling in to sleep. She refused to join them, but her body failed her—she drifted in and out, hunger preventing true rest. She lay suspended, nothing to place her head upon.

At least, lost among the watery cage, they wouldn't see her tears.

No one delivered breakfast. Tallora was not surprised.

Instead, when the heat of midday beat down upon her, her prison steadily growing close to boiling, workers wheeled in a series of steel beams, gilded and decorated with gems and silver. Dauriel was with them, shouting orders left and right—*The general herself will come inspect your work; if you've messed anything up, she'll personally—"*—and so on.

Though Tallora refused to succumb to intrigue, she watched from the corner of her eye as they assembled the beams into a hexagonal shape, far larger than her bubble. When the sun had left its position directly above, Magister Adrael joined them. "Exceptional," he mused, surveying the enormous stakes. "Continue. Best we bring the décor before it all wilts."

Tallora now openly watched, fascinated when entire wagons full of ocean plants were wheeled in, as well as a few stone structures, placed sporadically within the confines of the beam. Coral and other pastel life decorated the enclosure, and though Tallora refused to admit it was lovely, she appreciated the attention to detail—someone knowledgeable of her homeland had designed what she suspected was her new cage.

By nightfall, they had finished, except for the rather important detail of water.

Magister Adrael approached Tallora's bubble. "Brace yourself, Mermaid. Wouldn't want to lose you after all that."

Tallora's stomach lurched as her bubble floated away, the turbulent water forcing her from side to side. It settled between the hexagon, then expanded, filling the space but stopping abruptly at invisible barriers between the beams.

Tallora quickly studied this new environment, relishing the wall of seaweed blocking the outside world and the great stone tablet for her bed—although it lay in the open—admiring an plot of idle sand, perfect for a garden . . .

She swallowed her smile. This was Dauriel's plan. Instead, she bolted behind the blockade of seaweed.

Fury aside, she could have melted from the relief of touching something solid. Tallora's body relaxed for the first time in days, aching muscles singing praises to the soft sand.

She shut her eyes, not asleep but drifting. She heard the guttural accent of the general surveying the scenery, and later the empress, irate to find Tallora could *hide* within her own new home. No young princes, but Dauriel's voice passively trying to appease her, unenthused repetitions of, *"Give her time,"* and, *"We can't starve her forever."*

Damn them all. But at least Tallora could shit in peace.

23

Eventually, darkness settled. The voices disappeared. Despite her exhaustion, Tallora couldn't sleep.

Alone, or so she hoped, she peeked her head from the tangle of seaweed, savoring the feeling and scent of salt. Nothing but the typical inhabitants, the lifeless beasts she was deemed equal to. Tallora swam to inspect a beam, touched it, and felt nothing but smooth metal. Some enchantment must have been present, but Tallora held no talent for deciphering anything like that. She swam to the next beam, her hand trailing against the wall of water, like skimming the air.

The second beam was as the first. Tallora gripped it for support, then pushed against the wall of water.

It held, but it bent, moving with her hand as it pushed against the barrier. She swam to the top, realizing she could touch the sky, the air, and gasp for breath.

She had not felt the wind in days. It caressed her waterlogged locks of white, stinging her skin, yet she savored the sensation, relishing the pleasant chill after the heat of the day. The moon remained bright, prepared to slowly grow as the days went on. There, too, were the stars, breaking through the moon's light, ever-present.

Tallora swam to the side, head still above water. At the beam, she reached her hand across the barrier where it brushed past with ease. Nothing stopped her.

She was easily twenty feet above the ground, likely to break her neck should she jump. Death was well worth the risk.

She dried her hands in the air, praying it would be enough to secure her grip. Foolhardy or not, Tallora clutched the beam, hoisting herself up with her lingering strength and pure desperation. When she twisted, her arms already ached, but no use in crying now—not when her entire body dangled beyond her pen.

She gripped the decals of the beam, lowering herself in agonized motions. Her fingers burned, nails chipping as she went. Her tail dangled uselessly, reflecting the moon in distracting rays of light.

She swore it took hours. Tears seeped from her eyes. She wept, praying she was heard by only the gods and not those who would proclaim themselves among them. Her hair tangled around her arms and face, sticky as it slowly dried. Tallora released a whispered cry: *"Staella, grant me strength!"*

Her tail touched stone. Tallora collapsed, body smacking the slippery tiles, but she lived. Shaken, but not defeated, she began step two of her impossible plan.

She inched forward, using her tail to help push as she pulled herself along. She moved in painfully slow degrees, and her skin burned as it rubbed against the stone. Streaks of red shone beneath her pearlescent skin, her breasts and stomach and scales in agony.

She measured progress in tiles. Decorating the floor in sandy shades, the square pieces were nearly as long as she. Her burst of strength threatened to give out by tile five, but she pushed onward, prepared to die here.

Then, her hand touched a leather boot. Tallora looked up, only to face Princess Dauriel, who raised a patronizing eyebrow.

Exhausted, defeated, Tallora collapsed, weeping on the cut stone.

Dauriel stepped aside, a metallic clink echoing from whatever platter she held. "No, no—do continue."

Tallora knew she was being mocked. Cheeks burning, she spat at Dauriel's feet, making certain it splattered her perfectly polished boot, before inching forward once again, faster now with an audience.

"Tell you what—if you can make it to the sea, I'll let you go. It's only a thousand miles away. You're making excellent time."

Tallora ignored her, continuing her foolish quest. Let this bitch know her as spiteful above all else.

25

Dauriel's footsteps disappeared, following the path Tallora had crawled. The air dried out her sensitive skin, the stone chafing her stomach and breasts. But she could see the door. That much spurred her onward.

"You do realize you're leaving streaks of blood. Someone will have to mop."

Tallora held her tongue.

"Say the word, and I'll carry you back."

Tallora's arms failed her; she fell against the floor once more. "Touch me," she said, breathing labored, "and I'll bite."

"Bite me, and I'll pluck your teeth out. One by one."

Tallora's mouth ached at the mere thought. Her tears fell in droves. When she looked down at her chest, she saw streaks of raw skin, scraped by the floor. Dauriel's footsteps stopped beside her; Tallora curled into a ball, the shame of defeat settling upon her.

"Pitiful, truly. But I think it should stand to reason that tears won't draw any sympathy from me."

Tallora's arms covered her head, a vain attempt to block the hateful words. Callused hands against her back caused her to flinch.

She was surprised when Dauriel pulled back. "Let me pick you up. I'll take you back."

Leather-bound arms lifted Tallora's limp form. She wept, still covering her head, even after water enveloped her as she was pushed inside. The water embraced her as she gently floated to the bottom, sobbing all the while.

Hope seeped away with her tears. Tallora cried herself to sleep.

A voice spoke through the fog of her dreams, as clear and familiar as her own.

"Tallora, my child . . . do not lose hope."

Tallora felt nothing, saw nothing—simply existed within a void.

"Your prayers have been heard. My wife is displeased at your confines but will not interfere. It is not our place. It never has been."

Tallora wondered if she imagined the regret in the voice.

"But I have not abandoned you. You must save yourself, but I shall give you the means. At the new moon, await my gift."

The world erupted in a sea of stars. Tallora saw a woman of pure light, radiant wings bursting from her form. Kindness shone in her visage, her eyes as soft as her smile. Her arms wrapped around Tallora, embracing her.

Tallora felt divinity and warmth.

Chapter III 🐚

S he awoke to morning light, rested for the first time in days.

Tallora sat up, her vision replaying over and over, the burning touch of the angelic goddess still lingering. She'd witnessed a miracle. The goddess knew her. She'd heard her.

Tallora cried, but for hope and joy. The new moon was only a few weeks away.

When her wits returned, Tallora realized that upon a stone slab touching the invisible wall was . . . food?

Tallora swam to investigate. Blue flounder, chopped and prepared, though a few hours old now. Dauriel had brought this last night, she realized.

Had Tallora no hope, she would have dumped it beyond the barrier. Instead, she needed strength. Whatever boon Staella offered, Tallora had no guess, but with hope came the resolve to play a different game.

The day passed with little aplomb. No one visited, not until Dauriel made her predictable return in the evening. Tallora feigned indifference to the tray of food in her hands. "Isn't it demeaning for a princess to wait hand and foot on a prisoner—?"

Dauriel dropped the tray inches beyond the barrier. The chopped fish scattered across the tile, and Tallora's starving stomach lurched. "Glad we agree," the princess replied, and she walked away.

Tallora spent hours pushing past the barrier, trying and failing to retrieve her meal. When the crescent moon had risen high in the sky, she admitted defeat, quietly weeping from hunger.

She was awoken by an irate reprimand—*"What in Onias' Hell is this?!"*

Tallora peered through the wall of seaweed and saw General Khastra pointing furiously at the spilled platter of fish. Dauriel stood tall before her, but one could only stand so mightily before the behemoth. "She was disrespectful—"

"If this is your treatment of disrespect, then it is good you abdicated your throne. Clean it up."

"I'll call someone to—"

"You clean it up." The De'Sindai pointed at the mess; the incredulous princess gawked at her.

It might have been humorous, given Dauriel only barely stood as tall as the general's sternum, but the ensuing stare-down held more fury than a clash of gods. Silver flame rose at Princess Dauriel's feet, which she visibly fought to subdue; General Khastra became the immovable object, staring sternly down.

The fire remained as Dauriel knelt to pick up pieces of raw fish, piling them onto the tray. Tallora resisted the impulse to laugh, her cruel joy unparalleled for her torturer to be so subsumed. Again, she noticed the inked designs on Dauriel's wrists and realized it was writing—writing that matched the elaborate décor on the general's body.

"I will come back, and it will be gone." The general left, her hooves echoing across the stone tiles.

Tallora prayed her grin was shit-eating enough to further stoke the fire. "Abdicated your throne, huh?"

Dauriel spared her a glance, her skin unquestionably *glowing.*

"I wondered why your baby brother would be inheriting the throne instead of you. I'll bet it's a wonderful story, full of drama and intrigue. Did you kill a diplomat? Fuck the wrong foreign prince? I have to know."

A strip of meat squished as Dauriel tightened her fist. "I abdicated on my own accord," she spat.

When she relaxed her hand, raw bits of meat stuck to her palm.

"Realized you were bitchier than your mother?"

The princess brushed off her hands, her task hardly complete, but she turned her attention to Tallora fully now, and she wondered if she might die from Dauriel's fury. "I'm not any happier to be your keeper than you are. Yes, it's demeaning. I came home a victor only to be demoted to a mere servant—a *beast* keeper."

"Oh no. I feel so terrible for you," Tallora said, utterly straight-faced. "I'd cry a few tears, but I need to keep them for me."

"A mercy, then," Dauriel seethed, silver fire escaping from her mouth, "for a price."

Tallora refused to admit intrigue at this dragon-esque behavior. "You've already stolen my pride. Don't offer me pity—"

"I will free you."

Damn it all. Tallora listened now.

"Give me your name, and I swear upon my ancestral blood you will be freed upon my mother's death. I have no use for a menagerie, and my brother can be swayed."

The Solviraes famously lived to be centuries old. "Seems a paltry offer, for me to live most of my life in a gods-forsaken bubble."

Within Dauriel's hand sparked an idle flame of pure silver. She brought it up, staring into the fire as she whispered, "Given a reason, that time might not be so far away."

"What sort of reason?"

The flame rose and fell as she flexed her fingers, yet Tallora saw the tension in her countenance—as well as subtle glowing from the tattoos on her wrist. "I do not know. I only mean to give you hope. And perhaps make both our lives easier."

It wasn't sincerity she saw in Dauriel's flame-lit features, nor mercy—furious resolve, perhaps.

Apparently her name was worth its weight in gold. Tallora shook her head and swam back. "You think I don't know of magic that binds a person with their name? Whatever your plans, I'll keep my free will, thank you. I don't need your mercy."

"Perhaps you'll feel differently in a few more years." Dauriel closed her fist; the fire extinguished. "You'll have no kindness from me. Not then."

Kneeling, Dauriel resumed collecting the remaining chunks of meat.

"So you abdicated your throne willingly?" Tallora asked, content to poke what she saw was a wound. "Adolescent rebellion? Wanted to be a priestess instead?"

Dauriel continued in silence, but the grit of her jaw revealed her curtailed fury. Tallora reveled in her victory.

"Whoring around? Secret child—"

Dauriel slammed the tray with her fist, splattering bits of rotting fish onto the stone. *"Shut up!"*

Not what Tallora expected. "I see that this is a tender subject—"

"Don't. I abdicated because it was the noble thing to do when I was told I couldn't bear children. It's just as well; I've never cared for men. Would've never bent for one. I would have stepped down from my birthright either way—for my empty womb or my unwillingness to bear fruit from it anyway. So don't piss on what you don't understand."

Tallora wouldn't say she felt pity, no. But something else arose, something strange and foreign to feel toward someone she despised. She'd come across a complicated puzzle, one that joined to create the hateful princess she'd been cursed to meet. "I despise you. But I would be foolish to forget you have a soul, even if I haven't been granted the same kindness."

Tallora left Dauriel alone, contemplative even after the princess left.

Perhaps those puzzle pieces could be exploited.

Tallora recalled the first time she'd ever looked at a girl and wanted desperately to know her.

Ironically, she had been with a boy at the time—a beautiful boy with strong arms and a talent for making her laugh for hours on end—adoring the affection that came from young love. She had loved him with all her young heart; she had been a girl, then, not the grown woman she was now.

Once, as she'd held this boy's hand, a girl floated among a small group, giggling at their words, and Tallora's breath had caught—oh, how beautiful was her purple hair, as vibrant as the sky at sunset, her eyes the sun itself. Her lips had smiled, alluring and full, and the curiosity of what it might be like to kiss them passed through her head.

And when she and the boy had parted, both their hearts broken, she had found peace kissing those lips; they were as wonderful as she had hoped.

There were cultures who scoffed at such unions. But Tallora had always loved whom she would, and naysayers were uncommon among her people and other long-lived beings. The elves and the angels loved with no prejudice toward their peers, as did most Celestials.

Solviran culture certainly embraced lovers of the same sex, given two of their patron deities were women wedded and in love—and that was a rare thing, she'd heard, for angels to tie themselves together in matrimony.

But Tallora supposed she understood why the inability to bear an heir would destroy Dauriel's bid to the throne. She had read of the Solviraes bloodline, the inbreeding and murder used to keep the famed Silver Fire potent and exclusive to their family line. Should even one not birth the next generation, they risked utter ruin.

Dauriel only came at night, Tallora reasoned, because she saw nothing of her, but food awaited each morning. It seemed she'd pissed the princess off good, and Tallora reveled in glee at the prospect.

She felt like a new toy—forgotten within hours of her arrival. No one visited for days.

So accustomed she was to silence that as Tallora preened her hair one morning—rather, as well as she could, given her lack of mirror—she thought she imagined the voice from beyond her pen. "You'll want to present your best self, Mermaid. My mother is entertaining foreign guests; she plans to show you off."

Tallora slowly tilted her head toward the noise, realizing Dauriel stood beyond the wall of seaweed. She swam out of her barrier, frowning at Dauriel's palpable annoyance. "What is my 'best self?'"

"To not hide. To smile and wave. Perhaps present your name."

"What if I give a false one?"

Dauriel seethed a weighted sigh. "Better than nothing."

"Call me 'Staella.'" Tallora grinned at Dauriel's ever-increasing ire. "What, too blasphemous?" When the princess said nothing, she laughed uproariously— by Staella's Grace, she'd never tire of this game. "Sincere question," she managed through her amusement, "why not give me a name? I'm a beast, or so you've said. Beasts are given names, stripped of identity."

"Given names do not work for spells," Dauriel replied, resignation in her tone. "Has to be your real one."

Tallora's smile stretched wider than the barrier. "At least we're all being honest now."

"I say this as your caretaker," Dauriel said, her voice lowering. "Be careful with that sort of thinking. Khastra has my mother convinced to give you time to adjust, but you'll be held to a different standard sooner than later. Being tamed and being broken are merely a step apart, and torture will do the job either way. Whatever my feelings toward you, no one deserves that."

"Oh, so I'm someone now? Not a beast? Charming." Tallora swam away from the wall, content to hide until nightfall, when she heard Dauriel's reply.

"I ask you only to present yourself before my mother's guests. Be as stubborn a bitch as you want to me; don't piss off the people holding the axe."

Tallora poked her head out from the forest of seaweed. "That's quite the language for a royal, even a disgraced one." The insult hit its mark. At Dauriel's feet, flame simmered. Tallora feigned an oblivious smile and said, "And what must I do? Be a trained clownfish? Do flips above the water?"

"That would certainly do it." Dauriel stepped back, presumably to walk away.

Tallora poked the wound. "If a different tactic would endear to them more, I have nothing to lose. Your men certainly enjoyed ogling me on your deck; I could give your ambassadors a show." She swam forward, grinning as she cupped her breasts in her hands and squeezed. "Shall I practice on you?"

"Fuck you," Dauriel said, already leaving Tallora far behind.

"If that's what it takes to secure my freedom, please do."

Dauriel kept walking.

"Not even a rejection? I'm insulted."

"So am I."

"It's fine," Tallora cried, as Dauriel disappeared from view. "You're nothing to look at anyway—I'd have to close my eyes and imagine home to stomach you."

She heard nothing from Dauriel. Tallora hoped she'd struck a nerve.

As Dauriel said, Empress Vahla's guests followed her into the menagerie.

Two of them, both human men, wearing gold and white robes emblazoned with the symbol of the goddess Sol Kareena. As the sister to Neoma, her kingdom, the Theocracy of Sol Kareena, stood as tentative allies to Solvira. Tallora watched them from behind the seaweed, disappointed that Dauriel hadn't accompanied them.

". . . our newest addition, and our rarest—a beautiful mermaid, caught in the Tortalgan Sea."

Tallora saw mutual concern from the Theocracy's diplomats. "An odd choice of beings to keep in captivity," one said.

"I assure you, Lord Tiran, she is the loveliest creature you'll ever lay your eyes on." A pause; Tallora grinned at the empress' subtle, flickering ire. ". . . if she would appear, that is."

Tallora settled herself behind the barrier, feigning sleep, lest they catch a hint of her presence.

They remained a few minutes, casually discussing the décor, before the empress proclaimed that she must be sleeping and escorted them away, more quickly than they had entered.

Tallora laughed and stretched her limbs, her tail propelling her to the water's surface. Sunlight brushed across the waves, sparkling in opalescent hues, her skin illuminate.

Not so long now. Freedom tasted sweeter each day.

At nightfall, Tallora received her next set of guests. Dauriel approached, gaze cast to the floor. She carried no food, perhaps as penance for Tallora's disrespect. Following behind came a volley of guards and the empress herself, along with the sycophantic creature she called 'husband.'

Tallora bowed in mockery. "Good to see you, Empress."

A guard held what appeared to be a small harpoon. In the split moment after Tallora saw it, he shot it through the water.

Directly at the base of Tallora's tail.

She screamed, pain radiating from the mess of shattered scales. Gasping, she was heaved past the barrier, tearing through and flopping onto the stone floor.

Blood seeped from the wound. The guard ripped it from her tail, causing further pain and mess. Shock pulsed through her blood. Tallora whimpered at the leering eyes above her, helpless upon the floor.

"I don't take kindly to insults," the empress said. She snapped her fingers; two guards knelt beside Tallora, forcing her arms against the ground. A third crouched beside Tallora's tail, a knife in his hand.

She whipped her powerful tail about, panic stealing her voice. Another set of guards steadied her bloodied fin and tail. Overpowered, Tallora sobbed.

"I've read enough about fish and merfolk to know the damage won't be permanent. But perhaps this will prevent you from hiding for a few weeks."

Pain seared the base of her tail. Tallora looked down and saw the guard with the knife slashing strips into her fin, mutilating the sinew and muscle. She screamed, writhing in agony at each brutal slice.

It stretched for what felt like hours. Tears leaked from her eyes; she screamed all the while.

Though the pain lingered, the hold on her arms and tail released. Tallora realized the fin had been cut away. Her tail ended in a bloody, pointed stump.

"Lovely work," the empress cooed. "Place her back in the tank."

Tallora barely felt the rough arms lifting her from the ground, so great was her pain. Water enveloped her; Tallora floated to the bottom of her cage, lacking the will to move. Instead, she sobbed into the sand.

"You're lucky your insolent behavior didn't affect foreign relations—otherwise I might've offered you roasted on a spike to sweeten the deal. This is your warning, Mermaid. Take care your disrespect doesn't outweigh your usefulness."

The words faded. Tallora thought she heard footsteps but merely continued sobbing.

The great, gaping holes bled into the water. When Tallora dared to look up, her audience had left—all except Dauriel, no pride in her stance. Upon meeting her eye, the princess whispered, "I tried to warn you."

Tallora fell back into a supplicant's stance, weeping into her arms.

Chapter IV 🐚

When Tallora awoke from what she prayed was a nightmare, the lingering pain in her tail revealed the damning truth.

Tallora laid on the sand for days, occasionally summoning the will to pull herself along with her arms. She tried, in a single desperate moment, to swim with her stumped tail, no fins to propel her, to failing results.

She ignored her food. It piled upon the stone platform. She ignored Dauriel, who brought it every night and lingered, making vain attempts to talk. Tallora simply shut her eyes and breathed, content to waste away and die.

It would grow back. There was hope in that, distant and flickering. But that would be weeks from now, and Tallora had been promised the goddess' aid in mere days.

She prayed, when she felt the inclination. Her mindset remained dark, bitterness seeping into her thoughts. Staella promised aid, and that was a miracle. Tallora wondered, however, if this were a penance for a crime she did not know. She lay serene in hell, the pain in her tail settling to a dull throbbing.

In time, she picked at her food. To accept Staella's aid, as the goddess herself had said, would mean for Tallora to save herself, be given a fighting chance. Yet doubt threatened to ruin her resolve—what if it had been a dream and nothing more?

Visitors came. Eniah tried to speak through the barrier more than once, asking his mother why she languished. The empress said she was sick but would recover better than before.

Tallora's broken spirit. Better than before.

The new moon came, and Tallora had nearly forgotten. But when the sun set and no moon rose to replace it, she realized the day had come. She looked up to the sky, a sudden burst of hope spurring her to sit up. Clasping her hands, she whispered, "Goddess Staella—"

A tug in her soul cast her gaze to the sky, a streak of light calling to her in the night.

A falling star?

It grew brighter with each passing moment, twinkling against the radiant array of celestial lights. When it slowed, Tallora saw it was not a star, no—and it quite suddenly dropped into her pen, into the water, and gently floated down.

Tallora crawled toward it, inching forward with her hands and tail. A small vial, she realized, as she dug it from the sand. No instructions, no explanation; simply a bottle filled with shimmering liquid, stopped with a weighted, metal top.

Footsteps alerted her to another presence. Tallora buried the vial in the sand, heart beating rapidly. Dauriel's presence was no surprise, but Tallora wished, of all nights, the cursed princess could have been late.

They matched eyes, and the princess looked surprised, brow furrowing at the attention. "You seem to be feeling better," she mused, sliding the tray of food past the watery barrier. "I'll admit, I wondered if you'd lay in the sand and die."

No mockery in her words, but Tallora felt offense rise, nonetheless. "It would certainly make your life easier if I did. No, princess, it'll take more than mutilation to end me."

"There are healers to whom I could plead your case. My mother's wrath be damned—you'll have your fins regrown."

"How lovely. You'll mutilate me, then grovel to gain my sympathy." Tallora returned to the sand, laying down to face the stars, silently decreeing their conversation done.

"I tried to prevent this. I warned you of my mother's wrath. I pled with her to give you more time—"

"In your quest to tame me?" Tallora rolled over, the sand pressing against her torso. "To sway me with your unpleasant company? You're many things, princess, but I can't say charming is one of them."

Dauriel glared, but behind it, Tallora swore she saw a glimmer of regret, those silver eyes softer than velvet. "I could say the same."

"Forgive me. Captivity changes a girl."

"I can make your life comfortable—"

"Or you can make it hell, I know." Tallora waved her off, willing her to leave. "I'm a wild beast, remember? Can't be tamed. Now, kindly go away."

To her surprise, Dauriel listened, and once her footsteps disappeared, Tallora dug up her godly gift.

The vial radiated magic. Even Tallora felt it, with her limited awareness. She gazed fitfully at the surface high above; mutilated, she couldn't dream of reaching it. But a goddess wouldn't grant a gift only to let it fail. Tallora twisted the metal cap, and as she had hoped, the liquid stayed put.

Taking a breath for courage, Tallora drank the contents in one gulp.

Immediately, her throat closed. She gasped, her entire body suddenly wracked with pain. All her will went to subduing the urge to scream. Her vision glazed, dizziness stealing her focus. For a moment, her world went dark—

A warm voice sounded within her head: *Once submerged in the waters of your homeland, your form shall be restored.*

Tallora's eyes opened. The pain—all her pain—had gone away, save a burning sensation in her lungs. But when she opened her mouth, water rushed in to fill the space.

She could no longer breathe beneath the waves.

In the split second of panic, Tallora caught a glimpse of her lower half and saw she no longer had a tail, but two digits. When she tried to move them, like any limb, they reacted.

Tallora propelled herself to the barrier, reaching through with all her will and might—

And fell through.

Coughing, she gasped for air, her lungs singing at the influx of oxygen. Oh, pure air burned; it *burned.* Every motion felt staggered, these two new limbs clumsy and gangly, even prone on the ground. She turned on her bottom and inspected them closely. Scales remained at her feet, but soft, pleasant to the touch. They trailed up her legs, dissipating as they climbed her calves, disappearing entirely at her knees. Her coloring remained the same, perhaps more ingrained, less sleek—the color of sunset upon a white, sandy beach, pale and tipped with pink.

Unquestionably unique, but perhaps she'd be mistaken for a particularly exotic Celestial. Her hair remained white, clinging in sticky clumps to her face and back. Utterly nude, Tallora gripped one of the metal barriers for support as she pulled herself into standing. Her legs were strong, as strong as her tail, and though her first step stumbled, she did not fall.

Staella had delivered her boon. A fighting chance Tallora would have.

It would mean nothing if she could not escape the palace, however. The exotic beasts watched her as she slowly crept along the path, uneasy in her steps. The insect creature clicked in time with her footsteps, and she wondered if it purposefully meant to mask her awkward gait. She smiled at it, blowing a kiss as a silent thank you.

But past the door filtered light. No windows. No way to check what waited beyond. Tallora did as she'd seen the rest do and twisted the knob, stumbling back when it swung open.

When nothing pounced out, she peered through the door, noting the illuminate hallway and soft cloth covering the floor. Crystals hung from the immaculate, rich walls, lighting her path—a path stretching both left and right. A labyrinth awaited her.

Tallora stepped inside, the air cold against her sensitive, mortal skin. The hair on her arms—she had hair now?—rose, causing bumps to appear along her flesh. Water trailed behind, soaking the plush cloth beneath her feet, and when she heard voices, she ran the other away, wondering if the goddess had granted her balance as well as legs.

She passed doors, most closed, but some slightly ajar. Voices sounded in front now; panicked, Tallora ran inside one of the open doors, breathing unsettled.

Fire burned in a strange stone box set in the wall. Wooden shelves covered nearly every surface, filled with mortal books. The warmth in the room immediately soothed her skin, but then a voice said, "Who—"

Tallora gasped, frozen in the gaze of a young woman standing behind an array of furniture, a broom in her hand.

She held a finger to her lips. "Please don't—"

The girl screamed. Tallora nearly sobbed. When the girl held her broom aloft, prepared to fight, Tallora ran out, back into the hallway.

"You!"

Two guards stared wide-eyed at her appearance. She darted the opposite way, only to fall into the arms of two more as she rounded the hallway. "Let me go!" she shrieked, fighting with all her will, but her strength against four men was a mouse against a lion—pressed against their metal armor, she met a new sort of prison.

Still sobbing, she fought, despite her shattered hope. A swift punch to her face pulled a cry from her lips, her vision blurring.

"Is that—"

"How can it be—"

"What's this commotion? Release her, now!"

Tallora knew that voice, remembered that touch as it pulled her away from the men. She needn't see straight to know Dauriel supported her, laid her upon the ground. "What did you do?"

Tallora simply cried. Warmth stained her lip; a metallic taste assaulted her tongue.

"Don't stand there and gawk like a pack of animals—find a lady's maid and get this woman some clothing. And you! Fetch my mother. Tell her it's urgent."

Tallora's vision steadily settled, watching as the princess' features sharpened in her view. Something warm and rough covered her torso—she realized Dauriel had removed her leather coat and placed it atop her body. "So chivalrous," she spat to spite her tears.

"You're still a woman—"

"A woman now, am I? Not a beast in a pen?"

Dauriel ignored the bait—pity. Tallora so wanted to fight. When the princess pressed a white square of cloth to her bleeding lip, Tallora flinched at the stinging touch. Instinct rose, and she batted the cloth away; instead, Dauriel placed the blood-speckled cloth in her hand, silently bidding her to hold it to her lip.

Soon, the empress arrived, in tandem with a maid bearing a pile of dresses, and Tallora shut her eyes, prepared for the axe. They had no reason to keep her now, but to release her would be a blow to their pride. "What is this?" asked Vahla's voice, and Tallora felt Dauriel stand.

"I don't know what she did. The guards found her running down the hall and stopped her."

"This is witchcraft," the empress continued, and Tallora didn't presume to imagine the hate in her voice. "She should be burned for this."

"Perhaps, but we must decide what to do in the interim."

The tension in the air only grew with each shuddering, raw breath from Tallora's throat. "Get her dressed, for decency's sake. Then to the dungeons for the night. I shall converse with my council."

When Tallora refused to stand, Dauriel slipped her hands beneath her naked form and hauled her up.

Tallora had never pieced together, until that moment, how strong the woman must be, to lift her from the ground. With the lady's maid in tow, she was dragged to a nearby room—empty and filled with more books.

Tallora crumbled to the ground when Dauriel coaxed her to stand. "There's a time to be stubborn," the princess said. "But not when you're being offered the one kindness you'll get. Let the girl dress you, lest the men be tempted."

Tallora came from a society where all were nude—clothing only hindered her people's capacity to swim. No one gawked at her breasts beneath the sea. Merfolk physiology was often misunderstood by mortals who couldn't fathom that reproductive parts could hide behind a scaled sheath until aroused.

Here, every piece of Tallora lay exposed, and for the first time she felt fear for her humanoid body. There was truth in Dauriel's words. She offered back the blood-stained cloth, the bleeding in her lip finally staunched, but when Dauriel reached for it, she threw it to the ground with a sneer.

Soon, layers of cloth trapped in her a prison of fabric. Undergarments tightened with strings confined her torso, forcing her to stand straight. The white dress itched Tallora's sensitive skin, confining and annoying, tickling her legs as she walked. It might drive her mad, this added weight, and she missed the caress of the sea. The lady's maid brushed her hair, taming the crusted, salty locks. Dauriel looked away for all of it, facing the wall to preserve whatever dignity Tallora had left, or so she supposed.

Once acceptable, Tallora was pushed down the hallway, escorted by Dauriel and two guards she bid to follow.

They entered an odd room built into the wall, with clear windows revealing the outside. The Solviran Capital of Neolan spread out before her, luminous even at the late hour. The rich city boasted of money and power, those who lived in the upper districts prosperous and blessed.

The ground beneath her moved. Tallora gasped as the scenery outside shifted while the floor lowered, quickly moving them downward. "Don't touch the wall," was Dauriel's only comment, and Tallora obeyed.

The city disappeared as they traveled below the earth. Darkness engulfed them, save for crystals along the wall beyond the glass one encasing them, casting light and shadows across the small, moving room. When it stopped, a shrouded, underground path stretched before them. Dauriel grabbed her collar and pushed her out; Tallora stumbled, uneasy on her new legs, and collapsed.

On the ground, she noted the rough stone floor of the eerie hallway, dimly lit by similar crystal sconces. Dauriel's hand grasped her collar once more, forcing her up. Tallora coughed, choking on air once the grip released. "Keep walking."

Tallora obeyed, lost and afraid. They approached a great metal door, one that creaked in deafening tones as Dauriel shoved it open. She and the guards led Tallora to a longer hallway interspersed with windowless doors, spread widely apart.

From the rooms, Tallora heard quiet sobs, screaming, from some utter silence. Dauriel pushed open one and all but shoved her inside—to a vacant room with stone walls. "One cage for another," Tallora said, centered in the room. "Admittedly, I liked the first one better."

"How did you do it?" Dauriel asked, lingering in the doorframe. Her glare bore through to Tallora's soul, all softness having dissipated into the void.

"Witchcraft, as your mother said. Or perhaps divinity—depends on if my patron was a demon or angel." Tallora forced a smile, no joy in her eyes. "I took a chance, and I lost. But I'll rot here knowing I tried. Perhaps the gods will smite me quickly. It would be a greater mercy than your hateful company."

"I hold the key to your freedom," Dauriel replied, no kindness in her words. "My bargain stands. All you must do is give me your name."

Tallora spat at her feet. "My name is the only bit of value I have left. I'll die with it to spite you."

Dauriel said nothing. She simply slammed the door shut, engulfing Tallora in darkness.

In utter blackness, time flowed differently. Tallora lay on the stone ground, every part of her aching except her ego. There were small victories in her defeat. Perhaps she'd crack with time, give her captors all they asked, but today was not that day.

Time passed, but not enough for her stomach to ache from hunger. Footsteps sounded from beyond, and then the door creaked open. Blinded by the light, Tallora covered her eyes as she sat up, blinking at the unfamiliar pair of silhouettes in the doorframe. "The empress has summoned you before the council," a man said, and when she didn't immediately stand, he stepped inside and gripped her hair, forcing her to rise. Pain tore through her scalp; when he pushed her, she fell against the wall, biting back a sob.

"She's the prettiest thing in here," the other guard said, his leering eyes seeping discomforting cold through her limbs. "They'd never know if we—"

"If we're late and the general sees even a mark on her, she'll invoke Sha'Demoni law. Do you want a pike stuck up your shithole?"

The guard said nothing as the other grabbed Tallora yet again. "Move," he commanded, and Tallora obeyed, stumbling through the hallway with her arm in his painful grip.

This time, as she rode the lift, daylight rose upon the horizon, blinding as it pierced through the glass. They stopped at the first floor of the castle. Tallora was all but dragged through a spacious hall, then forced to stop behind enormous double doors. They parted at their entrance.

Within the round room, the Solviran Royal Council sat at an enormous, crescent moon table. Empress Vahla sat at the center with her husband to her right, his silver eyes a match to hers, and Tallora wondered, knowing the Solviraes' history of incest, just how much blood these two shared. General Khastra looked bored at the empress' left, and behind her was propped an enormous crystal hammer, taller than even the general by far. Beside her was the magister, and seated next to him was the priest to Ilune—Rel. A large, ugly bird ominously surveyed the scene beside him, its head almost reptilian, eyes black and beady.

Dauriel sat beside her father, her gaze fixed on Tallora. A woman sat next to her, bearing robes with star-like sigils—so this was Greyva, Priestess of Neoma. Upon her shoulder was a snow-white owl, gazing upon the scene with far more intelligence than any bird should have. Tallora knew of gods bestowing animal companions to their chosen servants and wondered if these birds were more than they seemed.

The guards shoved Tallora forward, then waited by the door, supervising the exchange.

Vahla glared from her throne, hands white as they gripped the other. "This is not a crime, but it is an insult, willfully done to spite me. We've decided you lack the power to have done this on your own. My question, then, is who aided you?"

Tallora shivered at the center of the room, still half-chilled from the dungeon. Her gaze traveled to each council member, their expressions ranging from awe to confusion to absolute distaste—save for the general, who looked merely bored.

"Who aided you, Mermaid?"

Tallora dared to face the empress and straightened her stance, realizing that to tell the truth might be to her benefit. "Goddess Staella."

"Oh?" Vahla said, skepticism etched into her face.

"I prayed to her for liberation. She gave me the chance to save myself."

"By turning you into a human girl?" Vahla studied her figure, raising an eyebrow. She spared a disparaging glance for Tallora's bare feet peeking out from her skirt. "Not quite useless, however. Still exotic enough to impress—perhaps more, now. Understand, I do not believe for a moment that Staella blessed you with legs, priestess or not. But I am willing to wait for a truthful answer, assuming you work for your keep."

Tallora wondered if her continued life depended on whether or not she was a priestess but decided to not correct them just yet. "Or you could release me, given I'm not fit to be a pet any longer."

"Not a pet, no. But perhaps a present to Moratham. Or Tholheim—dwarves are easily swayed by useless trinkets." The silence lingered, punctuating the threat. "Or simply entertainment for visiting ambassadors. We employ a few girls for that, and you're as pretty as they come. With the skirmishes going on at the southern border, I anticipate a letter from Moratham any day now—and they love to partake of our courtesans."

Tallora didn't dare to look away, though the words echoed in her head, weighing down her resolve. Perhaps this had been a mistake.

"My point," Vahla continued, "is you haven't won. We've prepared a room for you, in the interim. My daughter will continue heading your supervision, assuming she can be trusted to not nearly lose you a second time."

Despite the victory of Dauriel's humiliation, Tallora felt no joy.

"Dauriel, take her. You have your orders."

Dauriel stood from her chair, approaching with no ceremony. She simply grabbed Tallora's wrists, snapping a gold-plated shackle on each. A final one around her neck pulled tears to Tallora's eyes.

In silence, she cried before her captors until Dauriel tugged on the chain attaching the three cursed shackles to her body. Tallora stumbled forward, weighed down by gold and disgrace.

Chapter V 🐚

Tallora was shoved into a bath where a legion of lady's maids scrubbed her body of salt and grime, primped and preened her hair until it shone like a lustrous pearl. She no longer smelled of the sea and sand, but of . . . *jasmine,* as one maid had said. Whoever that was.

"Goddess Staella, grant me patience."

Now, chained to a bed fit for royalty, stuffed in layers of confining cloth, Tallora sat upon a cloud, sparing passing glances to the sunlight beyond. Though exhausted, her body trembled, the empress' words echoing through her mind.

It had taken all her will to stop crying. Were it not for Dauriel reading at the desk at the other end of the room, she might still be. The princess' leg bounced incessantly beneath her chair.

Restless, that one.

"You don't have to stay here," Tallora said softly, and she lifted her chains for show. The leash attached to the foot of the bed, so while she could comfortably sleep, she couldn't walk more than a few steps away. "I'm not going anywhere."

"You grew legs," Dauriel replied, her eyes fixed on her book. The symbols written on the cover meant nothing to Tallora. "Next thing we know, you'll sprout wings and fly away. My mother won't take that chance."

"So you're attached to me?"

"For a few days. Until you can be trusted elsewhere."

Tallora slowly fell backwards, her body sinking into the bed. The room was spectacular, with its gilded décor and velvet curtains. Though she was a prisoner, the suite was suited for a princess. "Like the whorehouse, right?"

"You won't be taken to the whorehouse."

Dauriel sounded almost bored; Tallora bristled in offense. "Your mother said—"

"The *courtesans* live in the palace. It's a comfortable life."

Tallora grimaced, the words souring any want for humor. "I'm sure you've helped them earn their keep over the years."

She felt Dauriel's eyes, but she couldn't summon a smile despite having stabbed a nerve. "They are not concubines—"

"Right, right. I'm certain you pay them handsomely for the honor of sucking their tits." Dauriel said nothing this time; Tallora dared to sit up and saw the princess' thinly veiled frown, trapped behind a blush as red as the velvet curtains. "If I let you suck mine, will it save me from being carted off to Moratham?"

Dauriel kept her stare at the book.

Tallora accepted that her next maneuver might get her thrown into the dungeon. With a coy twist of her lip, she leaned forward, letting a bit of the bodice fall open—as much as she could, rather, given that servant attire hardly lent itself to seduction. She'd try anything for the chance of gaining power over this hateful woman. "What would I have to let you do to me to gain a few favors? I'm going to die here; at least let me enjoy myself."

Again, Dauriel said nothing, but Tallora saw a twitch in her frown.

"Do you prefer your whores chained up?" She spared a glance for her shackles, then took the chain in her mouth, widening her eyes like a clownfish. "I couldn't fight if I wanted to," she said, teeth holding the chain. "Not that I'd try, unless that's what would get you hot—"

"What are you doing?" Dauriel glared from behind her book, eyes sharp.

Tallora let the chain drop from her mouth, coy gaze turning severe. "Better to face the demon I know than the demon I don't. You said yourself you like pretty girls, and I'd rather be fucked by you than an ambassador from Moratham."

"Funny," Dauriel spat, dropping the book, "because I seem to recall you'd have to shut your eyes and think of home to stomach me." The massive book reverberated against the table. "I could have any whore in this city, and she'd pay me for the honor of a Solviraes hand up her cunt—do you truly think I'd sully my bed with some fish-stenched harlot desperate for a favor? I can enjoy your tits from a distance, thank you."

She hadn't expected Dauriel's insults to actually hurt. "Not to correct you, but I smell like jasmine," she muttered. Her back hit the sheets, embarrassment paling to her fear.

Dauriel was quiet for a daunting amount of time, and the reality of Tallora's damning situation settled into her soul. She wished to hide in the blankets, like the seaweed of home, but that would require moving, thus jingling her shackles and drawing Dauriel's attention.

The princess finally did speak, though it held nothing but ire. "The plan is for you to follow me wherever I go for a few days, until my mother deems you fit to be left alone. My point is if you want to sleep, now's the time—I'll be training in a few hours, and you get to watch."

"Lucky me," Tallora mused, but she suspected after their rather uncomfortable altercation that she wouldn't be molested in her sleep. She shut her eyes, suspecting sleep would be a far-off thing, but passed out within minutes.

Clanking chains pulled Tallora from a fitful rest. Her eyelids held the weight of crushing ocean waves. When she managed to lift them, Dauriel stared down from above. "If I'm late, I'll be forced to run the entire perimeter of the palace. Let's go."

Tallora groaned as she sat up, head pounding, stomach growling from hunger. Her mouth felt . . . dry. She smacked her lips, grimacing at the stickiness of her tongue. "I don't feel well."

"Dinner will be after. You'll live until then." Dauriel offered some strange sort of sleeve. "Put these on. Your feet are probably sensitive."

Tallora studied the gift, touched its rough bottom, and said, "This is a shoe, correct? It's very small." Dauriel plucked it from her grasp and gently stole her foot, holding it up as she slipped the shoe on. Soft fabric enveloped her foot. "I've never worn a shoe before," she whispered, flicking her ankle about. "Why does it look different than your shoe?"

"Boots are for work. Those are slippers I stole from my mother." Dauriel's smile was not kind, but not quite wicked either. "She won't notice."

As Dauriel went to detach her chain from the bed, Tallora steadied herself on her feet, weighed down by these 'slippers.' Between clothing and shoes, she wondered if this were a greater torture than her watery pen.

Then, Dauriel yanked her along, and Tallora glowered as she trudged behind her, still unsteady on her feet.

She was grateful for the silence. Tallora put to memory the turns in the hallway, counted the time spent on the lift as they descended to the ground floor. The entry hall they appeared in was familiar—she recalled, staring at the double doors beyond, that the council chamber was behind them.

Sunset would be in only a few more hours. Fresh air caressed Tallora's face, lifted her hair, the familiarity of it soothing to her scared soul. Dauriel led her to what appeared to be a small coliseum, the stone walls round and wrapping to hide whatever lay inside. Dauriel pushed open the great wooden doors and beckoned for Tallora to pass through before letting them slam behind them.

She came upon a dirt clearing filled with the pungent scents of sweat and blood. The general sat idly upon a bench not a few feet away, cleaning mud from a longsword. Tallora heard the distant chattering of men behind the walls, but General Khastra sat alone, grinning at their entrance.

"So the mermaid is to join us?" Khastra beckoned them to her, and Dauriel followed, standing straight as a rod in the general's presence. "Have a seat; the chains look heavy."

Tallora obeyed. Dauriel moved to follow, but Khastra grabbed her shoulder instead. "Not you. Change and find your sword."

"I'm not supposed to leave her—"

"Dauriel, she would not be stupid enough to try and escape in my presence." Khastra spared Tallora a smile, even as Dauriel gave a swift, obedient nod.

"Yes, General." The princess jogged to another door, the one filled with the men, and disappeared.

Khastra sat, her massive bulk not quite touching Tallora as she said, "Are they feeding you?"

"They haven't yet. Dauriel said dinner is after training."

"You tell me if they do not."

Khastra returned her attention to polishing the sword on her lap. Tallora marveled at the handiwork—it had been etched in a filigree motif, subtle yet flawless. "You're the only one here who treats me like a person."

"As a half-demon among Celestial royals, I had to earn respect, despite being handpicked for this job. I understand what it means to be treated as lesser."

"A half-demon?" Tallora inspected her unique physique—her sheer size set her apart from others with demonic blood, but aside from the tattoos, nothing about her seemed particularly foreign among De'Sindai—horns and hooves and tails were common. "That's not a lineage many can claim."

"Nor is it a lineage I seek to. Wickedness runs in my blood. I do not aspire for righteousness, but there is merit in seeking good."

"I can't imagine your blood being any more wicked than the Solviran royals," Tallora replied, bitterness staining her tongue.

Khastra, however, laughed. "Take care how you speak. Empress Vahla is a volatile bitch. I can say that; I am many millennia older than her bloodline. You, however, could make life much worse for yourself if you said that to the wrong person." She lowered her voice, conspiracy twisting her elegant lips as she added, "You can say it to Dauriel."

"I've noticed some friction—"

Tallora stopped her words at Dauriel's return. She'd tell herself it was in fear of being overheard, but in truth, though Dauriel's musculature certainly paled to the general's, Tallora gawked like a fool at the definition of her arms.

She wore flexible breeches, boots, and a simple tunic revealing her shoulders and arms. Twin swords rested in scabbards on her back. Tallora hated her, which made the realization that Dauriel had an exceptionally well-built physique that much more aggravating.

Khastra stood up, adopting an aura Tallora shied from, standing taller than the sun. "In your stance," she barked, and Dauriel stood as straight as any soldier facing their superior. "To the center. Today, we run drills."

Tallora knew nothing of swordplay. Living in the ocean, weapons of choice were spears and harpoons, perhaps chains and nets to strangle an opponent. She understood little of it; her mother was a merchant.

But it mesmerized her, watching the duo. Dauriel stood as a statue at times while Khastra fine-tuned her motions, and other times moved with the fluidity of peaceful ocean waves, graceful and smooth. She held the swords with perfect control, though her muscles strained to hold so still as Khastra critiqued every minute shift in stance.

Tallora glared with perturb the entire time, steaming about those biceps.

In that hour, Tallora didn't see anything she would've called 'fighting,' but Dauriel returned drenched in sweat, and Khastra smacked her on the back. "Your foundations have grown lazy. We will drill this again tomorrow—if I do not see improvement, you will mop the armory. Now, go clean up."

Dauriel managed a nod, her breathing too heavy to form a reply. Once she'd left earshot, Tallora muttered, "I'll admit, it looked more like dancing than battle stances, but I don't know much of dancing either."

To Tallora's relief, Khastra chuckled. "I re-teach the foundational stances every few months. Soldiers get lazy, as do princesses. Everyone wants to fight; no one wants to learn."

"How long has she been training with you?"

"Since she was fifteen. Eight years. Long enough to not make foolish errors."

Khastra's scathing commentary filled Tallora's heart with spiteful glee. "In here, she's no better than anyone else," Tallora mused, staring at the door where the princess had left. "You don't show her any deference."

"I do, in her realm. But here, she is in mine."

The sky bore shades of indigo, yet bursts of light clung to the top of the coliseum. Tallora's stomach rumbled. "Is this normal for Solviran royals?"

Khastra shook her head. "I invited her to come and train, pushed her when she said no. There is a self-assurance that comes from building the strength and skill to fight. Thought it might help her body and spirit to recover. As always, I am right."

Tallora turned her attention to the general, curious at her words. "Can I ask what happened?"

"It is not a secret," Khastra said, softer now. She kept her proud stance even when sitting, though peace settled upon her elegant countenance as she faced the sky. "A sickness nearly stole Dauriel. It ravaged her body for years. Many times, healers would come, curing her or so we thought. It would come back, whatever curse was eating her. It was not until a chance visit from a Sun Elven refugee that her life was saved. He was a doctor in his homeland, one of the lucky few to escape the onslaught of The Endless Night."

"What's that?"

"A long story—do ask me some other time. But it was not magic that healed Dauriel—merely surgery. He saved her life, but years and years of sickness will break a person, and then after, when she was shamed by her own family for choosing to live."

"Why would she be shamed for living?"

In the distance, Dauriel emerged from where she'd left, hair falling in wet sheets down her back. Khastra replied, "Perhaps you should ask her. I was only privy to overhearing it; she would give a better account." She then turned to the approaching princess. "Your prisoner is hungry."

Dauriel wore different clothing—similar to her typical garb, but lighter material, her black shirt billowing where it didn't cling to her body from her damp hair. Tallora had never seen it down; the dark locks were longer than she had thought, nearly surpassing her own. "She's not the only one." Dauriel picked up the end of the chain from the bench. "I'm sure the kitchen will have something."

"If your mother objects, you tell me. I will make certain she eats."

An odd sort of ally, but an ally nonetheless. Tallora followed Dauriel out, her heart more at ease.

57

Someday, Tallora supposed she would be used to being treated like an animal. But as she sat on the floor beside the great table, her leash placed in the lap of her royal escort, she couldn't help but feel a little insulted.

Fortunately, while she didn't recognize the strange array of edibles before her, it all smelled delicious, and when she'd placed a cut of an unknown meat in her mouth, she'd nearly cried for its savory, delicious flavor. Some sort of soft, sand-colored brick sat beside it—bread, they'd called it. They most certainly did not have bread beneath the ocean, and she adored how it deflated in her mouth. Greenery accompanied it, as delicious as the rest. Tallora ate her fill, eavesdropping on mindless, petty gossip.

Dauriel said little. Little Eniah picked at his food while Empress Vahla said nothing. Instead, Dauriel's father—whose name was Ilaeri, Tallora finally overheard—told tale after tale of court drama. "The man had the audacity to plead for intercession—the *audacity*. There were countless testimonies to his character, most notably the heart-wrenching account from the little girl herself. But, law is law. To no one's surprise, Staella said absolutely nothing to that monster, merely stepped down from her pedestal to comfort the victim. When Neoma proclaimed him guilty, Ilune slew him then and there on the steps of the temple." Ilaeri 'huffed,' sounding almost perturbed. "The absolute audacity."

This brought a question Tallora had never considered the possibility of—but why would the goddesses appear in a temple?

The time for questions came that night, after Dauriel escorted her to bed. The stars outside offered only a paltry bit of light—the candle at her bedside illuminated the room, comparatively.

When instructed to change clothes, Tallora managed to unbutton her dress, letting it crumple unceremoniously to the floor. But she struggled with the strings at her back, trapping her in this *corset* or whatever they had called it, her rising frustration leading her to mutter curses beneath her breath.

Not quietly enough, however—from where Dauriel stood, facing the wall, Tallora heard a seething sigh, followed by a quiet, "Do you need help?"

Tallora's pride screamed *no,* but the part of her wanting a proper night's rest pushed it aside. "Yes."

Dauriel averted her eyes to the floor as she turned, visibly stiff when she approached and stopped behind Tallora. With expert skill, she made swift work of the strings tying Tallora into the undergarment, tugging here and there to quickly loosen it.

Tallora took a deep breath, her body relieved at the flood of oxygen. "You're good at that," she said, letting the undergarment fall to the floor. She was left in a simple white gown, and she wondered why in the world more layers were required for public decency. "Practice?"

She didn't have to see Dauriel's eyeroll to hear it in her words. "I've worn corsets. I know how to remove them."

To Tallora's surprise, Dauriel gathered her discarded dress, bundling it carefully as she placed it and the rest of her clothing onto a shelf on the wall. Tallora didn't envy her trousers—the bloomers around her hips and thighs were annoying enough—but she did wonder. "I don't think I've seen a single other woman in this castle dressed like you. Unless I'm counting Khastra, but she was wearing armor."

Dauriel's expression remained impassive. "I prefer dressing this way."

As Dauriel unbuttoned the front of her doublet, Tallora slouched on the mattress, grateful for the ability to bend her waist again. Rather than watch the princess undress, she thought of dinner, of Consort Ilaeri's odd tale. When Dauriel approached—still wearing her billowing black undershirt and trousers—Tallora asked, "What was your father talking about at dinner? Gods don't simply appear."

Dauriel sat on the bed beside her as she removed her shoes. "It's the right of every citizen condemned to death to plead for intercession from Staella, who may choose to mediate their case to Neoma herself. It's most often used by the falsely accused as a final hope, or for those with justified causes to beg for mercy."

"But they truly do appear?"

"They do. The temple holds a thin veil between Solvira and Celestière. They can manifest without a host."

It was rare that a mortal would ever host a god and allow them to use their body as their own. Most often, the host died during or after. Tallora contemplated the thought, curious at this foreign sort of justice. "And if Staella will plead on their behalf, are they acquitted?"

"Yes. Neoma serves as judge and jury, but the risk is the executioner, Ilune, the God of Death, who will whisper in her other ear for them to die. To be slain by Ilune means an eternity of undead servitude, but to be spared by Staella means to walk free. Some people find it worth the risk."

"And the man today—Staella wouldn't hear him?"

Dauriel shook her head. "He was foolish to ask, given Staella's nature. Crimes against children are among the greatest evils, in her view. Now he's Ilune's, and good riddance."

"I didn't realize she held such influence."

"Staella only whispers, but she whispers to a thunderstorm." Dauriel stood up from the bed, and approached a fanciful wardrobe, from which she pulled what appeared to be a thick, rolled-up blanket. She let it unravel, and Tallora realized it was a sort of bed.

"Are you going to sleep on the ground?"

"I am."

"Why?" Tallora was ignored as Dauriel laid herself down, content by appearances. "I'm your prisoner."

Dauriel stared at the ceiling, hands clasped over her stomach. "Chains can't be comfortable. You should have a fighting chance of getting some sleep."

"That's inordinately kind of you."

Dauriel chuckled as she caught Tallora's eye. "Chaining you to your bed is a kindness? By Neoma's Flame—you've already grown comfortable with imprisonment."

"Only a short time more," Tallora said as she fell back into her plush bed, unused to this concept of a 'pillow' but finding she rather liked it. "I'll be shipped off to Moratham, remember?"

The instant change in Dauriel's countenance drew Tallora's scrutiny; a glower overtook her features. "Solvira shouldn't be dealing with them anyway—rival gods. The Moon stole the Stars from the Desert Sands."

Tallora knew the story in passing—Neoma and Staella had not always been wed. Once, the Goddess of Stars had belonged to Morathma, Jewel of the Desert, though he wasn't a god Tallora knew much about. "Didn't realize he still held a grudge."

Dauriel resumed laughing, softer now. "Gods never forget."

"I suppose I'll do better as a courtesan in Solvira than a concubine in Moratham," she said joylessly. "Less hot. Mermaids don't like deserts, and I don't have to explain why."

The princess said nothing. Tallora listened for her breathing to settle, to fall into unconsciousness, but then a voice whispered, "Perhaps I have done you wrong."

Tallora rolled over, as well as she could with her chained wrists. Staring again at the ceiling, Dauriel's features flickered in shadow. "Because I have legs you can actually show a shred of regret? That's rather disgusting."

She was met with silence. When she moved to roll back over, Dauriel said, "I mean as I said. Upon my mother's death, you're free."

"We never agreed on that. I never gave you my name."

"Your name be damned; I'm committing now. It's my mother who wanted it, but it'll do her well to not get what she wants."

Tallora felt no gratitude, only fury. "Are you waiting for a 'thank you?' Certainly you'll spite your bitch of an empress, but defy her? Even when you're the one who's ruined my life? That'd be too much to ask, of course. You claim you're saving my life; you're only saving yours."

She fell back into bed. From below she heard a whispered, "I . . ."

And nothing else. The candlelight vanished, drenching them in darkness. Tallora shut her eyes, willing sleep to steal her quickly.

Chapter VI 🐚

Tallora was awoken by her day clothes being unceremoniously dropped beside her. "If you miss breakfast, it means I miss breakfast," Dauriel said as Tallora rubbed her eyes of sleep. "Don't make me miss breakfast."

Thus resumed the struggle of Tallora versus the damned corset. Thankfully, hunger made her forget her pride. "Help," she said, unable to even keep the boned garment from falling.

In silence, Dauriel made quick work of the undergarment, swiftly tugging on the strings in practiced motions, and though Tallora was jostled forward and back, she felt no discomfort as the corset molded around her figure. Not too tight; just tight enough, even if she couldn't bend over.

Dauriel held the strings taut, pausing before she tied them off. "How does that feel?"

"Um . . ." Unsure of what the proper answer was, Tallora took a leap and finished with, ". . . secure?"

"Good enough, then."

Following Dauriel around was dull, for the most part. She was taken to libraries full of books she couldn't read—about which Dauriel was appalled.

"You cannot read?"

In one such room, Tallora sat beside a roaring fire, mesmerized by its motions. Books filled the shelves, along with a couch and a desk and chair. "Almost no one can read below the sea."

"How do you communicate?"

Tallora frowned at that. "By visiting our neighbors? There aren't nearly so many merfolk as there are humans and Celestials. Our history is almost entirely oral, save for the few who take it upon themselves to sit on rocks and transcribe it. Some have befriended humans who were kind enough to write it as it was relayed to them. Writing on stone is taxing."

Dauriel stared, jaw agape. "We must teach you, then."

"I don't believe men care if their whores can read."

Dauriel returned to reading, lips pursed and pouted. Tallora loved it when she struck a nerve.

The princess owned her world, walking through the palace in a fighter's stance. She radiated confidence, yet Tallora saw it falter in strange moments—any mention of Empress Vahla, especially praise, brought a twitch to her lip. When crossing paths with men, she puffed up her chest, feathers ruffled until they had gone, but at the passing of a particularly pretty maidservant, Dauriel casually ducked into a hallway to avoid her.

Which Tallora couldn't help but comment on. "Oh, she's lovely. Do you know her?"

Dauriel frowned and shook her head. In the expansive hallway, Tallora peeked back at the girl, careful to lower her voice. Her plot was to embarrass Dauriel—not get herself thrown off the roof.

"Remember that thing about Solviraes hands in ladies' . . ." She trailed off at Dauriel's icy glare, her silver eyes frosted with warning. "I just want to see if they really do pay you."

Dauriel ignored her and instead stepped along the hall, tugging at Tallora's chain when she faltered.

"So you're all talk? I'm honestly heartbroken. Those poor ladies, denied the awesome power of your bedroom prowess. How will they continue their dreary lives if you haven't fucked them into—"

When Dauriel yanked on Tallora's chain, she stumbled into the princess' stiff back. "You're provoking me."

"It's my only joy in life lately."

Not entirely true. Tallora would never admit it out loud but she enjoyed watching Dauriel spar with Khastra.

More of the same. Khastra ran drills, kept the princess in stone-like stances until Tallora saw her arms and legs visibly quiver. The precision of her motions truly was impressive, and when Khastra grinned and said she'd done well, Tallora knew it was a compliment well earned.

After dinner one night, Dauriel presented a small golden key—and unshackled her locks.

Tallora stared at her chafed wrists, rubbed her sore neck. "Why?"

"You need a bath, and you need new clothes," Dauriel said, quickly undoing the strings of her corset—it was a ritual by now. She plopped a pile of cloth into her arms with little ceremony. "It would have been sooner, but my mother was remiss to part with the key. Bath is drawn. Knock if you need help."

For the first time in days, Tallora was utterly alone.

It felt wonderful to be submerged in water without the groping hands of lady's maids. Soap was strange, but it soothed her skin, leaving her smelling like upper-world flowers.

Not fish. She sneered at the memory, scrubbing harder at her skin in response.

Stranger still, though, was the chance to actually *look* at her new figure. Humans were an odd breed. Tallora inspected the soft scales on her legs, nostalgic as she ran her hand across them. She wondered if she were all human within or merely where it mattered, contemplating the merit of having an exposed vulva.

Try as she might, she couldn't look at it on her own, though with some contorting of her flexible form, she managed to take a decent peek in the mirror. Strange little thing—didn't look too much different. Smaller, certainly. But what was the use of having it be so open? Were humans so droll that they needed such simple access?

Not a question she particularly wanted to ask, and certainly not to Dauriel.

She tried to make sense of the chemise she'd been left with, knowing how human clothing looked, but kept getting lost even after sticking her head through the largest opening. She had managed to remove the old one but getting in was a different sort of beast to fight.

After a few trying minutes, a knock interrupted her struggle. "Please tell me you didn't jump through the window."

Tallora spared a glance for the tiny opening in the ceiling. "I'm not small enough for that, unfortunately. I . . ." She swallowed her pride. "I'm not sure how to put this on."

The doorknob twisted; Dauriel peeked inside as Tallora covered herself with the fabric. She hoped her grin hid the blow to her ego. Rolling her eyes, Dauriel gestured for the gown.

Tallora handed it over, feeling exposed in the intimate light. Dauriel had seen her naked before, but never alone. Not like this, and not since finding out her new, threatened role in this castle. Instinctively, she brought her arms up to cover her breasts, as well as a slight twist of her hips to hide what was between her legs.

Dauriel hadn't noticed, or so she prayed, given the princess actively gathered the fabric of the gown. "I'm going to place this over your head," she said, more patient than Tallora would have expected.

Tallora forced her breathing to relax as Dauriel did so. The princess touched her wrist; when Tallora flinched, she said, "I'll guide your arms through the sleeves. I'm not going to touch you anywhere else."

Tallora prayed the candlelight hid her blush. Dauriel did as she said she would, gently leading Tallora's arms through the confining sleeves, then she tugged at the bottom of the gown so it draped down to her ankles. "You'll learn," she said simply, and when she left the washroom, Tallora followed like a duckling.

Of course, the shackles returned. Tallora's wrists protested, but she stoically grit her teeth, refusing to show any weakness. The end of her leash was attached to the bed, and Dauriel lit a candle before setting up her make-shift cot.

"I take back what I said."

Dauriel looked up, visibly confused at Tallora's opener.

"You weren't awkward at all helping me dress. It's not new to you. You've touched women before."

"Are you known for being such a cunt back at home?"

Tallora winked as she laid herself down. "It's my name. You can tell your mother that."

When Dauriel didn't reply, Tallora realized she felt oddly uncomfortable. She watched the princess finish draping blankets over the cot and said, "You really don't care much for finery."

Dauriel didn't look at her. "I prefer adventure."

"I once snuck out of my bed and joined a boy I was hopelessly in love with on a quest to touch Yaleris' tail—well, as much as I could be in love at fourteen." She winked, but Dauriel still wouldn't face her. "We didn't make it even halfway to the Canyon of the Great Mother, but we did manage to creep back into our homes before sunrise. Does that count as adventure?"

"I . . ." Dauriel looked adorably confused. "I don't know what 'Yaleris' is."

"The blue dragon? He lives beneath the sea. Once a year, all my people go to pay homage to him and thank him for protecting us. If he weren't so shy, I think he'd be king." Tallora smiled, for she, too, had met the dragon and remembered how his great scales had glittered in the sunlight, sleek with water.

"I didn't think dragons were peaceful."

"Yaleris is."

Dauriel, again, fell silent, and this time Tallora let it be.

Dauriel eventually followed through on her odd threat—the next morning, she called for a writing tutor for Tallora. "Who knows how long you'll be here," she said, laughing at Tallora's bafflement as she inspected a quill. "Writing is the most powerful tool in the world, if you perfect it."

Oddly touched, Tallora accepted the strange offer, spending the afternoon clumsily scrawling letters and stumbling over syntax.

Later, Dauriel led her wordlessly to an enormous chamber in the center of the palace—one with walls to touch the stars, filled with books upon shelves as high as the ceiling. Breathless, Tallora longed to explore this strange new place but didn't have the opportunity to look for long. Dauriel escorted her along the wall to a door.

Within this new room, Tallora saw emblems of beauty. "This is the Hall of Relics," Dauriel said, gesturing to the pedestals. They filled the expansive room, evenly spaced in a grid-like display. Some bore swords and shields, others displayed art, and some were objects Tallora knew nothing of, perhaps trinkets of magic. Her eyes settled upon the side wall with a massive mural, filled with countless tentacle appendages and a great, golden eye in the center. "Thousands of years' worth of Solviran victories are celebrated here. Look up."

Tallora did, and nearly gasped as her heart skipped.

Above, in immaculate condition, perfectly assembled and displayed by ropes, was a skeleton dominating the ceiling. A dragon, Tallora knew, with a wingspan to rival the sky and in whose palm she might have easily sat.

"That was once Rulira, who inhabited the highest peak in the Mountains of Kaas, across the sea. I'm told she wielded storms and lightning and had a roar of literal thunder. My great-great grandfather led the battalion who brought her down. He wanted her treasure—one of the Old God's orbs, the same used to cause the Convergence. My family keeps it, but it's too dangerous to be displayed in here."

The tale felt more like a burden than a heroic exploit. "The Mountains of Kaas are across the sea, in Zauleen—well away from Solviran territory. Why would they hunt her down?"

"As I said, they sought her treasure." Dauriel joined Tallora's gaze, staring at the remains of the great dragon. "There are rumors of a dragon in a volcanic crater in Moratham. Politically, it would be difficult to reach but wouldn't that be a legacy? To be the second Solviraes to defeat a..." Her voice trailed off, and Tallora realized she looked at her alone now. "Are you all right?"

Tallora forced a smile, but truthfully she wanted to weep on Rulira's behalf. She did not know if the dragon had been wicked, but when she saw the skeleton, she thought only of Yaleris, wise and ancient... and patient and kind. "I've given away the secret of Yaleris' location. I suppose you'll be after him next."

"Not if you're going to make that face." Dauriel frowned, her thin lips turning stark white. "I was under the impression that dragons were wicked beings."

"Not Yaleris." Tallora, with her shackled wrists and neck, looked again to the dragon, though she struggled with the gold-plated weight.

"I apologize—"

Tallora nearly wrenched her neck at those words. "You what?"

The Solviran Princess' gaze held remorse—the same Tallora saw whenever Dauriel had the moral sense to feel the least bit bad about ruining her life. "I didn't mean to upset you."

"Honestly—" Tallora cut herself off, realizing that to insult Dauriel wouldn't bring her vindictive joy. Not this time. She swallowed her words and instead whispered, "Can we leave?"

Dauriel led her out. Tallora refused to look back.

A few days followed of tentative peace and boredom, with Tallora struggling to understand the difference between vowels and consonants.

"Every word must have a vowel? But not a consonant? That might mean something to me if I knew more than three letters by sight."

Training was the highlight of each day.

Power lay behind every move of Khastra's expansive musculature, each motion precise and perfect, yet fluid in a way her build should not have allowed. She wielded the same length of sword as her pupil, comically small at her size.

Despite what Dauriel lacked in experience compared to the general, her speed and precision was remarkable. Even Tallora could see that, watching as Dauriel slashed through the miniscule cracks in Khastra's armor, catching her at her weak points. Her curved blades became extensions of her own hands as they moved with unique grace. She kept her distance, nimble on her booted feet as she parried and dodged, only landing strikes she could assuredly make.

Khastra's sheer size forced Dauriel to stand away—but after a close call to her neck, near enough to slashing her throat that Tallora wondered if the general would *actually* kill her, she saw a familiar glow suddenly seep from the pores of Dauriel's skin. Silver flame rose to coat her swords, fire swirling as she parried and stepped closer, closer—

One step too close—*"Oomph!"*

Dauriel fell to the ground, swords dropped, fire dissipating. The dusty imprint of a hoof coated her leather armor. Tallora brought her hand to her mouth, not daring to laugh until the general herself cackled in the open arena. "Your whole body is a weapon,

Princess. As is mine." The half-demon offered a hand; Dauriel remained on the ground and moaned. "We will be done for the day. Now, get up."

Dauriel stumbled into standing, coughing blood onto the ground. "I need a healer," she groaned, and Khastra simply pushed her forward, no sympathy in the gesture.

"Cracked ribs will not kill you. Your mermaid will escort you." She looked to Tallora. "Kindly scream if she faints."

"More likely I'll let her bleed out and die."

Khastra chuckled as she stepped away. Dauriel supported herself against the wall and said, "You're enjoying this."

"Immensely. That aside, if I didn't hate you so much, I'd say you were impressive. That fire was spectacular."

"If I didn't hate you, I'd admit to being flattered." She managed a pained smile. "Come on. It's not too far a walk." Tallora held up the end of her leash, but Dauriel shook her head. "I need to hold my insides inside."

Tallora giggled and walked beside her, not an equal but at least a step up from where she was before.

It was as Dauriel said—not too far to walk, and only a floor up on the lift. Within minutes, Dauriel sat with her shirt lifted to her diaphragm as a woman 'tisk tisk-ed' at the state of her bruised stomach. Tallora would never say aloud that Dauriel had impressive abdominals for an uplander. For merfolk, lithe physiques were standard, save for their cousins up north who developed a layer of blubber to protect them from the chill. Tallora had seen every sort of body size in her short stay in Solvira, and she knew enough of beauty to realize Dauriel had worked for her imposing physique.

It did nothing to endear her to Tallora. But she did enjoy watching the minute motions of her stomach and obliques—human physiology was fascinating, more so since she'd adopted a human form of her own.

"The general is rougher with you than the men," the healer mused. "Plenty of bleeding cavities from them—never blunt-force trauma. That'll kill you quicker."

"She would never do it purposefully."

The healer simply snubbed her nose. Her hands glowed, and when she placed them upon Dauriel's bare skin, the princess stiffened, face contorting in pain until it quite suddenly relaxed, peace settling upon her countenance as the bruising disappeared. "Lucky you can't have children already—the internal damage nearly ruptured—"

"That's enough," Dauriel said, darker than Tallora had ever heard.

Odd.

A curious question tugged at her mind, the healer's statement having pieced together a hypothesis she hesitated to explore. But what more did she have to lose?

That night, when Dauriel settled in her bed, Tallora said, "Khastra once told me you were sick for years. You nearly died."

"I nearly died several times. What about it?"

"She said you were shamed for choosing to live. Why?"

She heard Dauriel's breath, could nearly feel her shudder. "The whole world knows. You might as well know too." Dauriel stared at the ceiling, half-shadowed from the candlelight. "Do mermaids bleed? To conceive children, I mean. Menstruation."

"We do. Every four months."

"Humans bleed every month, and I have enough human blood in me. When I was twelve, I had my first monthly—it lasted for weeks, and every second was agony." Dauriel laid an absent hand upon her womb. "My mother said I was dramatic, that this was a curse from the Old Gods every woman bore. But once I began fainting, the healers were called.

"I spent years of my life in bed," she continued, bitterness curling her lip. "No one knew what was wrong, deemed it a curse in my womb. Priests from the Theocracy of Sol Kareena were called, renowned for healing magic, but they met the same failure. I simply learned to live in pain, but then I started fading. By fifteen, I was dying."

She said nothing for a tense moment. Tallora feared she would cry, but Dauriel steeled her jaw instead. "Khastra told me," Tallora whispered, "you were saved by an elven doctor."

Dauriel nodded. "Elves have no magic. Instead, they understand the world in ways the rest of us simply don't, the convenience of magic crippling us, ultimately. He said if they removed . . . *everything*, I would be cured. It should have been an easy decision. Instead, the stigma of a descendent of the Goddess of Fertility and Creation being barren was too much for my mother to take; she begged for me to die instead."

Tallora thought of her own mother, surely worried to tears or worse beneath the sea. She thought of her mother who taught her to cook, to pray, to love by example, who had cared for Tallora's papa when he'd slowly fallen apart. Her mother wasn't perfect, no—she couldn't keep a proper count of wares, nor stay up past midnight without losing her temper.

But Empress Vahla had begged for her own child to die to spare *herself* the embarrassment.

"Needless to say," Dauriel continued, "I had the surgery. Recovery took no time at all—once everything was out, the healers did the rest, and I was running around the castle by evening. I was free. I'd hardly left my bedroom in years, and I wanted nothing more than to explore the world I'd missed."

"That's why you like adventure," Tallora teased, but Dauriel didn't smile. Her own joy faded. "Your mother never forgave you."

Dauriel shook her head, jaw stiff.

"She would have birthed Eniah after that—was it because you abdicated the throne?"

Dauriel's curt response of, "Yes," bespoke the end of their conversation, but Tallora took pride in her new reputation of being absolutely un-charming.

"What about your father?"

"You think my father cares? Better yet—you think he would stand up to *her?*" Dauriel scoffed, but a bitter smile tugged at her lip. "Adrael says it was like that when they were children as well. Mother would lord over him, tear his hair out when he said anything she didn't like."

Tallora again remembered the scandalous rumors of Solviraes marriages and dared to ask, "So they've known each other a long time?"

"Most of their lives. They're cousins."

Tallora chose to believe that they were seventh cousins, even though she knew the Silver Fire would have never diluted so far. Still, this stark taboo seemed absolutely normal, if Dauriel's nonchalance was to be believed.

"Theirs is a political marriage—they live very separate lives. Between you and me, I'm fairly certain having to conceive another child together was the real source of conflict."

Dauriel smiled to set a good mood, but Tallora saw it was forced. "She still made you feel like you were lesser."

Dauriel's hands fell to cradle her womb, protective of the barren space. She whispered, "It saved me from being sold into my own inevitable political marriage."

"But your mother still—"

"My mother did *everything* to destroy the miracle of my recovery," Dauriel spat, and Tallora realized she'd punctured a flood. "Cried that I was an embarrassment to her, that the whole world would've mourned my death but now laughed at the pitiful life I led. She conceived Eniah and never once shut up about how magical pregnancy was, how *blessed* she was to bear this child instead of me—"

Dauriel's mouth snapped shut. The hand at her abdomen tightened into a fist. She sat up, she blew out the candle on the table, and in the darkness fell back into bed.

"Her words mean nothing," Tallora whispered.

Dauriel remained silent. Tallora saw the barest hints of silver light flicker with each breath.

In the ensuing silence, Tallora's heart pushed her forward. Her hand brushed against Dauriel, who immediately stiffened. Tallora took her hand in hers and squeezed it, lingering at the touch as she said, "No one is worthless; certainly not you. I hate you, but even I can see your value."

Secluded in darkness, Dauriel wrenched her hand back. "We're done talking about this."

The conversation might have ended. Spurned, Tallora settled back into bed, the lingering ghost of Dauriel's hand in hers a daunting thing, but to her surprise, she heard a whisper. "I'm sorry."

"You've said that quite a lot lately."

"This isn't something I talk about. A word or two to Khastra perhaps, but I can't . . ." She sighed, and Tallora felt tension rise once again, the apparent internal battle made manifest. "You're easy to talk to. Your kindness is out of character, but not unappreciated."

Tallora smiled at that, realizing she felt oddly at ease, despite her chains and the woman she'd happily strangle with them not a foot away. "I think you secretly like being abused."

To her delight, she heard the princess chuckle. "Damn. Keep this up, and I'll let you out of your shackles by the end of the week."

"I didn't realize you were taking notes. Are you saying you like me now?"

Dauriel scoffed. "You're like a leech—no matter what I do you keep latching on."

"Terrible metaphor," Tallora said, shaking her head. "If I were a leech, I would have let you go

75

willingly. I'm more like a horse—the more you break me, the more I trust you."

She said it with a smile, but oh, the jest definitely fell flat. An awkward silence settled. To her surprise, Dauriel sat up. Illuminate silver flame rose from her hand as she touched the candle, sparking a flickering light, and from her trouser pocket she withdrew the golden key. She stared a moment, then sighed and said, "Do you swear you won't run?"

Tallora frowned. "I beg your pardon?"

"I'll release your shackles for the night. Do you swear you won't run?"

Tallora looked to the key, realizing she couldn't bear to lie. "I don't promise."

Nevertheless, Dauriel sat up and gently took her wrist, unlatching one, and then the next. At Tallora's hair, she brushed aside her white locks, tender in her motions. Those callused hands burned Tallora's skin, blood racing at the contact, but with a slight 'click,' the shackle came undone.

"Sleep well," Dauriel whispered. She blew out the candle, then settled into her cot.

Human bodies were strange, Tallora decided then. Thoughts were loud, consciences were quiet, and she hated Dauriel with all her heart, yet wished to hold her callused hand again.

Chapter VII 🐚

In the following days, Tallora smiled more often than not—so much so, she nearly forgot the looming shadow of Empress Vahla's threat.

One evening, after training with the general, a lady's maid stopped them as they approached the dining hall. She curtsied in the princess's presence, then said, "Princess Dauriel, the empress wishes to see the mermaid. I'm to escort her—"

"*I'll* escort her," Dauriel said, but the lady's maid shook her head.

"With all possible respect, the empress specifically relieved you of your duty for the time being."

Dauriel frowned but handed the end of the chain to Tallora. "Go with her, then," she said, and then added with a whisper, "and know I won't be far."

Tallora nodded in acknowledgement, yet her nerves had sparked to life.

The maid led Tallora to a corridor she had not yet seen, down a single flight of stairs to a wide, pillared hallway. The maid opened a set of double doors. Richly decorated in embroidered curtains and pillows, Tallora saw an ensemble of women in silken garb, lounging about as they ate and talked amongst themselves.

Empress Vahla stood among them, regal in her cape of furs, with Magister Adrael and two female guards at either side. "Holding your own bonds? Daring." She scowled at the lady's maid, who withered. "Dismissed. Welcome to your new home, Mermaid."

The maid scampered off, not needing to be told twice. Tallora, in her simple dress and slippers, felt exposed under the empress' scrutiny. "Adrael, kindly present the mermaid with her gift."

Adrael presented her with what appeared to be a small metal bracelet, crafted from gold and emblazoned with sigils Tallora couldn't read. When he knelt, Tallora was confused until it suddenly snapped around her ankle, fitting like a tight glove.

"We had that crafted for you, in case your willful recklessness led you to try and run away. If it's taken beyond the borders of the castle gates, it'll cause the most unbearable pain to the one wearing it."

Vahla smiled, and Tallora resisted the urge to spit on her feet.

"Adrael, leave us," Vahla continued, and the magister offered a quick nod before stepping out. "I wanted to give you time to acquaint yourself with this place and the girls here. Have you spent much time entertaining men?"

Tallora knew the threat, the implication, yet felt oddly muted in the moment, shock dulling her senses and freezing her tongue.

"Honestly, it's better if you haven't," Vahla said, ignoring Tallora's silence. "You're exceptionally beautiful, and men love to touch what's never been claimed. Still, I've instructed the more experienced girls to help you."

An older woman approached them, breaking off from the gaggle of gorgeous women lounging on the couches. No less beautiful than the rest, though she appeared old enough to be Tallora's mother, her sharp features and pointed ears set her apart. "Empress Vahla," the elven woman said, bowing low, "is this the new girl?"

"Mermaid, this is Lady Mithal Redwood. She spent many years in my service and now watches over the younger women. You'll be put in her charge."

The elf seemed kind enough, but Tallora still couldn't summon a smile, much less words.

"You'd best hope you loosen your tongue before you're put to work," Vahla said, her smile curt and vicious. "Serve your kingdom well, and you'll be rewarded. Otherwise, your accommodations won't be quite so comfortable."

The empress left. Lady Mithal Redwood watched until the door shut behind her and her guards, then whispered, "I stopped apologizing for her years ago. Absolute bitch, that one."

The audacity of her words pulled an easy laugh from Tallora's throat. Her fear melted, and she said, "Thank you. It's so refreshing to hear someone else say it."

"Only be careful who you say it in front of." She offered a hand, which Tallora accepted. "I'm Mithal Redwood, as she said, but you needn't refer to me as anything other than my first name. I hear your name is a secret only the Triage of Goddesses knows."

"Something like that. But you're in charge here?"

"As much as I can be." Mithal stole her hand again and led her forward, drawing the attention of the others—almost entirely women, but two ethereally beautiful men sat among them. "Surely you've heard of the mermaid in our midst. She'll be joining us. No asking for her name; it's the last secret she holds."

To Tallora's surprise, the women swarmed her, doting upon her hair and figure, complimenting her with a sincerity that shouldn't have shaken her so. She blushed and responded as she could, supposing it best to flatter them in return.

Perhaps she would find friends here, after all.

"Mermaid, you wouldn't mind meeting my son, would you? He's only just turned five and loves stories of other lands."

The woman who spoke held a figure even Tallora would admit to envying, and hair with the luxury of black silk. Around her eyes was some sort of black powder, enhancing her already alluring features. A slight broadness to her accent set her words apart from the rest of those speaking Solviran Common. Tallora nodded, following her to one of the many rooms surrounding the main area. "I didn't know you could keep children here."

"Many of us have children, and there's nowhere else for them to go." She tapped the door with her knuckle. "Mocum? There's someone here to meet you."

It wasn't only one child who came to greet her, but a whole flock who peered curiously from a room full of toys and bunkbeds. The boy who was Mocum came first and immediately clung to his mother, but a number of small children came to fawn over the scales on her legs and her shimmering skin. "May I braid your hair?" asked the oldest of the bunch, a girl no older than nine.

"Do your scales help you to swim?"

"Where's your tail?"

"Children," the woman reprimanded, "give her space to breathe."

Tallora smiled, smitten by her young admirers. "I don't mind in the slightest."

"Then perhaps after *dinner,*" she said, looking at the expectant children, "our new friend will be kind enough to tell you mermaid stories. Go wash your hands." The woman smiled as the last ones filtered out, including her son, then offered a hand. "My name is Leah. We'll be sharing a room."

Tallora accepted the hand, though her stomach dropped at the phrase, recalling Vahla's words. "Forgive me, but does that mean you will be . . ?"

Leah clearly did not understand, but she waited patiently for Tallora to finish.

"Sorry—the empress said I would be trained in . . . *this,* and does that mean you'll be the one . . ."

This time, Leah laughed, a hint of a blush on her cheeks. "The empress did say I should 'prepare' you, but never actually specified how. Frivolous pillow talk should be enough. Not much to learn, assuming you've been with men before. They're not difficult to please."

It seemed Tallora's nerves showed, because Leah lost her smile. Instead, she placed her hand against Tallora's waist, sympathy in her gaze. "I'm not saying what they're doing to you is right," she whispered, "nor will I say that everyone here would have chosen this life. Most of us are here because of poverty and because we have pretty enough faces to have gotten us out of the slums. But you'll be protected.

You'll be fed and clothed and have a comfortable bed to sleep in. The empress is terrifying, but this is far from the worst thing she could do to you."

Tallora didn't believe that, not in the moment, but she forced a smile and a nod, even if Leah clearly didn't accept it. She swallowed her discomfort, instead asking something she hoped wasn't too personal. "Do you enjoy . . . your career?"

Leah's smile held weight, much more so than her youthful self should carry. "It keeps me fed and sheltered, and my son is attending school on the crown's treasury." She pushed Tallora forward. "Now, let's get you set up in your room."

Soon, Tallora stepped into a windowless room with two beds on either side. One held semblance of a personality—a folded blanket at the base, a beaded tapestry on the wall. The other one awaited a personal touch, and Tallora wondered where she might find trinkets to decorate the boring walls.

"You'll be provided clothing," Leah explained. "We all share costumes, so you won't have to worry about that."

Tallora held up her shackles. "What about these?"

Leah frowned as she leaned against the doorframe. "No one has said anything about those."

Tallora's hope was a distant thing, and already she missed her bed with Dauriel on the floor beside her. She wondered if she would ever see the princess again—perhaps there was an element of truth to her teasing, and Dauriel might be a patron here.

She doubted Dauriel thought enough of her for that, and Tallora found the thought of her coming here to pay for her body discomforting.

She spent the evening forcing a smile with the others, eating her provided meal surrounded by surprisingly warm hearts. Perhaps comradery came from living in this gilded prison.

The men, she learned, were also for the servicing of guests, but often more discreetly—should a dwarven ambassador from Tholheim come, it would be a haven of sorts for him to spend an evening with a man with no fear. Solvira had no care to the gender of lovers, but not all the world felt the same.

And, cruel as it was, it gave Solvira a valuable piece of blackmail should there be any disagreements. Tallora wondered what Solvira's goddesses thought of that and realized the goddesses were worshipped, but they did not rule. Of their three goddesses, one was wicked, one was kind, and Neoma, the head of the Triage, was somewhere in between, a perfect balance of callused justice.

Afterward, Tallora distracted herself with the children, telling them tales of undersea trenches and sunsets that sparkled across the Tortalgan Sea. She said nothing of the dragon, though—lest someone other than Dauriel think ill will.

She excused herself to bed early. Leah followed.

The dark-haired woman sat upon her own bed as Tallora settled in. "This is how we spend most of our days. Oftentimes the men service Consort Ilaeri, but he has his own personal companion now, so unless there are visiting officials, our nights are usually quiet."

Tallora frowned at that. "Solviran royals have strange rules."

"Surely you know what they say? Years of inbreeding have resulted in an insanity that outsiders say will destabilize the empire. Not all of them are cruel, but Vahla, they say, is among the worst."

She couldn't stop her words in time. "What about Dauriel?"

Leah frowned, thoughtful in the ensuing silence. "I would've once said yes. But she's been absent in recent years, so I couldn't tell you if she were different. You'd know better than me, now. They say she was charged with watching over you."

"She was." Tallora swallowed the nervous lump in her throat. "Absent?"

Leah's nervous chuckle chilled Tallora's heart. "She used to come here every night."

Tallora merely nodded. "Am I allowed to leave?"

"You'll want to be discreet, but unless the empress catches you, I don't see why not."

Tears welled in her eyes. She rolled over, knowing it was rude, but couldn't bear to cry in front of her new friend. Leah apparently understood and left her alone, blowing out the candle as she stepped out.

Life had taken a wrenching turn, because it was only a matter of time before Tallora would be a slave in the arms of men while Dauriel bought services from the women around her, and this unnerved her to her core.

Tallora shut her eyes. *Goddess Staella, I don't think this is what you meant to happen when you gave me legs. I'm so afraid.*

In prayer, she fell asleep.

In the early morning, Tallora awoke before Leah and quietly crept from bed, still in her clothes from the previous day and with shackles at her wrists and neck.

A girl she didn't know sat leisurely on one of the couches reading and gave a brief smile at Tallora's entrance. Though frightened, the worst had already been done, and so she walked straight to the exit and stepped out the door.

Two guards met her, both women. "Where are you going?" one asked, sparing a glance for her hair and her chains.

"I've been summoned by Princess Dauriel, regarding removing my restraints," she said, wondering if this were in character.

"This early?"

Tallora offered an innocent nod.

The guards looked at the other. "Wait here," one said and left.

Tallora didn't shy away from small talk at home, but truthfully her nerves were much too frayed to be friendly to the remaining guard this early in the morning. Her wait wasn't long—soon, Dauriel appeared with the second guard, alert for the early hour.

Tallora's smile came unbidden, but Dauriel said nothing as she stopped before her and pulled a small golden key from her pocket. "The mermaid sees a tutor each morning," Dauriel said, ever the royal in her authoritarian tone, "and will be allowed to leave unhindered." She offered the shackles to the guards. "Give these to the Lady Mithal—my mother will want these kept somewhere, I'm sure."

Surprised, Tallora whispered, "I'm still to learn to read?"

"I've insisted on it. My mother doesn't know." Her stern gaze narrowed. "Come with me."

She followed as Dauriel escorted her away, and once down the hall, she whispered, "Thank you."

Dauriel stopped, her stoicism melting into sincerity. "I was relieved when you sent for me. It wouldn't be unlike my mother to throw you straight to the wolves. How is the courtesan's wing?"

"Everyone is very kind." She couldn't stomach to mention that perhaps Dauriel already knew that and knew it quite well.

Instead, the princess merely said, "I'm happy to hear it."

There was an odd finality to it, a passing of the torch of Dauriel's responsibility, but Tallora grabbed it and held it tight. "Do I still get to join you for training?"

"Do you want to?" Dauriel looked as startled as Tallora felt.

"I would," she said, truthfully. "I hate you very much, and watching General Khastra kick your ass has been the highlight of my days here."

Dauriel laughed, and Tallora silently thanked Staella for that. "I'll make certain no one stops you when you come."

They shared an awkward parting—no goodbyes; just a bumbling half-dance as they stepped apart. Tallora was left alone in the hallway, watching Dauriel and her silly, long braid and her walk like she owned the planet.

Tallora touched her burning cheeks. Swallowing back her smile, she returned to her new home, content to change before she went for her tutoring.

She joined Dauriel every night to watch her train, finding comradery with the princess and the general both. Afterward, she was invited to sit-in on dinner, whenever Vahla was absent.

Her tentative friendship with Dauriel became the subject of much gossip among the courtesans.

"Evanja says she heard you and the princess struck up a romance," Leah said one afternoon with a saucy wink.

Tallora scoffed, shaking her head in practiced disgust. "I think she tolerates me following her around like a guppy."

"Well, be careful what rumors start spreading—Empress Vahla is vindictive above all."

Tallora didn't take that to heart, though she should have.

One evening, after training with the general, Dauriel said, "My mother has guests. I hate them. We'll be taking dinner in your old room instead."

"Who are they?"

"'The Esteemed Amulon and envoy,'" she said in mocking tones. "Ambassadors from Moratham."

They entered Tallora's room, sunlight fading from the window. As Dauriel went to light a candle, Tallora said, "What does your mother want from them?"

"Border disputes. Solvira has expanded downward rapidly enough that a few of the southern cities are in limbo, as far as ownership—Moratham had been warring with the Onian Providence for years, but now Solvira owns it and we've inherited the dispute. My mother seems to think she can charm them with honey and lies." Dauriel shook her head, lip twisting into a deep grimace. "Still, they'll only see that as a weakness. We should stake our claim and be done with it."

"But are they right? Do the border cities belong to them?"

At that, Dauriel grew silent, contemplative features highlighted by candlelight. "Likely, yes," she finally said, "but in handing them back to their so-called rightful kingdom, we're dooming the De'Sindai populace living there to slavery. Surely you've heard what Moratham did to the giants?"

Tallora shook her head.

"Moratham stole the Urbon Mountains when I was a child. The entire population of giants was slaughtered or captured, forced to breed with human slaves to create more compliant 'half-giants.' Solvira saw this as an atrocity, but it was not our place to interfere. Law is law, but we harbor those who escape."

"By Staella's Grace," Tallora whispered, nauseated at the thought.

"Neoma is lawful above all else, teaches that you must protect yourself before you can help others, but she will interfere in the face of great injustice. She harbored Staella to save her from The Snake God, and so, too, should we for the De'Sindai on our border. The morals of their god spit in the faces of ours. This should not even be a negotiation—we should cut their throats and be done with it." A glower overtook Dauriel's countenance. "My mother claims if there's going to be

86

a war, that they should act first, lest we lose support from any countries who might ally with us. I don't agree—"

A knock interrupted her speech—at Dauriel's beckoning, a servant left two trays of food. "A pity you abdicated your throne," Tallora said. "Your goddess would bless you for your devotion to her will, and your people would as well."

Dauriel scoffed before swallowing her first bite of stew. "Is that a bit of faith, I'm hearing?"

"I hate you enough to be an unbiased party," Tallora replied with a wink. Dauriel laughed, and so did she, grinning as she stole a bite from her own tray.

"Well, I hate you enough to be flattered."

They fell into a banter of sorts, Tallora's merciless teasing pulling laughter from her princess captor. A knock interrupted their jests, and Dauriel frowned as she said, "Come in."

To Tallora's surprise, it was Lady Mithal, agitation etched into her elegant face. In her hand, she held the golden shackles. "Princess Dauriel," she said quickly, giving a bow. Then, she looked to Tallora. "Mermaid, a little bird told me you'll be asked to provide refreshments for the meeting this evening between the council and the ambassadors. You don't want to be missing when summoned."

Tallora nodded slowly, looking to Dauriel for an explanation. "What does 'provide refreshments' mean?"

"Exactly as it sounds, and nothing more," Mithal replied, beckoning for her to stand. When she obeyed, Dauriel stood as well. "It's commonplace for one of my girls to provide wine for visiting officials, and Ambassador Amulon was apparently intrigued when Vahla told him of the mermaid who transformed into a maiden."

Tallora's skin burned when Dauriel placed a gentle hand on her waist. "I'll be there," she said, and unbearable relief filled Tallora at the words. "As a royal, they won't besmirch me the right to sit in on negotiations."

"We really must hurry, Mermaid," Mithal said, hesitation in her words—perhaps Dauriel made her nervous. Tallora followed, but the smile she gave Dauriel was both unbidden and utterly beaming.

Dauriel returned it, and Tallora couldn't deny that she was awfully charming when she smiled.

Once the door closed, Mithal led her quickly down the hallway. "I say this out of sincere concern— you must be wary of Princess Dauriel."

The words jarred Tallora out of her joyous haze. "W-Why?"

"Her character aside, rumors spread quickly among the girls, and then to the servants and the nobles and finally to the crown. Your friendship with the princess is noteworthy for its innocence, but if the empress catches wind of a romance, I fear what she'll do to stop it."

"Like sell me to Moratham?" Tallora offered, her blood suddenly cold in her veins.

"That's the rumor I've heard, yes."

Tallora followed her rapid pace, though she struggled to feel her legs. "Forgive me, but what do you mean about the princess' character?"

Mithal glanced backward—when Tallora followed her gaze, the hallway was empty. "About two years ago," the elven woman whispered, "the Solviran Crown paid a considerable amount of gold to a lesser noble whose daughter died under mysterious circumstances—paid him to stay quiet. One of my girls was told the girl died at a tavern party—a party Princess Dauriel was also attending."

Tallora frowned, unsure of what Mithal was insinuating. "Attending the same party as a woman who died doesn't mean anything."

"I don't know quite what I believe, Mermaid," Mithal said, her voice lowering. "But sources say Dauriel and the girl left together, and then the girl was dead." Tallora's skin prickled at the words, the silent accusation lingering. "My girls have said she can be angry, but murder? I don't know. But I do know that Empress Vahla paid the girl's father to stay quiet; I also know the princess hasn't visited my girls since."

They reached the courtesan's wing, and Tallora's mind was reeling. Dauriel had a temper but . . . murder? And oh, that poor girl . . .

She didn't know what to think. She hardly thought anything until Mithal led her to her room and shoved an outfit into her arms. "This is as covered as you'll likely be able to get away with, tonight," Mithal said. "Would you like help?"

"Yes, please," Tallora replied, and the elven woman helped guide her into the odd attire. A brilliant pink, it matched her scales, but while the skirt was long despite the slit, the top only barely covered her breasts, the semi-sheer fabric leaving little to the imagination. Tallora arranged the gentle waves of her long hair to cover the rest. Under any other circumstance, she might've thought she looked beautiful, the top not unlike the decorations worn beneath the ocean for special occasions.

Tallora did not see herself in the mirror, but instead one of the daughters of King Merl. Yet, while she might look like undersea royalty, she did not feel like a princess. "You're there for decoration," Mithal said gently, "but nothing else. It's not out of the question that you'll be asked for more afterward, but if so, insist that you must return here first. I'll help prepare you."

Tallora nodded, actively fighting tears. Leah suddenly entered, smiling when she saw them. "There's a messenger here. They're requesting the mermaid at the ambassador's meeting."

Precisely as Mithal had said. Tallora had heard once that women of the night knew every secret to be known. Mithal might know every happening in this castle. "Leah," Mithal replied, "walk with her and explain the rules. I think she could use the company."

With a reassuring squeeze to her hand, Mithal left. Leah stepped up to take her place. "This is the simplest job you can have here," she said, offering a hand. When Tallora accepted, she held it like a sister. "You look lovely."

"Thank you," she replied, the words oddly reassuring, despite her fear. "So I serve wine and let them leer?"

"Yes. But they likely won't touch. Not in this kind of setting. In Moratham, sex outside the bounds of marriage is a grievous sin, so if they're going to disobey, which they will, it won't be in a formal setting."

Leah said this like it was perfectly predictable and acceptable. When she beckoned for Tallora to follow, she obeyed and asked, "This is how it always is?"

"Powerful men are the same wherever you go— the rules don't apply to them."

Tallora frowned, because everything about that rubbed her very wrong. She chose not to comment, instead studying Leah's complexion and features, her beauty unquestionably breathtaking. Surely not a mere human. "Is it . . . *rude* to ask if you're a Celestial?"

Leah's grin held amusement. "It's actually flattering. I am. Nearly every citizen of Moratham is descended from Morathma and one of his mortal wives—we all look very different, given he has hundreds, but we're all Celestial."

"You're from Moratham?"

"Yes, though I generally don't advertise it. My real name is Leahona, which is an iconic enough name that I can't really use it. Mocum and I came here five years ago, when he was an infant."

When a pair of guards rounded the corner, Tallora instinctively covered her chest and stomach with her arms, keeping her stare straight ahead until they passed. "Tell me if it isn't my business, but why would you come to Solvira?"

"My husband was . . . difficult." Leah's glower revealed far more than her words. "It's not impossible for a wife to leave her husband, but there are complicated steps to take. I would have had to present proof of infidelity or abuse to the Speaker himself, but I lived near the border, in Ablom. The capital was a thousand miles away. So we ran away here."

"I'm so sorry."

Leah shook her head, her lips a thin line. "Don't be. I was raised to be a good wife, like all the girls around me, but I never really . . . I wasn't good enough at tending to a home. But my husband was wealthy—lands for miles and slaves to toil the fields. I lived a luxurious life, so even though he was a brute, to complain would've meant I was ungrateful."

Tallora didn't wish to argue with a woman she'd only recently befriended, but the words wounded her, to hear Leah justify whatever awful things were done. "So why did you leave?"

"Because whatever my shortcomings as a wife, I am a good mother." Conviction returned to her voice—Tallora marveled at the change in demeanor. "As an infant, Mocum was difficult, and my husband once . . ." Her jaw steeled, forced stoicism upon her features. ". . . shook him so he'd quiet. My baby didn't move for hours, and I cried the whole while, praying to Morathma to wake him. It was a miracle that he did, and I ran away to Solvira that night."

Tallora looked closer at Leah, the realization that she had a five-year-old son suddenly starkly apparent. "You can't be older than I am."

"I've just turned twenty."

"You're younger than me."

"I was a few months shy of fifteen when I was married," Leah affirmed, as though this were entirely normal, and Tallora merely nodded, the thought making her sick. "Morathma is a strict god, but even though I didn't understand the purpose of all his teachings, I trusted that everything would make sense once I passed on and lived in his kingdom. We're all his children, and he loves us."

Tallora whispered, knowing where they were. "Do you still worship Morathma?"

Leah looked almost . . . forlorn. Her countenance fell, her smile suddenly painted. "Not anymore. It's difficult here." Her voice lowered further. "To worship the gods of Solvira feels like a betrayal to my upbringing. I don't know what to believe."

Tallora nodded, not understanding but realizing she simply couldn't. Morathma was a god to hate, or so she had been told by the people of Solvira. Beneath the sea, she'd heard little of him, but beneath the sea she'd heard little of the upper world at all.

Leah stopped before an ornate door, where a servant in simple attire held a tray with two bottles of wine. "You're to keep their glasses full and your ears open. It's our unspoken duty—to be the eyes and ears of the crown. Say absolutely nothing unless addressed—and even then, say as little as you can while still being polite. If they compliment you, say 'thank you,' and nothing more. Don't use titles, except to the empress—otherwise you risk insult to Solvira, and they're who you serve."

Tallora nodded, accepting the tray when the servant offered. "Can I ask something terribly stupid?"

Leah nodded.

"How do you pour wine?"

Leah laughed and explained it all.

"If money is what will smooth this negotiation, that's certainly no object."

In a lavish seating room, Tallora poured wine into Vahla's glass as she spoke honeyed words, noting that she drank at a slower pace than the rest.

Ambassador Lemhi, an indulgent, larger man, held up his empty wine glass, hardly sparing Tallora a glance as she approached—not until she stood beside him, at which point he spent a lingering moment ogling her near-exposed chest. His splotchy, red cheeks looked sickly on his pale skin. "Empress Vahla, the Speaker did not send us here to be bought. We hope for a compromise to be reached, and with due respect, money is also no object for us."

Consort Ilaeri had been paid little mind anytime he spoke, and Tallora found that odd. "That aside," he said, "we also wished to thank you for your esteemed gifts. The Speaker is generous to his allies."

At the word 'allies,' Tallora didn't miss Dauriel's sneer. She drank only water, and anytime Tallora came near, her gaze softened, a protective instinct clearly conveyed. Tallora might've fainted from fear without it.

"How much money?" Vahla said, ignoring her husband's words.

Lemhi named a number that meant nothing to Tallora, but even Dauriel turned her head to listen. Vahla smiled, her beauty unquestionably radiant, and she nodded. "You tease me, Ambassador."

"No jest. The Speaker is happy to be generous."

"And does this have anything to do with the rumors of Solviran citizens disappearing at my borders?" Vahla asked. "Numerous reports have been issued stating that slave caravans have been seen outside my southernmost cities."

"As I said, the Speaker is happy to be generous, with the promise of your continued discretion."

When Vahla smiled, Tallora prayed it was only an act to remain tactful, but Dauriel's glower suggested she might've been sincere. It seemed there was a price for her people's freedom and Lemhi had named it.

The second ambassador said little, but he watched Tallora nearly all evening. Ambassador Amulon was exceptionally handsome, his skin smoothly tanned from the sun, his cropped blonde hair starkly juxtaposed with his brooding eyes. She recalled Leah's words, that all citizens of Moratham were direct descendants of their god, and wondered how thick his angelic blood flowed. Like his counterpart, he wore a white tunic embroidered with amber thread, his dark trousers more akin to Dauriel's instead of the robes she saw many Solvirans wear. While she did feel his gaze, leering wasn't the word she would have used.

When she topped off his wine, he looked to her directly and said, "Thank you."

She simply nodded, recalling Leah's words.

"Empress Vahla, is this your mermaid girl?" Amulon continued, still looking at Tallora.

"Isn't she exquisite?" Vahla replied, her smile nearly . . . cute? "She's an absolute gem to the royal crown."

Amulon's smile held a subtle twitch. "What's your name, girl?"

"Staella," she replied, no hesitation at all.

To her relief, and surely Vahla's too, he laughed. "I must commend your parents, then—a worthy name."

Tallora nodded, unsure if she should continue engaging or try and leave.

He stared at her a moment longer, visibly contemplative, then returned his attention to Vahla, offering a flattering compliment regarding how lovely she looked in the crown gifted by Moratham.

There were others—Morathan guards and a few lesser nobles—but they stayed silent. Tallora merely kept their glasses full, nervous at their leering eyes, and at least once something brushed against her ass. Likely a hand, but she merely stiffened and moved forward. She returned to Dauriel, lingering in her corner until Lemhi finished his fifth glass. When she went to refill it, she anticipated his stare, noting that the more inebriated he became, the more shameless he was in his lustful gaze. "We're willing to offer the sea-side fortress of Kal'Far in exchange for Vaile."

"A tempting offer," Vahla replied, her smile far more drunk than her glass would suggest. "My council will likely feel similarly."

No consensus was reached, however—Vahla kept deflecting any true compromise, and Tallora couldn't fathom why. Instead, she clung to Dauriel's protective aura, standing beside her as often as possible. At least once, the princess' hand stole hers beneath the table, the reassuring squeeze drawing an immediate smile to her face.

Eventually, Amulon proclaimed the night must end and called for his envoy to escort the drunk Lemhi to bed. He lingered, however, even once Vahla bid them goodnight. Tallora moved to gather the wineglasses, uncertain if it was her duty, but it would at least make it easier for whichever servant was called to clean the mess.

As they filtered out, Amulon approached, his smile charming. "Staella, is it?"

She looked up, glanced to the door to confirm Vahla's absence, and replied with, "Well, no. But it's an attractive name in Solvira."

Amulon chuckled, and were they beneath the sea, she would have suspected he was flirting. But she was a courtesan and he was a foreign ambassador— there was an ulterior motive here, surely, but it may have simply been access to her cunt.

That . . . was likely precisely it, actually. She felt cold at the thought.

"It's uncommon to find a follower of the Goddess of Stars, even in this country," Amulon continued. "I was told you are a priestess. Did you know there is a small temple in Andiamen to her worship?" When Tallora shook her head, he said, "Morathma welcomes followers of the Stars with open arms."

Tallora smiled, unsure of what to say to that. "W-Well," she finally stammered, "I don't know that I'll have the opportunity to visit anytime soon, but I'll keep it in mind."

"If you're used to the ocean, it will be very different." Amulon's smile was kind, and that jarred her more than his company.

She stiffened when a hand suddenly settled at the small of her back. But then it was Dauriel standing beside her, and she could have wept for relief. "Ambassador," Dauriel said, giving a simple nod of deference. Then, she looked to Tallora, a dangerous glint in her eye. "I'm to escort you back. Come with me."

She kept her hand on Tallora's waist, possessive as she walked her out. It remained in the hallway, scattered members of the Morathan Envoy still lingering, some watching Tallora, others shying from the princess who puffed out her chest and looked prepared to breathe fire onto the next man who spoke to her.

When they turned the corner, Dauriel released her, perhaps deeming them truly alone. "I didn't want to leave you with them," she whispered.

"And I appreciate that," she replied, hardly audible. Then, she gathered her courage, an insane plot boiling in her head. "You don't have to escort me back, though. Rather, you could escort me somewhere else."

Dauriel raised an eyebrow, the slight smirk of her lips surprisingly adorable. "Could I?"

"In all honesty, I'm very wound up and liable to cry as soon as I'm alone, and rather than do that, might we just . . . talk? And laugh?" She cursed her own vulnerability, but under Dauriel's soft gaze, she felt no judgement.

"I'll take you to the roof," Dauriel said, her grin a delight after the anxious night. "Let's get you some clothing."

Tallora immediately brought an arm up to cover her near-exposed breasts, forgetting her own immodesty. "Right. I'm sorry—"

Dauriel shook her head, stealing Tallora's words. "As lovely as your breasts are, I don't want you to freeze outdoors." She winked, but Tallora struggled to smile—which the princess noticed. "That's not—I'm sorry. I swear I did all I could to not look at you during dinner—"

"No, no!" With her free hand, she grabbed Dauriel's, squeezing slightly as she lingered. "I know. I'm just feeling vulnerable right now."

Dauriel's hand fell away, her gaze apologetic. "Come with me."

Tallora did, and after a slight detour to grab a robe from her old bedroom, she was taken to the lift. They rode all the way to the top, and she marveled at the great height. She had swum down deep trenches but never been so high in all her life. So odd, to stare upon the world from such an elevated plane, and when it stopped and Dauriel beckoned her to follow, she did, escorted up a small set of stairs.

A door waited at the top, and Tallora was met with warm night air. Stone fencing prevented them from falling from the great tower, but she swore they were close enough to touch the stars. Thousands glittered high above, casting patterns she knew. She'd hardly seen them since her kidnapping, and she resisted the urge to sob for joy.

Staella smiled down upon her, and Tallora felt that love, kissed by the light of countless stars.

"I come here to think," Dauriel said softly, and Tallora smiled as the princess sat upon a precarious perch, only open air behind her.

The wicked thought came that she could easily push her down, slay the woman who had stolen her from the sea. But . . . no. Instead, Tallora sat on the ground, her back against the ledge beside where Dauriel sat. "At home, I would swim to the surface some nights and pray, sometimes simply bask in Staella's domain. It was why I was at the surface the night that . . ." She trailed off, unwilling to speak of the night of the storm. "Perhaps I shouldn't tell you this, but I'm not actually a priestess."

97

Dauriel frowned, bafflement in her furrowed brow. "But you were wearing a symbol of Goddess Staella."

"I want to be, but I'm still in training," Tallora said, her smile tentative and shy. "I actually wasn't supposed to be there that night. But I had missed the dark moon prayers because I was, um . . ." She cracked an embarrassed smile, heat filling her cheeks. "I was at a party. Met someone beautiful. Got a little carried away and forgot. So I came the next night instead."

Dauriel stared incredulously, though she just as soon chuckled and said, "I was scouting the waters the night of the storm. Preliminary preparations for war, in case the worst happens with Moratham. Not typical for a royal, but I'd had a spat with my mother and left with Adrael for a two-month sea voyage. I always feel . . . lighter when I leave Neolan."

"Do you not like living in Solvira?" Tallora dared to ask, curious at her melancholy.

"I love my country." Dauriel smiled, yet it held an ineffable shadow. "I love its forests and its fields, its mountain ranges. It's the greatest country in the world. I love my goddesses, and there is no grander destiny than bringing glory to their names." She gazed up at the sky and shut her eyes, the light beautiful upon her tanned skin. "But I have never been able to dismiss the dream of running away."

"Where would you go?" Tallora asked, curious as she studied the celestial light cast across Dauriel's face.

Exhaustion steadily weighed down her features. "If I knew, I'd be there."

Tallora placed a hand on Dauriel's polished boot, smiling unbidden at her joy. "You would have been a great empress." Dauriel's dimmed countenance suddenly looked taken aback. "I-I only mean," Tallora said, unable to hide her panic, "your mother doesn't care like you do. The way she spoke at that meeting? Forgive me, for I know nothing of politics, but her actions are awful."

Anger stiffened Dauriel's sharp features, and Tallora saw literal smoke leave with her exhale. "Perhaps I should run away. I'll take her head with me." The words chilled Tallora's blood. Before she could speak, Dauriel said, "I won't actually. I don't have the heart to swing the axe, and who's to say the next ruler would be any better? The whole world knows the Solviraes line is mad."

"Your brother seems very sweet," Tallora said, but Dauriel merely shook her head.

"Eniah is too young for us to know what kind of ruler he would be. Though with how my mother keeps sinking her claws inside his head, he'll be her spitting image."

Tallora's fingers brushed against the dirt upon the stone floor, cool despite the summer's warmth. "Did she try to do the same to you?"

"When I was very young, yes." Dauriel shrugged, but there was a change in her stance, her shoulders slumping when they had once been proud. Her words came with a scoff. "I still remember the first time she said I was ugly. I was five. She told me I looked like a fish in a bowl with how fat my cheeks were and wouldn't let me meet any visiting nobility for two years, when I finally slimmed out." Tallora's jaw fell to the floor, but Dauriel chuckled. "Turns out, my fat cheeks weren't the problem."

"I like your face very much, so she can shut up," Tallora said, her glower only darkening when Dauriel continued her laughter. But Tallora's heart hurt for the little Solviran princess, too young to laugh off something so cruel.

"It was bold of you, to claim the goddess' name," Dauriel said, blatantly redirecting the conversation. "Do your parents also worship Staella?"

"My momma does, yes. My papa did too, but he passed away years ago."

"I'm sorry to hear that." Dauriel looked up to the stars, contemplative as she added, "Well, I assume I should be sorry. It's terrible to say, but I don't know how sad I'd be if either of my parents fell dead."

It was cruel, and it brought a chilling reminder of Mithal's words—that perhaps Dauriel had less of a heart than Tallora thought. Yet, she had seen enough to know that Dauriel's relationship with her parents was far different than her own. "It was a difficult time," Tallora replied, and she looked inside herself, wondering if she could say the rest. Dauriel had been vulnerable to her—perhaps she owed that back. "I woke up one morning, and my momma was in tears. There were other people there, listening to what she said between sobs, and a few others cleaning up. I remember seeing blood in the water. He . . ." Tallora shrugged, the words painful, even fifteen years later. "My papa ended his life. He'd wished me a good night, he'd kissed me when I'd gone to bed, and then he was gone."

When Tallora looked up to Dauriel, she saw grief upon the Solviran Princess' countenance, her silver eyes as wide as the moon. "I don't know what to say. I'm . . . I'm so sorry."

"Papa was sick for a long time." Dauriel's booted calf shifted; Tallora leaned against it, taking comfort in the odd touch. "But not in his body; in his mind. I was just a little girl and didn't understand—he would lay in bed for days sometimes, and my mom would tell me he was sick. I'd hold a hand to his forehead to check for a fever." The memory brought a smile, sorrowful as it was. "I only hope he's found peace in the Beyond. I've heard stories of Staella taking our pain and sorrow upon herself, and . . . I hope it's true. I suppose I'll find out someday." She shut her eyes, willing her emotions to steady.

When she said nothing more, a tentative voice asked, "Forgive me if it isn't my place, but how did you move forward from that?"

Tallora rested her head against Dauriel's knee. "One day at a time. My mom said not to think about the rest of my life without him, but just today. And so on. Sometimes it still hurts. Momma never fully healed. I remember she told me once . . ." Tallora looked away from Dauriel, the words more difficult than she'd anticipated. Tears welled in her eyes, but she swallowed them back. "She told me that to love him was to hurt when he did, to feel joy when he did, to simply hold him for as long as she could and pray the sun would rise again. One morning, it didn't. I learned about love by watching them. Perhaps it ruined my view of it, I don't know. But my mother loved him every day as though it were her last. And my papa cherished her, gave all the love he had, when he could. And to me. He threw his whole heart into everything." She shrugged, her words finally fading. "I'm sorry. I've said too much."

"You haven't," Dauriel said, the gentleness in her tone jarring. There was affection in her gaze, and Tallora wondered what it meant. "I don't think you could."

"Oh, I don't know about that." Tallora smiled, though it had to be forced. "You wanted me to shut up more than a few times when I first came here."

"I've grown accustomed to your bitchiness." Despite the inherent cruelty of the words, Tallora's smile became genuine, especially when Dauriel matched it.

"A bitch, but a charming bitch."

"Endlessly so." Dauriel's gaze shifted up to the sky, to the thousands of stars above. They illuminated her skin and hair, shining light and love upon her—upon Dauriel, their progeny. "Tell me more of your home. I want to hear it all. Whatever you'll tell me."

For a moment, Tallora forgot she was a captive—she was simply a girl seated on the roof of a castle with a woman she hated, but might've also considered a friend. She spoke of home and all its beauty, and though she missed it dearly, she could smile.

For a moment, she felt safe.

It must have been for hours that they laughed beneath the stars' light. Tallora loved the lilt of Dauriel's chuckle, as well as her propensity to snort through her nose if she couldn't help it. When Tallora's eyelids drooped, she fought as long as she could.

She didn't recall when she fell asleep— sometime after Dauriel's tale of the time she walked in on her father with a male courtesan—but she did remember a shift in the light and the gentle rocking of her body. Her eyes fluttered open, surprised to see Dauriel's face, then realized she was being carried. "Dauriel?"

The princess looked down, her own sleepy eyes apparent. "Careful. I'll make you walk."

Tallora shut her eyes, feigning a snoring sound before bursting into subdued giggles. She looped her arms around Dauriel's neck, relaxing against her shoulder as the princess carried her through the castle to the courtesan's wing.

Two female guards stood before the doors, and Dauriel carefully helped her stand on her feet. Tallora lingered by her side, surprised at how lovely Dauriel's eyes were, half-lidded. "If there's trouble," Dauriel whispered, "send for me. Day or night."

Tallora nodded. "Goodnight, Princess."

"And you, Mermaid."

Dauriel left, unquestionable swagger in every stride. And Tallora returned to find a vacant common area—she supposed it was closer to morning than midnight. She crawled into bed, silent lest she disturb Leah, and drifted off to sleep, her final thoughts of Dauriel and whether they might steal time together tomorrow.

Chapter VIII 🐚

Tallora went to tutoring that morning, exhausted but oddly light.

When she returned to her new home, Leah greeted her while Mocum sat beside her, a book in his small hands. "Is it true you're learning to read?"

Tallora nodded. "It's not something we do beneath the sea."

"And is it also true Princess Dauriel returned you at an ungodly hour last night?"

Biting her lip, Tallora said, "Yes. We were talking on the roof."

Leah nodded, and Tallora's stomach clenched at the unsaid accusation. "Well, let me know if you ever need advice."

"Advice?"

Leah spared an exaggerated glance for the little boy seated beside her. "Just, advice."

"It's not like that," Tallora said, not wishing to argue in front of the child.

Leah smiled pleasantly, though too wide to be sincere. "How did the meeting go?"

She joined them on the couch, the plush fabrics enveloping her exhausted body. "Well enough. I served them, as instructed. Some leered—Amulon seems to have taken an interest in me. Kept trying to get me to talk."

"Sometimes they'll do that because they want free favors." Leah winked, all but confirming Tallora's suspicions. "Learn anything?"

"Moratham is stealing Solvira citizens by the border, and Vahla won't look twice so long as they keep paying her. Meanwhile, the border dispute seems like it won't come to any kind of consensus."

Leah's nod held approval. "Tell that to Mithal."

"Apparently there's a Temple of Staella in a place called 'Andiamen?'"

"That's the capital of Moratham. And it's true. Staella's worshippers are one of the few outsiders allowed as citizens."

"Why?"

"Don't you know the story? The Moon stole the Stars from the Desert Sands. It's a peace offering. Should she ever return to him, she'll be welcomed."

"That's . . ." Tallora words trailed off. Truthfully, she didn't know at all what to think of that. "Perhaps I don't know the story as well as I should. Why was she stolen?"

"In Moratham, I was taught that Neoma, the Goddess of Creation . . ." She glanced at Mocum as she lightly said, "*sought a vessel* for her . . . *spawn* and kidnapped the Stars to be the, um, vessel for her unnatural magic. But here I was told a very different story, that Morathma was cruel and Neoma harbored Staella to save her, and that they fell in love."

"Then why would she ever return?"

Leah glanced around, then looked to her son, voice lowered as she said, "Because there's an entire country's worth of people who think Neoma rapes her each night in a vain attempt to conceive a second child." She didn't say 'rapes'—she mouthed it lest the child hear, but Tallora understood. "There's an entire sect of priestesses devoted to her worship that believe the same."

"By Staella's Grace . . ."

Leah stopped a moment, visibly contemplative. "It was strange to me, coming here, because the only stories I had ever heard were that Staella was a prisoner. Neoma is hated there—but here, she and Staella are revered as a couple, no question to their love." Leah shrugged. "I'm inclined to believe the latter, truthfully."

"But does that mean Ilune is literally the child of Neoma and Staella both? How is that possible?"

Leah shrugged. "The Silver Fire can literally create life when wielded by Neoma, or so I've heard. One of those 'godly mysteries' we mortals aren't privy to. I'm surprised you don't know more about all this, though. You must have your own view of the gods, beneath the sea."

"Staella is revered for her star patterns. We don't speak much of Neoma or Ilune. Most people worship Tortalga of the Sea. I was always drawn to Staella for her teachings of kindness and gentleness, even if I'm not much of either."

"I think you're very nice," Leah replied, and Tallora couldn't resist laughing.

"Thank you. I'm glad someone here does."

Leah shrugged, always keeping one arm around Mocum. "The princess seems to think it."

"The princess thinks I'm an absolute bitch and isn't shy to let me know." Except she didn't say 'bitch'— she mouthed it, lest Mocum hear it and repeat it.

Leah's smile held conspiracy. "Whatever you say."

"You're ridiculous," Tallora teased, but the words unsettled her for reasons she couldn't quite bring herself to contemplate.

"Well, if you wanted to know more of the Triage, you could ask her," Leah said. "Dauriel despises Morathma and will tell anyone who listens."

Tallora had heard Dauriel's rants but felt compelled to ask all the same. "Oh?"

"She takes the old stories very seriously and hates Morathma for all he is. But even aside from all Solviran distrust of Moratham, Dauriel would never lie with a man, and it's a terrible crime there for two women or two men to be together. Morathma teaches that it's a woman's highest calling to bring children into the world, and while sex is a cherished act between married couples, it's frowned upon to avoid conceiving children. Men caught sleeping with other men are often executed. The women are usually given the chance to be rehabilitated and cured of their unnatural desires—Dauriel had quite a few words to say about all that."

Tallora cringed, horrified most of all at Leah's apparent indifference, and instead asked, "And how do you feel about it?"

Leah glanced to Mocum, who seemed pre-occupied enough, then faced Tallora, her lips a thin line. "I was taught that for most of my life, and I believed it. Were Dauriel the only woman I'd known to sleep with women, I might still hold to that belief, as horrid as that sounds. With due respect, I wouldn't say she's fully sound of mind—no Solviraes is." The words coursed offense through Tallora's blood, though she knew Leah was likely right. "But I've met other women besides her who favor woman, and they're as sane and good as anyone else. Solvira welcomes couples of the same sex and of different races, and all of that was so strange at first—in Moratham, to be anything other than a Celestial means to be thrown into slavery. And Solvira isn't declining as a country—they're thriving. I don't believe any of that anymore.

"But I think Dauriel, deep down, fears what Moratham preaches. Their beliefs are contrary to everything she is. She has bravado for miles, but it's difficult to hold your head high forever before people who think such a core part of you is evil."

The words were wounding, and Tallora knew in her heart that they were true. "She talks to you a lot," she said, happy to divert the somber mood.

Leah's blush spoke volumes. "Used to. She loosens up . . . after."

Tallora didn't want to hear any more of that. They drifted off into idle conversation, thoughts of the princess far behind.

Tallora spent a part of her day among the courtesans, telling stories of the sea, but then a knock came. When a guard peeked in and asked for Tallora, her breath caught in her throat. She wore normal attire, the sort she was comfortable wearing in front of children even if corsets and all the accompanying layers were an annoyance, and slowly approached, fingers tingling as her blood pulsed cold in her veins.

She expected the Morathan Envoy, anticipating Amulon and his charm and his probing questions, but nearly burst into tears when she saw Dauriel waiting in the hallway. Relief flooded her; she gathered her skirts and ran to greet her, her smile infectious when Dauriel matched it. "Good afternoon, Princess."

"I attended a meeting this morning," Dauriel said in greeting, "thinking you'd be there. Instead I wasted an entire hour listening to my mother kiss Amulon's ass."

Tallora laughed unbidden. "If I didn't hate you so much, I'd feel sorry for you."

"Come with me," Dauriel said with a wink, and Tallora followed, of course, curious to know what conspiracy the princess had concocted.

"You look awfully proud of yourself."

Dauriel's half-grin was nothing less than charming. Tallora's stomach fluttered to see it. "I am. There's something I want to show you."

"Is it a new bruise from Khastra?"

"Much more exciting than that."

To Tallora's surprise, she was led down the lift and to the outdoors. She'd seen so little of the sun and stopped a moment to absorb its rays, realizing how dearly she'd missed it.

A hand stole hers. "Come on," Dauriel said, dragging her along. She didn't let go—instead, her gloved hand held Tallora's and led her around the side of the castle, past foreign greenery and flowers of every shade.

But soon, cutting through the floral delights, something unsavory met Tallora's nose. "What smells like shit?"

"Shit, actually. Horse shit. We're going to the stables."

Suspecting Dauriel didn't have intentions to get her killed, Tallora followed along, content to hold the princess' hand. They came across a large wooden building. The smell only grew. "We aren't here to see the horses," Dauriel said, "though I'm happy to show them off if you'd like."

"I know nothing about them."

"Then I'll be certain to. My horse, Tycus, is here." Within, Tallora saw spindly, four-legged beasts, ones she'd previously only spotted from a distance. So these were 'horses'—admittedly she found them rather ugly, but they had large, kind eyes. Dauriel led her between the rows of stalls, to one at the back. "We have a dog here to keep watch at night. Her name is Mabel."

"I don't know what a dog is," Tallora admitted, and Dauriel grinned as broadly as the open windows.

"Well, she had puppies last night."

"What's a puppy?"

Dauriel chuckled, then pointed into the last stall. "She had babies."

A slight squeal left Tallora's throat unbidden at the large, fluffy creature lying upon a plush blanket. Surrounding this 'dog'—which Tallora found to be much cuter than the horses—were six lumps emitting precious little whines as they cuddled and suckled their mother. "Oh!" She covered her mouth, enamored at the scene, when Dauriel opened the stall.

"Would you like to see them?"

"Will she let me?"

Dauriel nodded. "She let me this morning." Her hand left Tallora's and instead beckoned her inside.

Tallora stepped into piles of prickly, yellow plants—some sort of dead grass with a smell strong enough to make her wince—and watched as Dauriel knelt before the mother dog and offered a hand. The dog licked it but kept her wary gaze on Tallora. Its tail thumped the ground, and Tallora didn't know what that meant. "Come slowly," Dauriel said. "Kneel and offer your hand."

Tallora did so, well aware of the dog's teeth as she presented her open palm. The dog sniffed it, then lapped its drooling tongue across it. She grinned as she withdrew, then gasped when Dauriel stole a sleeping baby dog—a puppy—from the mother's side. She held it to her chest, letting the puppy rest against her tunic. The little thing slept peacefully, perhaps unaware of Dauriel's presence. "Come closer. I'll help you hold it."

Tallora carefully sat beside her, cradling her arms so Dauriel could place the little thing against her. It could have nearly fit in her palm, this tiny, fluffy puppy, and it felt like pure joy against her skin. "It's blind, for now," Dauriel explained. "Their eyes will open in a few weeks."

With care, Tallora gently stroked a line down the puppy's fur—it opened its mouth and *yawned*, and she squealed with delight. "It's so peaceful," she whispered, gazing down upon the little creature. Her heart swelled when it emitted a tiny whine.

Dauriel carefully stole it back, placing it beside its brothers and sisters. She grabbed a different one and offered it forward—this one settled at the crook of Tallora's neck, where she cradled it with care. "It's so strange to me," Dauriel said softly," that you've never held a puppy."

"And you've never held a calf."

Dauriel frowned, though not unhappily. "I have held a calf. Cows are commonplace here."

"I mean a dolphin, silly. A baby dolphin."

Grinning, Dauriel said, "No, I suppose not."

"They make terrible pets, but I've met a few brave souls who dared to befriend them. A family friend had a tamed dolphin who gave birth—I was invited to watch it swim around and even managed to hold it."

"That's adorable."

Tallora hummed softly, shutting her eyes as the puppy curled around her. "Not as adorable as this. Dolphins are born . . . spunky."

"Spunky?"

"Spunky, yes. Puppies are peaceful. I like them much more."

Dauriel laughed and happily explained the lifecycle of dogs, how the puppies would be adopted out in a few more months, and Tallora listened with delight. Whatever peace the sweet puppies offered, Dauriel's radiant joy brought warmth to Tallora's heart.

She didn't know how long they remained, watching the puppies eat and yawn and sleep, but the sky had darkened, sunset falling, when frantic footsteps rapidly approached.

Tallora heard the door swing open. "Mermaid?!"

"Lady Mithal?" Tallora stood and leaned out from the stall, noting the elven woman's rapid approach.

"Mermaid, you'd best come quickly. Empress Vahla is furious."

Tallora tried to jostle the door to the stall, but Dauriel's hand on her arm burned. "Then I shall speak to her."

Lady Mithal glanced nervously down the path. "With every possible respect, Princess, I think it would be much worse for her if you did."

The gate swung open. With tepid steps, Tallora came forward, sparing a final glance to Dauriel before Mithal shut the door. "What's going on?"

Mithal beckoned her to follow, nearly flying through the open door; Tallora struggled to keep pace. "Empress Vahla brought the Morathan Envoy to see you—apparently you were specifically requested by Ambassador Lemhi. I told her you must have simply gotten lost while looking for dinner and volunteered to find you. She's waiting." Mithal stopped suddenly and stared Tallora directly in the eye. "She has half a mind to let them watch while she flays you alive. Be very careful. Feign innocence. Don't mention Dauriel."

"Why not?"

"If she realizes you've struck up a friendship with her daughter, she'll ship you off to spite you both. Now, come on."

When they finally entered the courtesans' wing, Tallora stepped into a flurry of activity. Everywhere, the women helped each other dress or darted out of the way of those that did. Tallora watched them inspect shameless attire, adjusting themselves with no regard for modesty as they threw on all sorts of clothing pieces and preened their hair.

Leah noticed their entrance and ran to them as Mithal said, "Did the empress leave?"

"Yes, and thank Staella's Mercy. The only reason she didn't throw us off the roof was to save face in front of the ambassadors. Instead, she's called for most all of us to service the entire envoy at once." Leah offered Tallora a small pile of clothing. "Except you. You'll be servicing Lemhi personally."

Tallora dropped the bits of cloth when her hands lost feeling. "I'm to—"

"The first time is the worst, but it'll only get easier. All men look the same with their trousers down. Just say what he wants to hear. I doubt he'll ask for anything weird. If Vahla gets a good report, she'll likely not bother you again until he's gone." Leah frowned as she leaned in and sniffed. "You smell like horse."

"Cover her in perfume, then," Mithal said, waving her away. She looked to Tallora, surely seeing her trembling lip. "I'll help you change."

Tallora managed a nod, dread welling in her stomach as Mithal helped her strip from her clothing. The woman shoved her bare breasts into a sheer, scarf-like top, as white as her hair. Leah returned, spraying her with a floral-smelling liquid, then helped in dressing her. They tied it expertly, the small knot appearing as a floral design, but a simple pull and the whole thing would unravel. A sort of tabard donned her hips, barely covering what lay between. All in white, purity embodied—Tallora looked into the mirror at her violated form and resisted the urge to sob.

"Put the shackles back on—Vahla requested it."

Tallora shut her eyes as Leah did, the gentle 'click' the most hated sound in the world.

"You'll be bringing him wine," she heard Leah whisper. "It'll be all right. We were all new once."

"It's not—" Tallora gasped back a sob, actively fighting tears. "It's not being new that—"

"I know." Leah pulled Tallora close, and she clung to the offered comfort, realizing that after these past few weeks, a hug from a friend was a treasure. "I know. I do it for my child. Find your reason."

For the mother Tallora longed to return to beneath the sea, she swallowed her tears and followed the women out.

Dauriel had always warned Tallora against wine, even when the servants delivered it. Said she needed her wits about her, that alcohol would dull her instincts for survival.

When she stood outside the envoy's door, one of the other courtesans offered her a flask. "For luck," she said, and Tallora hesitated, hand trembling as she grasped it. She stole a breath, cringing as she brought the metal to her lips and forced the bitter liquid down her throat. Coughing, she returned it, then steadied her hands around the open bottle of wine and two glasses. They entered the suite.

Ambassador Lemhi sat among an array of pillows, dressed in loose clothing patterned in green and gold. He caught her eye immediately—he and the other men around him. Girls were already attending to them, doting upon them with food and wine, some seated in their laps and kissing their ears. No sign of Amulon.

The visiting ambassador beckoned Tallora forward, and she obeyed, her stomach in knots. She swore she felt her pulse in her throat. "You are prettier every time I see you," the man said, grinning as he studied her. The words were foreign to him, a broad accent on his tongue. "Join me."

Tallora's legs suddenly failed; she all but fell against his side.

He helped steady her, placing an arm around her shoulders. "I'm told you turned into a Celestial girl." His other hand skimmed her bare skin, glossing over her scaled calves like a treasure chest of gold. "Astounding. You might be the rarest creature in the world." His rough hand stroked her shoulder; tears brimmed in her eyes. "Any other tricks I should know?"

"Oh, I can turn into other things besides a Celestial," she said, unable to even fake a smile. Fear screamed to run. Instead, she simply lied. "I once turned into a shark and ate a man alive."

He only looked more intrigued. "Have you?" His leering grin came much too close to her hair. His lips brushed the locks. "Tell me more."

She heard gentle moaning from beyond— looking past him, she caught a glimpse of a woman she didn't know leading a man behind a curtain, his hands actively groping her body.

"I can become a sailfish," she heard herself say. "Dart away at any danger—no one can catch me."

"Except Solvira, it seems." His hand traveled up her shin and to her thigh instead; she trembled and swallowed tears, reality rapidly descending, crushing her soul. "But you are all woman now, yes?"

Beyond, she saw a woman in an open-mouthed kiss with a man while another knelt between his legs, and although Tallora couldn't quite see the act, she imagined it well enough.

Fingers at her shoulder dipped down enough to pluck the string holding her top together. It unraveled like a present, and Tallora gasped to hide her sob. "Even prettier than last night," he whispered into her ear. The hand at her thigh came up to stroke the thin garment between her legs. Fear rose, utter violation causing her entire body to shudder. Apparently, he misinterpreted. "I'm more than happy to move this along—"

In a moment of daring, or perhaps stupidity, Tallora dumped the bottle of wine onto her bare chest and tabard.

Lemhi released her, likely from shock, and Tallora bolted up, lightheaded as she covered her breasts with her hands. "Clumsy me," she said, nearly in hysterics. Tears welled in her eyes; a few escaped unbidden.

The ambassador seemed startled but not unhappy. "I will gladly clean you up myself—"

"No, I couldn't possibly—I'm so embarrassed—I'll be back!"

Tallora ran from the room, past men and women in varying states of undress, bursting through the door—

Right into the arms of Ambassador Amulon.

He stood beside a baffled pair of guards stationed beyond the door—which clicked shut behind her. She wrenched herself from his grasp. "Where are you going?"

"As you can clearly see, I need a change of clothing," she managed to say through her tears. She forced a smile, surely a sight with her wine-stained, nearly naked body and tear-streaked face.

One of the guards stood in her path when she tried to step away. "Empress Vahla said you were not to leave under any circumstances."

Amulon's hand on her shoulder nearly pulled a sob from her throat. "Surely the empress wouldn't object if I escorted her?"

"*Mermaid!*"

Tallora looked up, as did the guards and Amulon. Dauriel stood strong, shoulders puffed up as she approached them. "Mermaid," she spat, "my mother would have words with you."

When none of them moved, Dauriel strode forward and snatched the chain trailing from behind Tallora, yanking her along. She yelped, forced to expose herself before the men, tears and wine staining the floor as she was pulled along.

Dauriel kept her bravado all through the halls—it wasn't until she'd shut the door to Tallora's old room that she dropped the chain. When she turned, her eyes scanned Tallora's trembling figure, her countenance falling to sorrow.

Nearly naked and terrified beyond her nightmares, Tallora burst into hysterical sobs, falling to her knees as she released soul-aching cries. Safety was tentative; still she felt his leering eyes and his hand skimming her intimate parts. Her very core revolted, and she wrapped her arms around herself, curling into a ball on the floor as her breathing grew deep and much too quick.

When a hand lightly touched her arm, she flinched and wept.

Then, a knock sounded at the door. "Princess?"

Tallora could not try and quiet herself.

"Have you seen the mermaid? Your mother wishes to know."

Tallora heard scuffling beside her. "I have. Tell my mother she's sick."

Surely the servant heard Tallora weep. But she was met with silence; the servant had gone. Beside her, she heard Dauriel say, "I don't wish to startle you. But we should move you to the washroom in case my mother comes to confirm the tale."

Tallora managed a shaky nod, weeping all the while. When Dauriel helped her to stand, she collapsed into the princess' side, desperate to find safety somewhere, anywhere—even in the arms of the woman she hated.

Dauriel held her—and by the Goddess it was with all the tenderness in the realm. Protective and tight, and then came a whisper in Tallora's ear: "They won't take you back. Not tonight. Let's get you cleaned up."

She was acutely aware of her bare chest against Dauriel's tunic. Shame filled her. She pulled away, covering her nudity with her hands. Never as a mermaid had she cared; as a human girl, her own body was something to fear.

Dauriel was a lover of women as well, yet Tallora didn't feel leering eyes—only sincere concern, a desperation to console.

Tallora pulled her gaze from the floor, noticing Dauriel's helpless stance. "I-I'm sorry," Tallora said through her tears.

"May I touch you?"

Tallora nodded, resisting the instinct to flinch when Dauriel placed a hand on her waist. "I'll draw you a bath. The wine will be sticky sooner than later. We'll get you clean. We'll get you something soft to wear. I swear upon my honor, as a Princess of Solvira, you will not be left alone tonight."

Tallora let Dauriel lead, numb as she sat upon the floor of the washroom. Through misted vision, she watched Dauriel fill the tub with water she knew would be warm. Bubbles frothed from the brass edges—soon, Dauriel offered Tallora a hand. "I'll leave you to bathe and guard the—"

"No." Tallora gasped, forcing her panic to settle. "Stay. Stay, please."

The princess nodded, shying her gaze away as Tallora peeled the ruined garments from her lower body. Exposed, she slipped into the tub, letting the bubbles hide her nudity. The water embraced her like a mother's hug, enveloping her in comfort. Tallora's tears still fell, but less now, quiet. Dauriel tentatively peeked, and once she saw Tallora was covered, she approached, kneeling beside the tub with a gentle smile. "Do you need to talk about what happened?"

Tallora shook her head. "I wasn't raped, before you worry. I was simply touched enough to feel as though . . ." Her voice trailed off, soft cries stealing her words.

Dauriel watched helplessly from the side, but she assisted more than she realized. Whatever Tallora's fear . . . she trusted Dauriel at her word. "What do you need?"

"To talk about literally anything else. I want to forget."

Dauriel immediately launched into a tale, some anecdote of years ago when Khastra had offended a diplomat from Tholheim. She conveyed such kindness, such light, and Tallora managed to smile.

When she'd grown wrinkly from the water, Dauriel held Tallora's towel. Wrapped in luxury, she was taken back to the bedroom, led by Dauriel's touch and voice. She babbled all the way, and Tallora clung to it, finding comfort in her attempts to talk about, well, literally anything.

Dauriel offered a nightgown, pausing only to say, "This one is new. I hope it fits," before resuming her story. She turned around when Tallora dropped her towel.

Tallora managed to navigate her way through the fabric, letting it hug her, protect her from perverse advances. When she sat on the bed, she beckoned for Dauriel to join her.

She fell into Dauriel's side as the princess sat up at the headboard, clutching her arm as she listened. Whenever Dauriel caught her eye, Tallora noticed something tender in that soft, silver gaze, an elusive kindness she had never seen from the princess. Dauriel was fierce, malicious at times, her cleverness punctuated with cruelty.

Tonight, there was warmth, and for hours they spoke. Dauriel's eyes drooped but she never faltered, even as the moon rose and fell, and when the first speckles of light bled from the horizon. Tallora clung to her words like a rock in a storm.

The sun rose. Tallora's eyelids grew heavy. She slipped down into the covers, Dauriel's words swirling together like water turned to steam and dissipating just the same . . .

Tallora drifted off to sleep.

Chapter IX ✽

When Tallora awoke, her body insisted it must have been years, though her mind said it was, perhaps, a few hours. She sat up, vision groggy and muddled, and realized she was alone.

Confused, Tallora yawned deep enough for her head to spin and chose to wait, hoping her escort might return sooner than later. Her stomach growled, and she went to entertain herself by stumbling through books.

Words were strange, artistic compilations, and though she could understand specific names—there, at the top of the page, was scrawled *Neoma*—Tallora could make little of the foreign script. Time with a tutor hadn't quite set any lessons into stone.

After an hour, Tallora's impatience led to nerves.

She slipped a robe over her nightgown, hoping she might creep about unnoticed. Her occasional glance to her pearlescent skin tragically dissuaded her of that, but if anyone asked, she would simply inquire of Dauriel's whereabouts.

From her bedroom, Tallora could navigate the path to the training grounds well enough. However, when she stepped into the room bearing the lift, she realized she had no idea how it worked. She stood awkwardly for a few seconds, then said, "Down."

Nothing happened. With a sigh, she left, resolving to find the stairs instead.

She passed one of the many libraries sequestered in the castle, recalling that Dauriel often spent time in those as well, but stopped when she heard a familiar voice practically spit the very name she sought: *"Dauriel!"*

Not loud enough to be a yell, but certainly not quiet—Tallora pressed herself against the wall, realizing Khastra had continued speaking. "You will *not* speak to her of this. This woman was nearly raped last night, and you would burden her with your feelings?"

Tallora couldn't hear the whispered response, only that it was Dauriel's muted reply.

"Furthermore," Khastra continued, derision in every pointed word, "she is your prisoner. She *cannot* consent to you. She would reject you at risk of castigation or worse, but should she say yes, it is more likely out of fear than sincerity, given her new duties in this castle. You do not even know her name because it is all she has left. You and your family have taken everything else. The power imbalance is sickening, and you would be dishonorable to exploit her."

Whatever this feeling gripping Tallora's heart, it paled to the shattering she felt when she heard Dauriel's tearful reply. "Then what do I do?"

"Nothing." The space after that single word felt boundless, infinitely expansive and lonely. "When I say you have done her wrong, I do not cast judgement. You have done what you thought was right for your kingdom. But reality has no moral lens; this girl has been displaced from her lands and surely lives in constant fear." Khastra stopped again, and when she resumed, the tone she took was not soft, no, but it lacked the virulent anger of before. "I disagree with the empress' treatment of her, but it is not my place to defy Empress Vahla. If you wish to give the mermaid girl a comfortable life, leave her be."

Tallora pressed closer to hear Dauriel's response: "I understand."

"You are young, Princess, and I know to swallow your feelings feels like a fate worse than death. But it may be the noblest act you do upon this earth. Be her friend. Offer kindness amidst the hell that has become her life—"

"General, do you have to call it that?" So much guilt in those words. Tallora felt fury rise in her heart at Dauriel's absolute misunderstanding of her crime.

"She is a slave to the Solviran crown." The finality of the words filled Tallora with dread. "You have delayed her fate for one night, but you cannot protect her forever."

Tallora had to step away, risking exposure from swallowing back her emotions. Damn Dauriel. Damn her and her charm and idiotic view of the world, and damn her most of all for forcing Tallora to confront her own complicated and tumultuous feelings.

She left them, returned to her room, and sat on the floor before the door, blocking it with her body. She stared in silence at the lavish décor, her thoughts far louder than her mind could bear.

Oh Dauriel, Dauriel, with her soft, silver eyes and misguided intentions. She'd ruined Tallora's life. Destroyed it. Shattered her future and every hope and dream.

Tallora's head fell into her hands, wondering if her ever-softening feelings were because Dauriel was the only peace in this storm or because she might've loved her in another life, one where they weren't at odds from the start.

She could exploit this. Seduce Dauriel. Ravish her. Touch every inch of her beautiful, strong body . . .

Tallora angrily snapped her eyes open and looked back out to the room. She could seduce Dauriel *with the intention* of manipulating her, saving her from a lifetime of fucking men for a foreign crown, perhaps even securing a way home.

But could she? Tallora's posture fell as she slid onto the floor, facing the ceiling. She recalled Dauriel's gentleness, the light in her eyes when she'd held Tallora all night long.

What did she truly want?

Dauriel came to her room not an hour later, carrying a tray full of food. "Are you feeling more rested?" she said, her smile as soft as her eyes.

Her smile had been kinder lately.

Tallora sat on the bed, patting the space beside her as she said, "I am. Did you sleep at all?"

With care to not jostle the array of bread and fruit, Dauriel placed the tray upon the table beside the bed. "No. But I haven't been tired. Been thinking too much." She sat down, at Tallora's insistent beckoning. "You had a horrible ordeal last night. Are you all right?"

Nothing but sincerity in her tone. Tallora spared a glance for her lips and braided hair, marveling at how the dark locks shimmered in the sunlight, revealing subtle shades of burgundy. "I'm shaken," she admitted. "And fearful, because I know this is a temporary haven, the eye of the storm, you could say." A bitter smile stole her lips as she reached for the food. It tasted of ash.

"I will speak to my mother. Beg her to spare you. You're beautiful, yes, but your intelligence and wit could lead to something great. I'll convince her to educate you—you could be an ambassador within a year."

Disbelief raised Tallora's eyebrow. "An ambassador?"

"Foreign countries love beautiful people who speak pretty words. Goddess knows I'm terrible for both, but you could be spectacular."

Tallora's face fell at the implication, and she wondered if this were a festering wound. "I would appreciate it if you didn't insult yourself to compliment me." Before Dauriel could speak and object, Tallora sat up on her knees, close enough to reach over and touch the princess' face. No, she was not beautiful; she was fierce and cold, her strong jaw and sharp features from her plain-looking father, not her mother whom the gods would cry to look upon.

Yet Tallora, if she were being truly, sincerely honest with herself, found Dauriel striking nonetheless.

She leaned forward, demure as she gazed into Dauriel's eyes. Oh, she was nervous, the fluttering in her stomach as nauseating as it was exciting. The stakes were high, but she swallowed her fear, realizing how dearly she desired this. "My name is Tallora," she whispered, and Dauriel repeated the word like a prayer to Neoma herself.

"Tallora—"

Tallora stole the name back from her lips, kissing her with all the gentleness of the sunlight against her ebony hair. Absolute bliss filled her, her stomach fluttering like a bird. When she pulled away, Dauriel's blush rivaled the pinks of Tallora's skin. The princess shied away, wide-eyed as she asked, "What was that?"

"It was a kiss." Tallora smiled, finding it easier than she might have thought. "I'll do it again, if you'll let me."

"Your name—"

"Is proof of my trust. I'm giving it to you, but I hope you'll keep it safe and secret."

Dauriel stared, mouth agape. "Tallora, we can't . . ." She shut her eyes and jaw, visibly struggling with her words. "I can't violate your trust by sleeping with you."

"You pompous ass." That pulled Dauriel back from the pit of self-loathing she'd fallen into. The princess' eyes shot open, offense on her tongue. Tallora grinned, mischief in her smile. "You'll have to earn my bed. The kiss was free, and I'd happily do it again, but don't flatter yourself into assuming you have the honor of touching my lovely self without working for it."

She failed to bite back laughter at Dauriel's bafflement. Amidst her riotous fit, she heard the princess shyly ask, "Are you mocking me?"

By Staella's Grace, she'd never heard Dauriel sound *demure*, and it was both endearing and a little pitiful. "Only as far as your adorable thick-headedness." Tallora came forward and cupped Dauriel's cheek, her features softening as she added, "It's as odd to me as it surely is to you. You've been an absolute bitch, but I've also seen you become . . . softer." She placed a light kiss on Dauriel's cheek, feeling heat beneath the princess' skin. "And it became startlingly clear, when you stayed up all night to comfort me, that there could be something more between us."

"You're my prisoner," Dauriel whispered, her blinking much too heavy for Tallora's heart to handle; Princess Dauriel was strong, yet here she was a fragile bird, too frightened to move. "There can't be anything between us."

"Tell me to stop, and I'll stop."

Tension settled between them. Tallora thought for a moment she might actually be rejected, unprepared for how much that ached, when Dauriel finally pressed their lips together, tender and sweet.

Tallora's mouth parted for her tongue. She sighed at the contact, relishing the touch, her heart racing when Dauriel cupped the back of her head, her rough hand stroking her hair. When Dauriel pulled away, Tallora ended with a quick peck on her soft lips then smiled, a blush burning her own cheeks. "I don't know what happens next," she whispered, "but I'm more than happy to simply let it be."

"I have a crass idea," Dauriel replied, her blush managing to spread to her neck. Tallora found it adorable. "You have full rights to reject it, but at least hear me out."

Tallora agreed, her grin growing ever wider as Dauriel spoke of a scandalous conspiracy.

The statement was so startling, in fact, that Empress Vahla was reduced to mere blinking.

In the throne room, Tallora marveled at the spacious walls, the great paneled windows stretching impossibly high. She saw the lake beyond and wondered, not for the first time, just how far they were from the sea. Weighed down by her shackles and chains, she couldn't quite lift her head high enough to see much more.

"You mean to tell me," Empress Vahla said, startling Tallora back to the present, "you stole her last night from jealousy."

"Correct," Dauriel said, her stance tall, lips pursed in a lurid smirk. "I don't want them touching my property."

"She'll be your personal whore?"

"She showed me last night she'll do anything to avoid a beating."

Gods, Dauriel spoke lies well enough to chill Tallora's blood.

"And here I thought she was a gift to me." Empress Vahla's lips twitched, itching to twist into a frown. Tallora feared she would reject the plot, even if it spited her own presence. When she turned her fierce gaze onto Tallora, she flinched, living the act of the abused maiden. "She'll be kept with the other courtesans to spare you the trouble of supervising her, but I accept this. For now. Past emperors and princes have kept pretty girls and boys to warm their bed—it fits your character."

"I appreciate you sharing," Dauriel replied, her wink nothing less than salacious. Tallora wouldn't have spoken to her mother like that in a thousand years. She gasped when Dauriel suddenly gripped her chin, cooing sardonically in her face. "For fairness sake, show her off all you like. She's a pretty little thing and still a good pet for impressing guests, but only I'm to touch her."

Forced to meet her wicked gaze, Tallora saw a shark on the prowl for meat. When Dauriel released her, she feared her skin had bruised.

Vahla's scoff precluded a chuckle. "Try not to get this one too drunk. The last thing you need is more of those ghastly tattoos."

Cold filled the room, though Tallora didn't understand, only saw Dauriel match her mother's smile, no joy in it at all. "If you'll excuse me, I'd like to play with my new toy." She tugged on Tallora's leash, dragging her away. When Tallora stumbled and fell, nothing changed—Dauriel pulled her along, uncaring of the stone floor chafing her legs.

By Staella's Grace, she'd actually be upset had Dauriel not immediately helped her to rise the moment the doors to the throne room slammed shut. Hesitation showed in the princess' countenance, a stark contrast from the predator not five seconds prior. "I am so sorry," she whispered, offering the chain to Tallora.

Tallora forced a smile as she shook her head. "It would be suspicious if I held it."

Dauriel cast a glance down the hall, then pulled Tallora into a tight embrace. Tallora's heart raced, but not for fear this time. "My mother's cruelty is to spite you. She has to think you'll be worse off with me than the men from Moratham." With a glance to the door, Dauriel placed a hand on Tallora's back and led her away.

"What was she talking about? When she mentioned your tattoos, I mean."

"Nothing," Dauriel replied, but her touch stiffen against Tallora's back. "She simply hates them."

Tallora nodded, though she didn't accept that for a second. "Well, I'm amazed you'd speak to your mother like that."

Dauriel's sneer could have withered the flowers outside. "We have an odd relationship."

"My mother would have slapped me for insinuating that I'd ever had sex. I . . . kept a few secrets from her." Tallora smiled, hoping to lift the mood.

"I'm surprised she'd give a damn at all."

"She's protective, to say the least. What matters is I'd rather be your whore than Lemhi's."

"At least this means I'll get to sleep in my bedroom again," Dauriel replied, her wink holding much more innocence than the one she'd graced her mother. "I'm due for the training grounds, and afterward, you'll likely be taking dinner with the other courtesans. But you won't sleep there. I wouldn't dare let you as long as the ambassadors are here."

Tallora followed, eager to watch Dauriel train with no filter to her thoughts.

Predictably, training was a delight.

Each glittering drop of sweat at Dauriel's brow seemed as fascinating as the motions of her musculature. Dauriel glowed, silver fire swirling at her swords, but it had been countless minutes and Khastra would not fall.

The general remained a teacher above all. "Do not let your power control you, Dauriel," she said as she parried a blow from the princess' swords. "That is a weakness."

The fire at Dauriel's feet dwindled but would not die; Tallora wondered how the Silver Fire could possibly be thought of as a weakness. Still, Khastra pushed her and pushed her—never had they gone so long without a break. Tallora feared she would collapse, but anytime she looked near fainting, Dauriel would cry out and rush Khastra once more.

And it was so strange, for Tallora to watch and feel so utterly enamored. She fought her grin but couldn't stop her blush after a particularly bold attempt to swipe at Khastra's digitigrade knees—Dauriel's biceps were too attractive for words.

Dauriel suddenly fell to the ground, Khastra's training sword against her calf downing her in a single blow. Tallora gasped; Khastra relaxed her stance as she stepped forward.

Light burned from Dauriel's figure—her entire body exploded into silver flame as she jumped to her feet. An angry cry left her throat as a burst of fire left her body. Tallora feared the general would fall—

instead, she cried, "Dauriel, you will calm yourself immediately."

The figure within the flame held Khastra's gaze, breathing heavily as the time slowed and stopped. But the standoff eased; Dauriel's silver flame dwindled. She threw her weapons upon the ground.

"I highly encourage you to use your blood powers for an enemy you intend to kill," Khastra said, smiling easily as she approached the glowering princess. "But you must learn to control it. Otherwise, it will control you."

Dauriel had said nothing, merely picked up her swords—real steel, unlike Khastra's—and offered her a nod and nothing else. To Tallora's surprise, Khastra let her go.

Tallora stood at Dauriel's approach. "For what it's worth," she whispered, "I think your silver fire is hot."

The silence between them stretched long, but Dauriel finally released a silly, scoffing laugh. "She's right. It's dangerous."

"It's something, that's for certain."

Drenched in sweat, Dauriel nearly touched her—her hand brushed Tallora's waist but fell instead to her side. Such a strange mortal habit, to release water from their pores. Tallora didn't care for it, didn't like how sticky she felt, but there was something tempting in Dauriel's shined face, her flushed cheeks, even her smell as she stood so close—not vile at all. Merely stronger. Tallora idly grabbed a lock of her own white hair and twirled it with her fingers.

The princess glanced to the coliseum, vacant save for the general who seemed preoccupied wiping dirt off a fallen sword. "It's the most powerful magic in all the world," Dauriel said, "or so I'm told. I have little finesse, but when my blood is pounding, I can summon a torrent." She held out her arm and pointed at the tattooed design along her wrist—thick but unquestionably foreign writing. "These are Demoni characters, a written spell to help me focus. I've noticed a huge difference. Khastra has a contact who inscribes them; she has them all over, but this is as much as I need, for now."

When Tallora tried to look closer, Dauriel pulled away. "But is it real fire? I was taught it was pure creation—whatever that means."

"As far as I understand it, it's energy," Dauriel replied, watching as Khastra disappeared toward a door leading to the inside of the outer wall, "and so it can burn as flame if it catches on something." Alone now, Dauriel's hand settled against Tallora's waist—she leaned into the touch, uncaring of her glimmering sheen of sweat. "Neoma's power is a mystery to us all, but it's a responsibility every Solviraes must master. I'm doing as well as I can." Tallora adored the princess' sincere smile. "Some of us can rip holes through the planes, like my father—it's how we travelled here, from Tanill. Some can absorb magic and shoot it back, while others can simply summon the energy within themselves."

Tallora spared a glance toward the grounds and deemed them alone. Though it was daring, she pressed her lips against Dauriel's, just for a moment. When she pulled back, Dauriel's cheeks had reddened. "Tell me more. But find me food."

Dauriel grinned, and Tallora felt she might be utterly smitten.

Chapter X ✸

O f course, Empress Vahla made it her business to spite Tallora however she could.

Dauriel had escorted her to the courtesan's wing, implication bleeding into her voice at her farewell of, *"See you tonight."*

Tallora offered a nervous nod, but once Dauriel left, she was immediately stolen by Leah. Her friend inspected her, glossing aside her hair to inspect her neck. "Are you all right?"

"I am," Tallora replied, concerned at Leah's frown.

"I presume the rumor that Princess Dauriel violently raped you after you ran away from Lemhi is false, then?"

Taken aback, Tallora said, "What? Who would say that?"

"Apparently you were overheard sobbing after she took you. I didn't believe it, but I had to be certain."

"She and I—" Tallora bit her tongue, realizing that for her protection, and for the women she would be asking to risk their lives to lie for her, she must maintain the façade here too. "I'm to be hers alone. But I'm fine with the arrangement—much more so than I was servicing the Morathan Ambassadors."

"We heard that too." Leah's apologetic grimace said enough. "The empress was quick to inform us that you were merely not to be *touched* by anyone except the princess, but insisted you still be put to use. It's the ambassadors' last night in Solvira, and Empress Vahla has requested a number of us serve dinner to them and the royal family. They'll be eating in one of the private chambers."

"Of course they will," Tallora replied, bitterness sneering her lip.

"Come. I'll help you dress."

And so, within a few minutes, Tallora's hair was done up with pins, lest it touch the food or cover her assets, and at her waist was a split skirt that showed nearly all of her legs. The layered jewelry around her neck reminded her of home—for grand occasions, merfolk would drape themselves with beaded shells, perhaps even clip their ears and tails with jewels. And of course, like home, she wore nothing to cover her breasts, a fact which was commented upon by the equally bare Leah. "Do you wear clothing beneath the sea?"

Tallora shook her head.

"Then it must not bother you to have men's eyes on you."

"Men don't leer beneath the sea, because it isn't a scandal to be naked. Call it animalistic if you like."

"To be quite honest," Leah replied, "it sounds refreshing."

Leah and a few others escorted her through the hallways, whispering instructions as they walked in a line. "You're to keep their wine glasses filled."

Tallora would have thought they'd learned their lesson about trusting her with beverages.

"Say nothing at all, simply smile."

"Unless they prevent you from doing your job, let them do what they like."

They entered a small dining room, lavishly decorated with velvet chairs and jeweled sconces. A chandelier cast soft light upon the patrons at the table. Tallora was grateful Eniah was not among them, but there was Dauriel, unquestionably surprised to see her, but her face just as quickly shifted to ire as she shot a glance to Vahla, who was busy charming Ambassador Amulon. Dauriel's father spared the women no mind, instead laughing at some jest from Ambassador Lemhi. Coldness seeped through her veins when he cast his eyes on her—she purposefully averted her own, recalling his wandering hands.

No one acknowledged them otherwise, instead continuing their idle conversations about wine and other frivolous, non-political things. Only one remark caused her pulse to spike, from Lemhi himself.

"Perhaps you'll be a little less clumsy tonight," he said. Though highly tempted, she resisted the urge to spill the bottle into his lap as she filled his glass. When she merely smiled, he added, "Come to my chambers—I want to hear all about your secret mermaid powers. Perhaps even experience it myself."

Dauriel's chair scraped against the floor, and Tallora feared what she might do. But to her surprise, Vahla waved off his words. "The mermaid has already been spoken for this evening," she said, though not without a glance to Dauriel. The princess glowered in the corner. Under different circumstances, Tallora might've laughed at her petulance, but it was reassuring for someone to fight on her behalf.

Lemhi looked visibly disappointed; she avoided his corner of the table as much as possible.

When the wine bottles had emptied and dessert was delivered, Tallora excused herself under the pretense of finding more. She chose to simply not return, instead covering herself with her arms as she traversed the halls alone.

At the courtesan's wing, Mithal laughed at her entrance. "No one in here will give a second glance to your nudity," she said, her own robe just a shift away from revealing her body.

"Habits develop quickly," Tallora replied. "Where are my clothes? I'll be expected in the princess' chambers soon."

The elven woman pointed to her shared bedroom, her knowing gaze unnerving Tallora's resolve.

She swallowed her memories, unwilling to entertain thoughts of groping hands and cold eyes. Instead, she sat on her bed, knowing it would hardly ever be used, and offered a silent prayer. *Goddess Staella, I'm so afraid. Yet, I've found an unexpected joy.* She opened her eyes, surprised at the sudden rise of emotion. Savoring this rare moment alone, she shut her eyes again, hands trembling as they clutched the other. *So why am I still afraid?*

Perhaps because Tallora still lived and died by her word? Yet, despite Dauriel's boorish bravado in public, she'd shown nothing but kindness alone, at least in recent days. She trusted Dauriel . . . She hoped.

There, Tallora stayed in silent prayer until Leah came in and said, "I'm to show you the way to Dauriel's chambers. Change into something enticing, and we'll go."

Tallora was about to object, given that Dauriel wouldn't have a single care regarding what she wore, but stilled her tongue, recalling her ruse. With a nod, Tallora went to the closet of scandalous things, picking something that at least covered her top half, praying Dauriel would let her borrow something more comfortable.

When she'd left with Leah, the woman said, quite knowingly, "So, the princess is fond of you?"

"It seems so." Tallora struggled to identify the coldness in her limbs.

There was victory in Leah's smile. "As I said, don't be shy if you want advice on how to please her."

Oh. Right. "Do tell."

"She's rather aggressive," Leah continued, still doing well to keep her voice lowered, "but doesn't want you submissive. She won't hang you from the stocks for a bit of teasing. Very crass though—loves to insult you right back. You've probably noticed that out of the bedroom too. Don't try and fuck her; she'll get angry. And be prepared—she loves using her tongue."

Her cold nerves were suddenly replaced by pulsing heat, and Tallora realized she was jealous. "You know a lot about this."

"Evanja and I were her favorites—don't know if you've met her. But she and I would keep her busy all night, sometimes."

"Together?"

Leah had the audacity to chuckle. "Don't be so shocked. We perform in groups more often than not. Men love to watch two women, and so does the princess."

"I don't know if I could do that," Tallora said softly. She'd been with men she hadn't loved, certainly not one to shy from a bit of fun. Women too—Tallora loved to be gazed upon and adored. But to kiss someone for another's entertainment . . . for *Dauriel's* entertainment . . .

Tallora thrust the thought aside, feeling sick at the prospect.

They came upon a set of carved double doors, the dark wood bearing the crest of Solvira—a full moon with the emblem of a skull, surrounded by a perfect circle of stars. The holy triage, and Tallora could have admired it for hours had Leah not knocked and twisted the knob. *"Good luck,"* she mouthed.

Tallora stepped into what appeared to be a small entry hall, windowless and dim. Before her was a door slightly ajar, and when she peeked inside, she saw an enormous bedchamber, filled with finery beyond what Tallora had seen thus far. An enormous window bathed the room in moonlight, while the stone tiles bore a subtle motif of stars.

Centered was a large four-poster bed—empty, for its owner sat at a writing desk, a single candle lighting her scribbling. She looked up at Tallora's entrance, immediately standing and rushing to her side. "Tallora, I'm so sorry. I didn't think my mother would—"

"You gave her permission," Tallora said, marveling at how Dauriel's eyes reflected the moon. They shone as bright as her progenitor's light. "And you had to, to keep up the ruse. I'd rather be looked at than touched." She took both of Dauriel's hands in her own, squeezing tight but not quite able to meet her eye, staring instead at the floor, studying the patterns etched within.

"Let's get you out of those clothes. I have some you can borrow."

Dauriel released her hands and went to an enormous wardrobe, which she fully stepped inside of. Curious, Tallora realized it led to an entire room filled with an array of rich gowns and accessories. Every manner of shoe and hairclip, yet she'd seen Dauriel wear none of them. "These are magnificent."

"Thank you," the princess replied, riffling through a drawer.

Hidden among the trove of fine, feminine things were emblems of Dauriel's true self—a small row of doublets hung in the back, leather boots by the door, and a folded pile of trousers sat neatly in the corner. "Why do you keep them if you don't wear them?"

Dauriel withdrew a pale green dress from a drawer. "My mother gifts them to me, perhaps in hopes that I'll stop embarrassing her at every public function. Getting rid of them would be more trouble than it's worth; at least this way, she thinks there's hope. And I do like looking at them—but I'd like them much more if someone like you were wearing them."

Tallora smiled at that, the idea of being admired for wearing something beautiful instead of provocative rather refreshing.

"This may look sickly with your skin," Dauriel continued, offering the green dress, "but it's the most comfortable nightgown I own."

"I don't care much for looks right now, assuming you don't either."

She accepted it when offered, and Dauriel said, "Never worry about what you're wearing. Not with me."

"Because you'd prefer me naked anyway, right?" Tallora teased, but for Dauriel, it seemed, she'd struck a nerve. "Princess—"

"I swear, I tried not to look at you at dinner," Dauriel said, immutable guilt in her words. "Tallora, I would never take advantage of your situation—"

"Stop," Tallora said gently, grateful when Dauriel obeyed. She kept her soft tone, a smile gracing her lips. "You're so funny, you know that? So brave and confident, but all it takes is a pretty girl to get you flustered."

Dauriel's light blush came with a shy smile. "I only want you to be comfortable."

"I am," Tallora whispered, yet the hesitation in Dauriel's stance wounded her heart, and she knew there was more she had to say. "Is this because Khastra yelled at you?"

Visibly taken aback, Dauriel opened her mouth . . . then shut it again, a frown pulling at her thin lips.

"I overheard," Tallora continued, "and it's honestly why I had the courage to even mention my feelings toward you, knowing you felt the same way. You can't take advantage of me, because I want to be here. I like you, and you don't need to feel guilty for liking me or thinking I'm beautiful. She's right, but she's wrong."

Dauriel's breath escaped in a pained sort of sigh, and Tallora offered a smile as she asked, "Where is the washroom? I'll need a minute to take out the pins in my hair."

Dauriel placed a tentative hand against Tallora's waist as she escorted her out of the bedroom and to one of the closed doors in the entry hall. "Take a bath, if you feel like you need to. And don't be shy if I can help with anything."

Tallora placed a slow kiss at the side of Dauriel's mouth, trailing her lips to the center and letting it linger. Warmth filled her, a reminder of her blossoming feelings, and when Dauriel's other hand cupped her cheek, she cherished the sensation, a bit of security in the storm of her life.

When she pulled back, Dauriel's gaze was nothing less than adoring. "I'll be quick," Tallora whispered, and she drifted away.

Tallora didn't feel the need to bathe, but it took what felt like hours to procure all the pins from her hair. In hindsight, it might have been smart to ask Dauriel to stay and assist, but she was stubborn above all else and committed to victory.

Soon, her white locks fell in sheets around the pale green gown—which, yes, did look vile against her skin, but Dauriel's room was dark anyway, and the texture was absolutely divine. As it was the first outfit she'd worn without wanting to pitch herself into a whirlpool, she decided to keep it.

When she returned to Dauriel's bedroom, the curtains had been drawn to cover the moonlit window. Unlike time past, the princess wore a maroon robe tied around what Tallora assumed was a nightgown. Her hair fell in waves, the braid having twisted curls into what would otherwise be pin-straight hair. Odd, to see Dauriel looking anything less than powerful, but odder still were the cushions she piled upon the floor. She looked up at Tallora's entrance and said, "You take the bed."

"Don't be ridiculous," Tallora said, grinning as she approached. "The bed is enormous; we'll share."

"Only if you're certain."

Tallora stole Dauriel's face in her hands, holding it level with her own stare. "I am." She dared to smile, hoping it softened her words. "I want to be here. I've spoken my mind from the moment you plucked me from the sea, and I don't intend to start lying now." She leaned in and kissed Dauriel's lips, grinning against them when her companion's hands slid around her waist. "And you're disgustingly attractive when you're ready to murder a man for me."

"Lemhi has it coming," Dauriel said, and she smiled. "I'll try to relax."

Tallora dragged her to the bed, content to simply bask in the feeling of safety. As she settled herself in the center of the embroidered covers, she said, "I should clarify that I'm absolutely not having sex with you tonight." She patted the space beside her, amused when Dauriel removed her robe, revealing a rather low-cut nightgown. "But I would adore being held and kissed."

Dauriel's wicked grin was the one Tallora knew and secretly loved, and now that she'd admitted it, she realized it excited her. Perhaps she would be easier to convince out of her clothing than she'd thought. But, she had stated her terms, and when Dauriel joined her in bed, she pulled Tallora against her chest and touched only in chaste places, then planted a kiss on the back of her neck.

A few locks of Dauriel's hair draped against Tallora's shoulder. She turned within the embrace, lying on her back as she said, "You have lovely hair, did you know?"

Dauriel scoffed. "I despise it."

"Really?" Tallora reached over to touch an errant lock. "I can hardly believe that."

"It's impractical. Always getting in the way. In a fight, it can be grabbed. Tangles against my tunic. Not useful at all, but it's fashionable."

"If you ask me nicely, I'll cut it for you."

Disbelief looked rather handsome on Dauriel's features, even if Tallora wanted to smack it away. "You cut hair?"

"We do have razors of sorts beneath the sea. I know how to cut hair." She grinned at Dauriel's grimace. "You'd look dashing with it short. Think about it."

"Is this a ploy to set a razor against my throat?" Dauriel teased, and Tallora shut her up with a languid kiss.

"Perhaps," she whispered, but then she smiled against Dauriel's lips. "My life is already in your hands. The dynamic would turn."

Dauriel kissed her again, wasting no time in slipping her tongue between Tallora's parted lips. Oh, how delightful she felt, more so when they pressed their bodies together, the thin fabric doing little to hide the feeling of warm skin and lithe curves beneath her hands.

Yet, with arousal came a surge of unwanted remembrance, of her jealousy of time past. Tallora gently pulled away, hating how her face betrayed her vulnerable thoughts. "There was something I wanted to talk to you about."

Dauriel nodded, brow furrowing in concern.

"You used to visit the courtesans in this palace often, or so they told me." Shame flooded Dauriel's features, and she quickly added, "I don't mind. I merely want to understand. And I wanted to know if this was something that might happen again. We haven't had a chance to discuss what this is, and I'm realizing now that we need to. If I'm to be on the side, I do understand. We're secret. We're forbidden. And if you have to sleep with other women to maintain the illusion, or even marry one . . ." Tallora's stare fell to Dauriel's collarbones, reality settling of how damned she truly was. Spots of joy, perhaps, but only in a life of slavery, and only until the empress decided to sell her body to the highest bidder.

"Tallora . . ." The name still sounded so foreign and tentative, like a fragile shard of glass. To even speak too loudly would break it. "No," Dauriel finally finished, her grip growing tight and then slack. "I won't be going there."

Tallora brought a gentle hand up to caress Dauriel's hair. "Tell me. You can be vulnerable to me."

Dauriel stole a stiff breath, but each word she spoke grew steadily less pained. "After my surgery, I suppose I felt I had to compensate for my broken self. I slept with many women—too many women. The courtesans were convenient, but I often left the castle and found a quick fuck at the tavern. I . . . wasn't happy."

"No matter how many holes you filled, you were still empty?"

Dauriel's melancholy vanished under a fit of laughter, to Tallora's relief. "You aren't wrong." She cupped Tallora's cheek, her laughter fading but leaving a smile. "I don't quite know what we are either, but I have no intention of having anyone else."

Tallora turned into the touch, kissing her hand, very aware of how Dauriel's pupils expanded at the gesture. Yet there was still a distant hesitation in the princess' gaze, a breath she hadn't released. Tallora dared to ask a dangerous question. "Forgive me if this is out of bounds, but why *did* you stop going to see the courtesans?"

Dauriel's guilt of before flooded her countenance; Tallora immediately regretted the inquiry. "It's a long story."

Tallora recalled Mithal's words, yet while she knew Dauriel was capable of violence, she couldn't fathom that the rumors were true. Instead, she smiled and kissed the princess once more. With a wink, she said, "If any good came out of all this, the girl who brought me here gave all sorts of advice on how to please you."

Dauriel's face immediately paled, much to Tallora's delight. She laughed and kissed Dauriel's nose and cheeks, unable to stop even when she spoke. "Leah loves to talk."

"Oh, so the whole castle knows you love your tongue between a woman's legs?"

Dauriel covered her face with her hand, blushing behind her fingers. Tallora gently pulled it away. "Tonight, you'll kiss me here," she cooed, pursing her lips. "Perhaps tomorrow we'll talk about the lips between my legs."

Their lips met, and oh, what a joy it was to feel her, for Dauriel to slip her tongue into Tallora's mouth and make her idly long for more. Her hands were rough from work when she brushed against her arms, and Tallora ran her fingers through Dauriel's hair, enamored by the dark locks tangling in her fingers.

When they finally parted for air, Tallora grinned as she placed their foreheads together, her smile unflappable.

They spoke of idleness and joy after that, lazily kissing until Dauriel drifted off to sleep. Tallora recalled that she hadn't slept the night before and tucked the princess into bed, settling beside her before sleep stole her as well.

Tallora awoke to a slight rustling of the bed.

When she slowly blinked awake, the window was still dark. The curtains covering it shook, however, recently disturbed.

Tallora was alone. When she ran her hand across the sheets, Dauriel's imprint was still warm. She sat up, frowning until she noticed movement beyond the window.

Tallora stood and approached, realizing that behind the cracked curtain was a larger window than she'd thought—it led to a balcony.

Frozen beneath the moon's light, Dauriel stared upon the kingdom she had given up her claim to. Tallora twisted the knob, the warm night air caressing her as she stepped out. Beyond, she saw an expansive lake and a kingdom of prosperous people, though they lived in the shadow of an empress Tallora knew was cruel. Dauriel met her gaze, the bags beneath her eyes deep.

"You have a beautiful view," Tallora said softly, joining Dauriel by the edge. A short, stone fencing, similar to the roof, stood between her and a plummet to her death.

"I couldn't stay asleep," Dauriel replied. "I'm sorry if I woke you."

Tallora shook her head. "Don't be. Are you all right?"

Scrutiny filled Dauriel's gaze as she slowly looked her up and down. Tallora felt like a cut of meat, inspected for flaws at every angle. But she met Dauriel's eye at the end, though her stomach twisted. When Dauriel spoke, it was hardly a whisper, carried away on the wind. "So many times, you offered your body in exchange for freedom and favors. I want so badly to believe you, but you heard me talking to Khastra. You knew I was weak and falling for you." When she faced Tallora fully, the vulnerability in her gaze was enough to break her heart. Dauriel's pleading stare begged for answers, and Tallora didn't know what she could say.

With care, she took Dauriel's hand in hers, grateful the princess let her, and stroked gentle lines across her palm. "You're not weak. It isn't a weakness to care for another person," she said, letting her heart guide her words. "And . . . I understand why you would think that. I'm sorry—"

"Don't." Dauriel swallowed, each word plucked unwillingly from her tongue. "I don't care for people. I've never cared to know a woman. I've only ever wanted to have them in my bed. But . . . I want to know you. I want you to know me and that terrifies me—" She shut her mouth, jaw stiffening as she looked back to the beyond.

In idle motions, Tallora's thumb caressed the princess' hand. "It's as surprising to me as it is to you," she said, echoing her previous sentiment. "I think it defies fate for us to have even met. But I love the way you look at me, whether it's with adoration or when you're trying and failing to not think about my body." She smiled, letting the words come as they would. "I'm a tease by nature, but I don't hate you anymore. Forgive me if it's bold to admit, but I think we might be friends. I want to know you too, just as you are."

Dauriel squeezed her hand. They dwelled in silence, until the princess said, "I have a cruel question."

"I highly doubt it'll be the cruelest thing you've said to me."

To her relief, Dauriel smiled at the remark. "Have you been with a woman before?"

Tallora's soft laughter filled the balcony. "That's not cruel, and yes, I have. Not so many times as I have with men, but I like women's bodies very much. Men tend to be more forward with what they want, in my experience."

Dauriel nodded, her expression unchanging. "It's cruel because I didn't think you actually liked women at all for most of your time here. I thought you were just a bitch willing to fuck me for favors."

"Little did I know I'd have to pay you for the honor of having a Solviraes hand up my cunt." Tallora laughed, grateful when Dauriel kept her smile, but saw her lip twitch at the remark. "I'm sorry. I only mean—"

"I know what you mean. You're very funny." Dauriel's expression fell fully at that. She pulled her hand away; Tallora released her. "I struggle to be introspective. I only know that I have a complicated view of myself. My mother made it very clear after my surgery that I was lesser, and when I was caught in bed the first time with one of the courtesans, she mocked me, saying I chased what I couldn't be. But it was just as well because no man would have wanted me either, for what I lacked."

Not for the first time, Tallora wished so badly to wring Vahla's neck.

"I think she meant to shame me but instead I embraced it because, well, I was already disgusting so why not enjoy it? I paid women to fuck each other while I watched. I paid them to let me fuck them any way I liked. I don't like being touched, but I can still enjoy myself. And then I started going to taverns and parties—for years I would drink until I passed out and wake up surrounded by girls I didn't remember meeting. Khastra disapproved, but she couldn't stop me."

Dauriel looked to the sky, eyes shut, and shuddered as she breathed. "You asked me why I stopped and I . . . About two years ago, I met a girl at a party. She and I flirted all through the night, and when she kissed me, we found our own private place to fuck." Though her face remained still, Tallora saw the tension in her arms, fearing her nails might break skin as her hands clutched her forearms. "We fucked. We drank until even I couldn't see straight. And when we went to rejoin the rest, she passed out. That's when I realized she was turning blue. By the time help was called it was too late—she died as I was holding her, poisoned by too much ale."

Tallora's hand slowly rose to cover her mouth.

"My mother paid the girl's father so he wouldn't talk," Dauriel continued, unequivocal shame in her countenance. "But word spreads. She told me I was a stain upon my lineage, that it was a damn good thing I'd abdicated my throne because I was a disgusting embarrassment to her and my family—" She stopped herself, visibly pained. But just when Tallora might've spoken, she softly said, "That night I . . . I tried to end it."

Tallora felt the words like a knife to her stomach, and when Dauriel offered her arm, she gently took it, the tattoos illuminate beneath the moon's light. She saw, for the first time, the distorted skin beneath the runic designs on her wrists, jagged and scarred. "Dauriel—"

"It's a damn miracle that I didn't succeed," Dauriel interrupted, pulling her arm back. "Khastra found me. Managed to get me to the healers in time." She smiled, but it held only sorrow. "The tattoos were my idea. Can't have a woman of my station showing weakness to the world." She traced the runic symbols, and Tallora watched them faintly glow, yet could not unsee the brutal history hiding beneath them. "I stopped drinking. I stopped finding girls in taverns. I couldn't even visit the courtesans in the castle without remembering what it felt like to have that girl grow cold in my arms. I was empty, but at least I was alive."

"You didn't kill her," Tallora whispered, the stars gently casting love across her skin. "It was a terrible accident, yes, but it wasn't your fault." Dauriel said nothing; Tallora said more. "You aren't disgusting. You're a mess, but you aren't disgusting. I think you throw your whole heart into every endeavor—into fucking girls and drinking, but also into your fighting, your kingdom, even . . . even into me."

Dauriel blinked, her eyes shut a moment too long as she shuddered. Slowly, deliberately, Tallora took Dauriel's hands and brought her wrists to her lips. She left a lingering kiss on each, then wrapped her arms around the disgraced princess, holding her tight, feeling her stiffen and then crumble.

Dauriel didn't cry, though she actively fought it. But she clung to Tallora like she had that fateful night beneath the ocean's surface, when Tallora had saved her from a watery grave.

Tallora placed a gentle kiss into her hair. "I want to know you, all the good and bad. You're not weak; you're wonderful."

Instead of speaking, Dauriel stole her lips, content to consume her beneath the moon's light. She gripped Tallora's hair, and Tallora felt no tenderness here—only desperation and lust. Heat rose with each passionate touch, though their hands stayed chaste. But Tallora felt power in both Dauriel's veins and her body, and within herself she craved domination.

When she released a soft whine, Dauriel suddenly pulled back, breathless as she gazed into Tallora's eyes. Her silver eyes were but a ring around a pool of black. "You said not tonight."

She had. And though her body wanted more, she knew it was too much, too soon, too fast. Tallora held her close again, this time in an innocent embrace. "You need sleep."

Dauriel held her tight, her breaths steadying. When they returned to her bedroom, they kept the embrace as they fell into bed. Tallora loved it so, to feel Dauriel breathe in her arms.

Chapter XI 🐚

When Tallora awoke, sunlight shone on the horizon, though thankfully not through the window—that would have been devastatingly blinding. As she rubbed the exhaustion from her eyes, she noticed Dauriel still fast asleep, blissful in her unconscious state. Tallora let her be, recalling how dearly she needed rest.

Instead, she stood and stretched, letting her bones crack and awaken. In the light, she saw the finery of the princess' bedroom, a collection of splendor and beauty upon the walls. Tallora wondered at that, surprised to realize there was little luxury in it aside from the bed, but delicate beauty, live flowers and crystal statues as thin as paper, even jewelry perhaps never worn but displayed with pride, and a small crown meant for a child—treasures to be adored and protected.

She'd expected something sparse and militant. Instead, it stole her breath, the meticulous care put into the decorations.

She shuffled to the washroom. In Dauriel's personal bath, all manner of luxury lay tucked away— soaps that smelled of foreign floral life, dried petals, bottles with labels she tragically could not yet read, as well as further bits of beautiful decorations, motifs of flowers upon the walls, jeweled trinkets, and more.

One small ornament stood out among a collection on a shelf—a mermaid, fully nude, balanced on her tail as she waved at an invisible crowd. She chuckled at the audacity of it, then rolled her eyes and focused on the gorgeous main attraction—the bath itself, large enough for her to submerge her whole body and imagine she were lounging upon the seafloor. Perhaps even she and Dauriel together.

She blushed at the thought, and began undressing, idle thoughts of sex and curiosity dancing through her head. She'd never fucked as a human girl and wondered what the difference would be, how different the air would be than the sea.

Though her very existence had become fear, Tallora felt peace. Dauriel's chambers were a different plane, where they could speak as equals, where Tallora was safe.

As she'd learned from the other bath, Tallora twisted the strange knob, letting blessed, gushing water burst from the pipes. It was all magic, Dauriel had explained—a rather clever bit of planar manipulation, and Tallora hadn't understood it at all. She dropped a smattering of petals on the surface and stepped in, the very core of her soul delighted to return to the water.

She let all but her head submerge, content to sleep in the blanket of warmth. A pity her lungs could not breathe beneath the peaceful waves. Instead, she stole one of the fancier soaps—if it was colored gold, it was expensive, right?—and ran the slippery luxury across her arms and neck, amused at the lather of bubbles collecting along her shoulders.

A quiet knock interrupted her tentative peace. "Tallora?"

"I'm here," she replied, sitting up to see the door. "Come in, if you'd like."

The knob gently twisted, and Dauriel peeked inside, diverting her eyes at Tallora's nudity. Tallora couldn't help her laugh. "Oh, look at me, you precious idiot." She lifted herself enough to rest her breasts on the side of the tub, water steadily dripping down, and felt heat rush her cheeks when Dauriel's eyes shifted oh-so-classily between her face and the peaked buds. "Yours are the only eyes I want on me."

Dauriel shut the door behind her, eyes sunken and grey. Poor princess—she needed more sleep. She knelt before Tallora, keeping her eyes firmly fixed on her face, and kissed her tenderly. "Good morning," she whispered. "How did you sleep?"

"I've always slept better with a warm body beside me," Tallora teased. She pulled away, resettling back into the water, but let a peek of her breasts bob at the surface—Dauriel was much too fun to tease. Merfolk weren't so worked up over breasts, and Tallora found Dauriel's palpable weakness delightful. "Forgive me if this is rude, but your bedroom isn't what I expected. It's absolutely beautiful, but I won't lie and say I didn't imagine something more utilitarian."

Dauriel's hand dipped below the tub's edge, her finger idly skimming the water's edge. "I love beautiful things," she said simply, no weight in the words, yet Tallora realized something precious and heartbreaking to consider.

For Dauriel, who did not see herself as beautiful, cherished the beauty around her in quiet and subtle ways. Tallora studied her, this woman she had once hated, who she had kissed and would happily give herself to, and thought her wonderful. "Explain one thing, though," Tallora said, failing to hide her smile. She pointed at the collection of small statues on the shelf. "That."

At the front was that silly nude mermaid, and the moment Dauriel's eyes settled upon it, they widened; she blushed. "That was something I received years ago when I was young. I-I can take it down—"

"Don't you dare," Tallora teased, adoring her flustered companion. "It just means I was always your type." She laughed as she leaned forward to steal Dauriel's mouth, overjoyed to feel her relax.

When their lips finally parted, Dauriel said, "I accept your offer."

"Which offer?"

"Cut my hair."

Tallora's grin could have widened the walls. "Bring me shears, then. Sharp as you have."

In the few moments Dauriel spent riffling through drawers, Tallora contemplated her next move, wondering if it were too forward. When Dauriel stood tall, a pair of shears in hand, Tallora dared to say, "Clothes off."

Dauriel looked merely amused, raising an eyebrow as she said, "Less blood to clean from the fabric?"

"I only know how to cut wet hair. Let me wash it."

With an easy sensuality, Dauriel slipped her nightgown from her body, slowly revealing her lithe, magnificent figure, the muscles of her back shifting as she tossed her garment away. Tallora shamelessly admired her ass and thighs, strong and built from years of training, and grinned at the hint of vulva lips between her legs—and though none of that was found among her people, she found it all unbearably attractive. When Dauriel turned, she was just as splendid, the hard muscles of her abdomen nearly as enticing as the small curves of her breasts. Centered between her hipbones, a scar remained, a perfect line no longer than Tallora's hand. Dauriel's smile was nothing less than wicked, staring down at her like one of the fierce sea monsters of the depths.

"Are you going to stand there staring like a fool?" Tallora teased, enamored at the slight raise in Dauriel's eyebrow.

"I'll stand as long as you need to properly admire me."

"There's the asshole I remember," Tallora replied, grinning as she beckoned her down. "Join me."

Dauriel grabbed the shears and offered them first, and once Tallora had plucked them from her grasp, she gracefully joined her in the warm bathwater. Seated opposite of her, Dauriel sighed as the water caressed her figure, and Tallora wondered, truly and sincerely, if she were ready to claim this striking woman as her own. A part of her wondered if they'd even leave this bathtub without claiming the other.

"Still admiring?"

Tallora realized she had spaced out while staring. "Only thinking." She beckoned her closer, their bodies touching as Tallora kissed her, sprinkling water into the dry locks of Dauriel's hair when her hand cupped her face.

Beneath the water, Dauriel's hand grazed her bare waist, the other skimming her thigh. "Sorry," she whispered, suddenly drawing back. "Too forward."

"No." Tallora grinned against Dauriel's lips, adoring her curtailed passion. "I like that."

Dauriel's hand returned to her thigh, her thumb gentle as it soothed little circles against her skin. "How did you do it?" she whispered, her pupils expanding when Tallora inched closer, their legs slowly entangling. "Your legs, I mean."

The water hardly shrouded Dauriel's naked body, and heat steadily rose within Tallora at the sight. She prayed the princess felt the same. "I told the truth—I prayed, and Staella answered. In a dream, she said she'd give me the means to free myself." Tallora shrugged, the mood dampened by the words. Still, she craved their intimacy, longed for Dauriel to press her against the side of the tub and, well, do whatever the hell she wanted. Tallora had never been so weak beneath anyone's gaze. "I'll return to my true form when I'm submerged in the water of my homeland. That's what she said."

Dauriel's nod held a tragic sort of resignation. The reminder surely brought guilt—rightfully so—but Tallora couldn't say she cared. Not here. Not now, with the gentle water caressing them, and Dauriel's sleek figure tempting and unbearably perfect.

"Dunk your head in, silly," Tallora said, desperate to see that smile again. "If you turn around, I'll wash it for you."

She set the shears on the small table beside them as Dauriel disappeared beneath the water. When Dauriel sat with her back to Tallora's chest, the intimacy of it broke some wall around her heart to watch this woman, once her enemy, willingly show her back to her. Tallora could grab the blade and end it all . . . but no.

Instead, she lathered what she hoped was the correct soap through Dauriel's hair, gently rubbing her fingers against her scalp. At Dauriel's contented moan, her heart soared, and she placed a kiss on the back of her jaw, uncaring of the soap on her face.

In absolute silence, there was bliss. Only the water and the faint sound of her hands against Dauriel's hair, and Tallora adored it so, the innocent sensuality of it. With utmost care to spare her eyes, she rinsed the soapy residue, leaving only shined onyx flecked with hints of burgundy. "Dry yourself with me," she whispered, unwilling to disturb the glorious peace. "Then sit in front of the mirror. I have a plan, if you'll trust me."

Dauriel stood from the tub, shining and naked, and helped Tallora to rise. Once she'd left the tub, she stumbled into a slippery embrace, their naked bodies pressed together. A surge of heat filled Tallora's abdomen, settling low between her legs at Dauriel's slick touch, their breasts brushing against the other.

Perhaps she'd reconsider her timeline. Tallora recklessly kissed her mouth, shameless as her hands slid up Dauriel's back, savoring the lithe musculature beneath her fingers. Dauriel moaned against her lips, her fingers daring to skim along Tallora slick skin to her ass. "May I?"

Tallora managed an eloquent, *"Uh-huh,"* and gasped when Dauriel squeezed, giggling before smashing their mouths together against, the heat between them boiling—

Sudden banging against the door beyond pulled them apart. *"Dauriel!"* a voice cried, fury in the single word.

"Khastra?" Dauriel said, and she immediately slipped into a robe hanging from the ajar closet. She tossed one to Tallora. "Stay here."

Dauriel left the bathroom, and the moment she'd shut the door, Tallora heard that same anger simmer, threatening to rage. "Is it true, what I am hearing? Is the mermaid in your bed?"

"Yes, but—"

"What am I saying? Not a day ago, *what am I saying?"*

"General, it's not what you think!" Tallora heard actual fear in Dauriel's voice. She ran to the door. "I meant to do as you said, but then—"

"But then you are taking her as your personal whore?! I have taught you better than this—"

Tallora threw open the door. "General Khastra, please listen!"

Khastra had Dauriel backed to the wall, towering over her with all the menace the half-demon could very easily conjure. Her glowing eyes settled onto Tallora, fury etched into her elegant features. "Mermaid," she said, a dare in disguise.

Tallora spoke as quickly as her tongue could move. "I understand what this looks like, but it's a ploy. Dauriel and I haven't slept together—she wanted to protect me from the ambassador by telling her mother she was keeping me to herself."

Khastra looked her up and down, skepticism in her raised eyebrow. "Why are you bathing together?"

"She asked me to cut her hair. I washed it—*after* I'd finished my own bath."

A seamless lie, and Khastra seemed appeased for the moment. She returned her stare to Dauriel. "Anything else?"

"General . . ." Pain crossed Dauriel's face, or rather the anticipation of it, given her next words. ". . . we did kiss. But!" She held up a hand, before Khastra could interrupt. "In my defense, she kissed me first."

Khastra returned her stare to Tallora, who said, "It's true. And it was sincere."

"I do not like this," Khastra replied, and to Dauriel, she added, "and you already know why. But I will tell no one." She crossed her arms, managing to somehow look even more terrifying. Tallora kept a grip on the doorframe. "I am choosing to trust you, Dauriel. Do not get this woman killed."

She left, yet her presence lingered, settling as a weight upon their shoulders. Tallora finally held out a hand. "Come on, before your hair dries." She smiled, placing a small kiss on Dauriel's cheek as she led her back inside.

Soon clothed in a fluffy robe, Dauriel sat in a chair before the mirror.

Tallora was naked, a set of shears in her hand. "Ready?"

"Are you really going to do this nude?"

"You can't be nervous if you're distracted by my tits." At Dauriel's scowl, she laughed, purposefully letting the aforementioned tits bounce in the princess' view. "And it'll be easier to clean me off after. This is very different than cutting hair beneath the sea, but I have a reputation for being good at a few things." She winked as she set the shears aside, instead running a brush through Dauriel's shined, slick hair.

She braided the long, dark locks, nearly black when wet. Tallora's own hair dried to her shoulders and back, sticky in the damp air. "Last chance to change your mind."

Dauriel shut her eyes. "Do it quickly," she squeaked, and when Tallora brought the shears to the base of her head, she tensed when the metal caressed the back of her neck.

She giggled nervously, and it might've been the most darling sound Tallora had ever heard. She snipped—Dauriel *squeaked* as the first bits of hair fell to the shears, and Tallora steadily cut through the thick rope. "It sounds like you're cutting flesh," Dauriel said, and when she peeked, she gasped when Tallora held up the severed braid.

Tallora handed the lengthy rope to Dauriel and said, "How do you feel?"

Dauriel stared at the braid. She held it up, letting it dangle like a snake. "Lightheaded," she said curtly, and Tallora laughed as she tussled the short locks. "And like I should have done this years ago."

Tallora continued her work with the shears, planting kisses between each snip.

Dauriel, with her newly cropped hair, escorted Tallora back to the courtesan's wing.

Tallora shamelessly admired her work, finding it much too handsome for words. She'd styled it so both sides collected at the top, Dauriel encouraging her to use one of the many bottles to manipulate the hair with some sticky substance. Dauriel walked taller, apparently quite confident in her new masculine style, for she held herself grander than Tallora had seen before.

She adored it, just as she was coming to adore Dauriel. Grinning like a fool, she blushed when Dauriel caught her eye. "What?" the princess asked.

"Nothing," she teased, unable to help her girlish giggle. "I did an excellent job, that's all."

"Are you calling me pretty?"

At the devilish glint in Dauriel's eyes, Tallora glanced backwards and forward, then pushed the princess against the wall, meeting no resistance— merely a startled, breathless visage. Casually, she slid her hand up her leather doublet, fingering the buttons as she bit her lip. "I'll call you anything you like with the promise of feeling your naked body against mine again. Tonight, perhaps?" She unlatched the top button, revealing a hint of Dauriel's collar bones; the princess' breath hitched.

Dauriel spared a look to either side of the hallway, then thoughtlessly stole her lips, impassioned enough to stir fresh heat within her. Just for a moment; Tallora whined as the princess pulled away. "Tonight," the princess repeated, and Tallora's blush flared across her cheeks. "I'll make certain everything is perfect."

Tallora grinned as she released her light touch, freeing Dauriel from her sensuous prison. "I have no doubt," she said, unafraid to loop her arm around Dauriel's.

Yet Dauriel wouldn't face her, despite Tallora's grin. Something new shadowed her countenance, and Tallora slowed, then held her back as she stepped in front and stopped. "What's on your mind? Because it isn't my breasts—not with that glower."

"Nothing. Just not looking forward to . . ." Dauriel sighed, her previous bravado seeping away. ". . . seeing my mother."

"Fuck her and her opinions on your hair. Leave the braid on her pillow and be done with it."

Dauriel chuckled, though her smile lacked sincerity. "It isn't the hair. You mentioned last night not knowing what our future could be, and while I know you meant it regarding us, I'm more worried about you. I won't pretend to understand my mother's mind, but she isn't stupid. I . . ." With boundless trepidation, Dauriel took Tallora's hands in hers. "I need to talk to her."

"What are you not saying?" Tallora asked, and when Dauriel shook her head, she dared to touch the princess' cheek. "What are you not telling me, Dauriel?"

"Tallora . . ." Still, Dauriel spoke the name with such reverence, like the precious thing it was. ". . . I swear to tell you everything tonight."

Tallora glanced back, then gently stole her lips in a kiss.

When they reached the door to the courtesan's wing, the princess placed a lingering kiss on her knuckle. "Until tonight," Dauriel whispered, and Tallora grinned like a fool as she stumbled into her new home, drunk from exhilaration.

She was immediately accosted. Leah met her at the door and took her arm as she escorted her inside. "That good?"

"Hmm?"

"You're grinning like an idiot."

155

Tallora merely shrugged, and apparently that was enough.

Leah patted her hand. "Falling for our clients isn't encouraged, but it does make for a fun night."

"I'll bear that in mind, given I'll be going back tonight."

Leah's laughter stole the other women's attentions. "You'll be in love before the week's out with that kind of thinking."

Perhaps she would.

Flocked with interest, Tallora invented a rather elaborate tale of last night's liaison, the newer girls enthralled at the prospect of serving the Princess of Solvira. "It was as I was warned—the princess is rather shameless in her affection. Likes to leave little bite marks." With a wink, she added, "But not on your neck."

Tallora reveled in the attention, only stopping once breakfast was delivered.

She adored the children, spent most of the day telling more innocent tales to them, of her adventures below the sea. Leah's son, Mocum, seemed the most enthralled of them all, but a flock of wide, innocent eyes listened with rapt attention. "I once had a pet named Leona—does anyone want to guess what kind of fish she was?"

"A dolphin?" one little girl asked.

"Dolphins aren't fish, actually," Tallora explained. "They breathe air just like you and make terrible pets. Though I did know someone who befriended one—managed to squeak at just the right tone, I think. No, no—Leona was a clownfish. She lived outside our house when I was a little girl, where my mother tended to the sea anemones."

She described her colorful home and missed it with all her soul.

Chapter XII 🐚

In the early evening, a pair of guards came. "Mermaid?" one said, then spotted her speaking with Leah—as enthralled by Tallora's stories as the children, constantly peppering her with questions she was happy to answer. "You've been summoned."

She nodded and bid Leah goodnight. "I needn't change, trust me," she told the guards. "I won't be wearing it long enough."

When she'd left the great room, one of them brutally clutched her arm, a grip threatening to bruise. "I beg your pardon? Princess Dauriel will—"

"You've been summoned by the empress."

She was dragged away. Both of them held her, though she wouldn't have tried to escape—as she continuously insisted. "I don't have a hope of outrunning you."

"We have our orders."

"I won't tell."

They ignored her.

Thus was her journey to the council chamber. In the narrow room, Tallora was released and stood before a smaller array of council members. Empress Vahla sat in the center, her husband beside her, as well as Magister Adrael, and the two priests of their respective goddesses. Khastra did not sit, but she stood at the back, more focused on what appeared to be an enormous crystal hammer than whatever was about to unfold.

"Congratulations, Mermaid," Vahla said, a vicious smile gracing her lips. "You've managed to earn your keep."

Dread filled her.

"As I had hoped, the Morathan Envoy was absolutely smitten with you. They've convinced the Speaker to make an offer—all the border cities in exchange for you. You'll be sent off tonight."

Panic rose in Tallora's blood. She glanced rapidly to the door, to General Khastra, indifferent as she polished her weapon, and finally back to the empress, her voice surely erratic. "Empress Vahla, your daughter has staked her claim—"

"Then Dauriel shall learn a lesson," the empress spat. "Duty before heart. What other use do you think you ever had, than to be sold? Take comfort in knowing your captivity has saved countless others."

Manacles clasped onto her wrist. Tallora flinched from the hands on her shoulders. "Please don't send me away—"

"Adorable, to finally see you beg." Empress Vahla's smile widened, a wicked joy twisting her lips. "A pity we never learned your name—I'd etch it in a collar around your neck. Take her away."

The guards dragged her back, but she fought, one last hope tearing from her throat. "Khastra! General!"

The general glanced her way but did not even grant her the honor of interest—utter apathy colored her stare.

"Tell Dauriel! Tell her where I've gone—" Her words ended with a brutal slap to her face. Metal gloves scraped her chin. Tallora tasted blood. "Please!"

The guards grabbed her by the hair this time. Tears welled in her eyes—Khastra returned her attention to her weapon. Tallora sobbed from pain and betrayal. With a final wrenching of her body, she yanked herself free—

Only to hear a voice—Magister Adrael's hated voice—mumble the word *sleep* in her head.

Tallora's vision spun. Her feet stumbled. Unforgiving hands caught her before she could collapse against the stone floor, yet her sight failed.

Darkness overtook her.

❧

Tallora awoke feeling ill. The ground beneath her moved. Nauseous from the motion, she vomited on the wooden floor before her, sickened and weak. Beyond, she heard a foreign tongue. Dim sunlight cast light into her pen.

At her ankle, the bracelet was gone. Her same, simple gown adorned her figure. She stumbled to her feet, falling against one of the wooden walls surrounding her. At eye level was a small, barred window, revealing the source of sunlight. She peered through the bars and saw armed horsemen riding alongside her. The scenery was lush and green but entirely foreign. No sign of castles or cities, no landmarks to find her way back to Neolan or to home.

How long had she been unconscious? Tallora collapsed on the floor and sobbed, crippling reality settling. In all her weeks of hopelessness, never had her soul felt so dark. Whatever new prison awaited her promised to be a hellish fate.

The carriage suddenly slowed and stopped. Tallora braced herself, lest she fall into the spreading pile of vomit. She heard clinking metal beyond, then the door swung open, revealing Ambassador Amulon.

Surely she was a pitiful sight, fighting tears, hair tussled from forced sleep. He was handsome and hated and when he smiled, she flinched. "I'm happy to see you awake. It's been two days—I was worried this was permanent."

She said nothing, merely stood at the back of the cage.

"We can clean up the mess, if you'd like to come out."

Again, she merely stared, fear suffocating her.

"Tallora, you have nothing to fear from me."

"Nothing except a lifetime of fucking the leader of a foreign land—" She stopped, realizing what he'd said. He . . . He knew her name?

Amulon gently shook his head. "Though I presume it would be better than being molested by the Solviran Princess, Moratham is only a temporary stop."

Oh, by Staella's Grace—of course he would have heard that.

"We are taking you home."

All feeling left her limbs at once. Tallora nearly fainted—instead, she leaned against the wall, refusing to collapse. "W-What?"

"I have been in quiet correspondence with King Merl of the Tortalgan Sea," he said, voice calm and soothing, "ever since news came of a mermaid girl being held captive by the Solviran Empire. They came to us, imploring for aid, and we agreed. Morathma has proclaimed this his will."

Tallora sought a lie in his countenance but saw only earnest sincerity. Trembling, she could not staunch the flow of tears spilling down her face.

"Come out, please. I won't have you travelling in filth."

Her body moved on its own accord, a puppet to which Amulon pulled the strings. When her feet touched the grass, she sank to her knees and sobbed, fear and relief and sorrow flooding her at once. She would go home. She would see her mother again.

But what of Dauriel? Dauriel and her bleeding heart and hot-headed antics—what would she do, to think Moratham held her prisoner?

Servants moved around her, lesser members of the envoy. Amulon stood by her, stalwart as she wept. "My associate, Lemhi, travels in his own party back to Moratham. He did not know my intentions for you. You'll be safe from him as well."

Tallora and her tear-streaked face dared to look at him, the sun blinding, casting him in a silhouette. "You have to take me to the sea."

"In due time—"

"No, listen," she pled at his feet. "Goddess Staella transformed me into this. For me to change back, I have to be submerged in the water of my homeland—that's what she said."

Amulon knelt beside her, the kindness on his face a betrayal to his words. "Are you quite certain it wasn't just a dream?"

Tallora frantically nodded. "How else would I have transformed into this? Staella said she couldn't interfere, but she would give me the means to free myself. She gave me legs."

Amulon kept his smile, and Tallora wanted to scream at that infantilizing stare. "Perhaps that's true. But the Speaker would like to meet with you personally. He will do all in his power to restore you—"

"I told you—"

"I have my orders, Tallora. When Morathma speaks, the thinking is done." Curtness stiffened his tone; the negotiation was over. "This is for your own good."

Frustration rose in tandem with fresh tears. "Then you have to write to Solvira."

"That wouldn't be wise—"

"Dauriel will think—"

"Shh," he soothed, and he reached forward to stroke her hair from her face. She hated his touch but could not speak of it. "You're safe from her. She will never touch you again."

Tallora shook her head. "It's not . . . She never— We never—"

"You've been through a horrible ordeal," he said softly. "The Speaker worries for you, as does the world. Perhaps you feel conflicted, but let me reassure you that this hysteria is curable. What the princess did was depraved and unnatural. You need time to heal, and then your mind will be unclouded."

"You . . ." The words were too awful to contemplate. Tallora shied from his touch this time, though innocent it might have been. "You don't believe me."

Amulon shut his mouth, his gaze the sort reserved for a small child. "The Speaker is wiser than us all. We shall speak to him."

Tallora's gut clenched; shock stilled her tongue. When Amulon offered a hand to stand, she accepted, though her conflicted heart wept for the princess who had ruined her life.

"Now, while you are welcome to ride in your cage, I'd be just as inclined to have you ride up front with me. It's much more comfortable."

She nodded slowly, merely a body and not a soul as she climbed into the comfortable carriage. Amulon sat across from her. "Would you like food?"

She nodded, her stomach as empty as her hope. When she was offered bread, she ate it slowly, ignored as he withdrew a book.

When the carriage moved, she shut her eyes. She whispered a silent prayer in her mind. *Goddess Staella . . .*

She knew not what to ask for. Perhaps all might be well. But fear gnawed at her core, this new unknown she had been plunged into somehow more frightening than the last.

. . . help.

Sobs overcame her, her heart aching for freedom and for the woman she'd left behind.

Tallora sat beside a campfire that night, silently eating a ration of bread and dried meat.

The Morathan Envoy wasn't small, but it had been split. Tallora watched a moderate ensemble of guards and servants hustle about setting up tents. Despite the promise of freedom, she was still a stranger among them, a vulnerable girl in the midst of foreign men, and so she quietly kept to herself until Amulon joined her.

"How are you feeling?"

Tallora swallowed her bite, apprehension on her tongue as she said, "Exhausted. Emotionally and physically."

"You have been through some terrible things."

Tallora clutched the bowl tight, watching the color drain from her fingers. "So terrible that I've apparently lost my mind?"

"As I said—"

"We'll talk to the Speaker, I remember." Tallora stared at her food, her appetite delicate and easily startled away. "Since you refuse to drop me into the ocean, what will you do instead?"

Amulon looked to the campfire, contemplative as the fire reflected the dark pools of his eyes. "We have priests prepared to cast a number of spells to try and restore your legs. But if that fails and you cannot return home, the Speaker has already promised that you shall be cared for in his home."

She smiled, wondering if it showed any ounce of sincerity at all. "And be his wife?"

"The Speaker has one wife. But the highest honor in the land would surely be yours, should you be unable to return to your home."

Tallora stared a moment, confusion stilling her tongue. "I beg your pardon?"

"Morathma has spoken of accepting you as one of his wives," Amulon said, and Tallora was shaken at both the words and his sincerity. "Perhaps you see yourself as sullied, but he does not. You would be protected for the rest of your days from Solviran tyranny and live a blessed life—you might even bear him a child and be exalted."

Her gut clenched in horror; the words meant nothing and yet everything, the sudden threat of being given to a god at odds to her own—worse, to submit to him—more terrifying than all her days in Solvira. She set her bowl of rations onto the ground, head light, hands trembling, breath shallow as she absorbed this new reality.

And reality, it would surely be. Staella had spoken, but no one believed her.

Amulon must have seen it. "Tallora, you will be given time to adjust and heal, whether it be before you are returned home or granted a place at Morathma's side. There are Priestesses of Staella in the capital trained to aid in soothing confused minds. You will be well in time."

There were Priestesses of Staella below the sea trained to soothe emotional wounds, yet her skin bristled at his words. "Your flowery words are very cryptic," she spat. "Say what you actually mean."

"I don't wish to cause you distress—"

"Too late for that."

"I only mean to give you hope." His hesitation spoke volumes; Tallora glared as he gathered his thoughts. "What Princess Dauriel did to you has likely left you . . . confused. She has turned her back on her divine purpose, but you can still be cured and live a normal life. Morathma has grand hope for your recovery."

Tallora looked away, watching the flickering flame slowly consume the stacked wood, and wondered when she'd become a child's toy, stolen and tugged until she fell apart. "Why?" she whispered, teeth grit to staunch her fear and fury. "Why do you even care about me at all? I'm just a girl. I'm not royal. My mother doesn't have money. What am I worth to you?"

Amulon's hand settled upon her hair, lightly stroking the fine locks. Tallora's nails dug into the skin of her arms. "It is true that one girl is not worth giving up an entire city for, or several. But if I may be so bold, what you represent means everything. The world is watching Solvira, and you've become the face for their atrocities. Your kidnapping showed the world Solvira's true colors."

Tallora's head grew suddenly light. "So I'm a political pawn?"

"Tangentially, yes," Amulon withdrew his hand, returning it to his lap. When Tallora shuddered, locks of hair fell to veil her face. "I cannot lie and say otherwise. The Tortalgan Sea has offered a treaty in exchange for your safety, with the understanding that your legs might be permanent. We in Moratham accept all the allies we can against Solvira's tyranny. But you are also an innocent girl, and Morathma does not condone kidnapping and torturing innocent girls."

Tallora recalled her fear when the guards had stripped her tail of her fin, the pain and agony, and couldn't deny his claim. But that had been Vahla's doing.

She smiled idly, unable to stomach her food, despite her hunger. "Forgive me, but it's a little sick of you to talk about Solviran tyranny when your kingdom is the one stealing their citizens and selling them into slavery."

"It's extreme perhaps, but it's a form of salvation."

Tallora merely stared.

"Should they accept Morathma's will, either in this life or the afterlife, they may still be saved, rather than live out eternity among depraved gods."

She clenched her jaw, frustration growing at his words, but bit back her reply nonetheless. He could still put a knife to her throat or leave her to die—though it might not be a worse fate than the one ahead.

There remained a more pressing matter. Words rose in her throat; Tallora held them in her mouth, contemplating their bitter taste before she finally let them free. "Say what you will of my apparent hysteria, but may I ask for one thing?"

"Please."

"Empress Vahla is wicked," Tallora said. "She is the one who threatened me, who tortured me, who forced me to live among the courtesans—she did it all to spite me, because I wouldn't fall under her will. Throw her name around as the face of evil—I don't care. But . . ." Tallora shut her eyes, swallowing tears at the memories. "...but say nothing of Princess Dauriel."

"But she's the one who—"

"Who stole me from the ocean, I know. But though she never said it in so many words, I know she would undo that if she could. She never hurt me. All those rumors were only that—she never raped me. It was a ruse to protect me from your envoy and any others. I swear to you, Amulon, she never touched me. She was my friend. And since she was willing to sully her reputation to protect me, if there's any way to leave her name unspoken in the inevitable defamation of Solvira, please do so."

Amulon stared as though she'd spoken Demoni. "That is not what I expected," he said slowly, "considering previous rumors of Dauriel's character."

Tallora shook her head. "She's gone through some horrible things, but her heart is good."

She was suddenly privy to distant hooves, rapidly approaching.

The only warning.

The camp erupted in silver flame.

Screams rose as half the encampment burst in blinding light. Tallora felt no heat as she gazed into the silver inferno, but pure power. It could consume her just the same. Amulon grabbed her arm and wrenched her into standing. He drew his sword.

From the flames emerged Dauriel Solviraes, standing tall as she wielded her curved blades. Those who ran to her met a swift end—with a ferocity Tallora had never seen, Dauriel parried and slashed, removing limbs, slitting throats. She fought with her body as well as her blades, landing at least one kick square into a man's chest. Flame burst from her swords. Men screamed. Yet she remained silent, her gaze hardened from focus.

"Dauriel!" Tallora cried, held behind Amulon. She fought to escape his grasp—perhaps it was from surprise, but he released her.

She ran forward. From a pile of dead men came Dauriel, her face dirtied from sweat, smoke, and blood, her chopped hair disheveled. The silver flame steadily turned a blinding orange, true fire the longer it burned. Dauriel's gaze drifted from Tallora to Amulon and the few men standing with him, her stance stiffening.

But Tallora came close, fearless before her beloved dragon of a princess. "Spare them, please," she said softly.

Dauriel stared beyond her. When Tallora followed her gaze, she saw that Amulon and his guards took slow steps forward. Tallora held out her hand, silently pleading for them to stop—they did.

Anger burned in Dauriel's eyes. "They would give you to Morathma."

"There's more to this than you know. I didn't know either."

Dauriel still stared at the envoy, smoke filtering from her nostrils with every breath. Tallora dared to touch her and felt her burning within. "Take me away from here," she whispered. Dauriel slowly put one sword away and pulled Tallora to her chest, holding the other sword ready in case they struck.

Tallora kept her gaze to Amulon as Dauriel escorted her away from the burning camp. But he never once looked to her—only to Dauriel, and she saw quiet rage.

Once far enough away, Dauriel whistled impossibly loud; an enormous horse appeared from the darkness, ebony and speckled with umber. Towering over them both, it lowered its head at Dauriel's behest, content at her touch. "You've never ridden a horse, correct?" Dauriel said. When Tallora shook her head, she offered a hand. "Tycus is strong enough to carry us both—not the fastest horse, but once I knew where you were going, I knew I would need to take us both away as quickly as possible."

Tallora's fingers interlaced with Dauriel's. "Your mother told you?"

"Khastra did."

Tallora could have sobbed from relief. Her pleas had been heard.

"She whispered it in the hallway the night you were taken. Told me to wait until you were far enough from the city, in case someone saw." Dauriel's grip tightened, exhaustion steadily overtaking her features. "She'll be sent to find us, once my mother knows I've gone. She warned that if she did, she would have no mercy to show."

Split between duty to the crown and kindness to her ward, it seemed Khastra had done what she could. "Aren't you taking me back?"

"I'm taking you home."

The words panged like a heartbeat in Tallora's stomach.

"Set your foot in the stirrup, here. I'll steady you." Tallora wobbled as Dauriel helped her to mount the enormous beast, but she didn't fall. She clutched the saddle as Dauriel came up behind her, grateful when strong arms embraced her.

When Tallora turned, Dauriel caught her lips. Relief flooded Tallora, and she pressed against her, tears welling in her eyes. The horse began a smooth canter, but it quickly increased to a run. "We're going to the ocean?" Tallora asked, finding it difficult to speak as the horse sped along its unknown path.

"It's a hard day's ride to the sea—we're close enough to where we made port that I think you may be able to find your way home. Depending on how you're feeling, we'll stop to rest in Kent. Tycus could use the break."

Something stifling swamped Tallora's heart, threatening to drown her resolve. Home?

Tallora knew a conversation needed to be had, but not here and now. Dauriel said, "But were they not taking you to the Speaker?"

Tallora carefully reached backward to stroke the skin of Dauriel's neck. "They were. They didn't believe me when I told them I needed to be returned to the sea." The relief of Dauriel's company settled against her skin, sinking down to her bones, and all the fear she'd held to threatened to spill from her eyes. Tallora swallowed her sudden rise in tears, but Dauriel's arm tightened around her shuddering form. "I'm sorry—"

"Did they hurt you?"

Tallora shook her head as she pressed herself closer into Dauriel's doublet, savoring the smell of leather and sweat. After a stabilizing breath, she said, "Listening to self-righteous men talk about my supposed divine purpose is enough to make anyone mad. If their attempts to turn my legs into a tail hadn't worked, I would have most likely spent my life spreading them for Morathma so ..." Her clever tongue tried to find humor in it, anything to lighten the weighted mood, but instead she clung to Dauriel's arm, fighting fresh tears. "I'm just so thankful you're here."

Dauriel curled around her, as well as she could while directing her horse. Tentative peace settled between them, but Tallora feared it was as fragile as glass. Nothing was said, but the princess' protective embrace remained.

In the ensuing silence, Tallora recalled Vahla's words, her implied meaning. "I was stolen from the ocean for this. That's it, isn't it? You stole me to barter for the border towns. You knew I was a follower of Staella, and you knew Moratham wouldn't sit idly when Neoma's country mistreated one. You manipulated them." A secondary wave of realization washed over her, leaving her suddenly cold. "And you knew that all along."

"I was going to tell you. The day you were taken, I approached my mother to bargain for you, but she said it wasn't necessary—that the envoy hadn't mentioned you at all in their final negotiations. I realize now she lied." Her grip on Tallora tightened; she felt Dauriel's hesitation in her held breath. "The greater good said if we became the monsters they thought we were, we'd be able to save those towns from Moratham's rule, or so said my mother months ago, when she bemoaned having nothing to barter with. I didn't know she was willingly turning a blind eye to our own stolen citizens. But it hardly matters; I wasn't thinking of the greater good when I grabbed you from the sea. Just my own idiot self—that for perhaps one gods-damned moment, I would do something right in her eyes."

Though the words hurt, it came with no anger— instead, it brought the closure of *knowing* the cause of her great crime. Anguish lay in Dauriel's voice, no hint of the princess bearing godly blood, but a little girl who had spent all her life living in a cold and distant shadow, burdened by a shame thrust upon her from years of crying herself to sleep, of living in pain, of being told she was fundamentally wrong for existing, yet still gathered every discarded scrap of love she could cling to . . .

Perhaps it was Tallora's own misguided notions of love that drove her to turn and embrace Dauriel— or, as well as she could, given her legs were set around a horse. Perhaps it was foolish to feel sorrow for her captor. And perhaps she should have kept her next words to herself, but Tallora set them free, nevertheless. "For what it's worth," she whispered, half-held in Dauriel's returned embrace, "I'm so glad I know you."

Dauriel said nothing, merely held her despite the jostling pace of the horse. After a long stretch of silence, Tallora said, "Amulon and I spoke by the fire. He has been in correspondence with my people. You should hear this."

Tallora savored Dauriel's arms around her body, appreciating the breeze and the thundering hooves beneath her as she told her of Amulon's words.

170

They reached Kent at sunrise.

The small village bridged the path from Neolan to the sea, Dauriel explained. It prospered in trade and held a richness betraying its size. The dusty road through town brought them into a bustling scene, even at the early hour. Merchants yelled to advertise their wares, children ran about the alleyways, and Dauriel kept her head down, though her horse drew attention enough. Those silver eyes would be unmistakable, Tallora realized.

At the first passing of an inn, they stopped. "Stay with Tycus," Dauriel said, as though Tallora had a choice—Dauriel slid off with ease. Tallora might as well have been stranded in the desert, trapped atop the gigantic horse.

She dared to touch the great beast's muscled neck. "You're a good creature," she said, realizing a damp sheen of sweat covered its slight dusting of fur.

As though in response to her words, the horse turned its head, a single, enormous eye looking back to her. It held an intelligence that surprised Tallora, and she smiled, hoping it understood she was a friend.

Dauriel emerged with a young boy at her heels. "I'll help you down," she said, and did so, catching Tallora when she collapsed beside her. The young boy led Tycus away. "I requested a room with a bath—both of us could use it."

"Together?" Tallora teased, and Dauriel's wink spoke volumes.

"Oh, that it were large enough. Most people don't have baths quite so nice as mine."

Their room held two beds and a large window, one with blessed curtains to filter the sunlight. Tallora stumbled inside, exhaustion threatening to overtake her. "Which of us first? To bathe, I mean."

"First one to bathe gets to collapse into sleep," Dauriel said, opening the single door at the corner. It led to a small washroom—and it was, as she said, the tiniest tub Tallora had ever seen. "Go on. You've suffered enough."

The water pulled grime and soot from Tallora's skin. Though her sullied clothing would have to be dealt with eventually, for now she watched her skin turn from ashen grey to pearlescent pinks and whites, and all the while she contemplated Dauriel's promise. She would be taken to the sea. All she ever wanted, to go home—it was right before her on a platter.

So why did she hesitate?

Tallora emerged with a towel around her body, surprised to see a folded nightgown on one of the beds. Dauriel sat on the other, removing her boots. "I purchased spare clothing from the innkeeper—plus a tip for him to stop staring so closely at my eyes," she added with a wink. "It's yours. I thought you'd rather sleep comfortably."

Tallora could only manage a nod, the crushing weight in her chest threatening to consume her lungs.

"There's something else," Dauriel said, her bravado fading into something shy. From her riding pouch, she withdrew something of infinite worth—Tallora's heart leapt.

Her vestment of Staella; the necklace of sea stars and pearls. Repaired like it was never ruined.

When Tallora didn't speak, Dauriel gently grabbed her hand and placed the long necklace in her grasp. Tears filled Tallora's eyes as she stared first upon her precious necklace and then into Dauriel's gentle gaze, the unspoken apology freeing some of the weight in Tallora's heart. With infinite care, Dauriel closed Tallora's fingers around it, then released her, her smile as soft as gold.

When the princess disappeared to take her own bath, Tallora clutched the vestment to her chest, a strange finality settling upon her shoulders. Her mind buzzed as she changed into her nightclothes, the necklace tucked carefully in the nightstand. If Vahla learned the mermaid hadn't reached Moratham, she would only have Dauriel to blame, with her disappearance.

Dauriel had thrown away everything—her family, her title, even her freedom if she were caught . . . perhaps even her life.

Tallora settled into bed, wondering why there were two, but exhaustion from days' worth of fear had taken a toll. Sleep stole her, unwilling as she might have been.

Tallora awoke at sunset, as told by the faint maroon light shining around the edges of the curtains.

Below her, for they were on the second floor, Tallora heard the muted sounds of patrons bustling about, but the quiet breathing beside her sounded so much louder. Dauriel slept, having ridden for days straight to find her, and yet had still let Tallora bathe first, putting her happiness before her own.

In the dim light, Tallora saw the princess' strong features, the peace in her countenance as she slept. Silently, she slipped from her bed. The floorboards creaked beneath her feet, but Dauriel did not stir—not until Tallora settled in beside her. With a sleepy groan, her eyes fluttered open, silver reflecting the fiery light beyond. "Tallora?"

Tallora cupped Dauriel's cheek and pressed their lips together, as languid and slow as their sleepy minds. Warm hands wrapped around Tallora's waist, holding her close, and she loved it so, this security and tenderness. When she pulled away, emotion threatened to choke her. She managed to say, "Why did you do it?"

Dauriel's fingers laced into her hair, smoothing over the locks of snowfall. "Do what?"

"Rescue me. They'll know it was you. You've thrown away your life for me—why?"

Softness settled upon her princess' countenance. "I stole everything from you." Dauriel's embrace tightened at Tallora's waist. "I stole you from your home, condemned you to a hellish fate—so it was not a decision. I had to save you at any cost."

Tallora searched her soul and realized, to her surprise, that a new feeling had settled in beside the warmth she felt for Dauriel. "I forgive you," she said, and the truth of it set her brutalized heart free. "And so you'll take me back?"

The question brought tears to her eyes. Dauriel watched them fall, quiet when her own lip trembled. "Yes."

"And you'll never see me again?"

"Likely not." Dauriel's smile held joy, yes, but of the bitterest sort. "I've taken so much, but perhaps you can still salvage a life—"

"Don't." Tallora kissed her once more, rougher now, desperation driving her touch. She pulled away unwillingly, knowing there was more she must say. "You have proven your sincerity over and over. I've forgiven you; please, don't hate yourself."

Freed of her words, she kissed Dauriel, deepening it with her tongue. A sudden spike of longing struck her—by all the gods, she would be gone soon, and the thought was too wrenching to consider. With their lips sealed, Tallora removed herself from Dauriel's embrace, straddling her instead, desperate to silence the voice screaming that this must end.

When her touch threatened to take an amorous turn, Dauriel clutched her hands to still them. Tallora pulled away from her mouth, realizing the princess' eyes were rimmed in red. "Tallora," she whispered, the name a holy, blessed thing, "if we do this—" She shut her eyes, and Tallora's heart broke to see her tears. "We shouldn't do this. To have you now will only make goodbye unbearable."

"Heartbreak is inevitable, when you've felt true love," Tallora whispered, hand trembling as she brushed a tear from Dauriel's face. Her own still fell freely, and she could do nothing to staunch them. Dauriel stole her hand, but Tallora gently brought it back, placing a tender kiss upon the princess' palm. "I want nothing more than to have loved you with all my body and soul, if you'll have me."

Dauriel pressed their mouths together, and they kissed with all the passion their tears had summoned. Tallora touched Dauriel with reckless abandon, first above her clothes and then below, her hands desperate to write her body to memory. Dauriel gasped when Tallora's hands skimmed her breasts, but when she moved to take them in her hand, Dauriel stopped her, idly shaking her head.

"Sorry," Tallora said, but the words were stolen from her lips, and instead she reveled in the strong muscles of Dauriel's back, adoring when they shifted with every subtle motion. "You don't like to be touched."

When Dauriel pulled away, a subtle twitch of abashment settled upon her countenance. "Some is fine. Depends on where. I will say I love it when you . . ." Dauriel blushed, something darling in that shy smirk of hers. ". . . touch my hair."

Tallora's lips brushed Dauriel's, praying her smile would reassure her. "For what it's worth, you can touch me however you like," she said, giggling at Dauriel's reddened face. "Stop me if I do anything wrong."

Dauriel's hands caressed her clothed waist, and when their eyes met, Tallora removed her gown with no hesitation. She wore nothing beneath and delighted in the sudden widening of Dauriel's eyes. Her hips ground against Dauriel's, wanting nothing more than to be taken, to be owned. She would leave; her heart would stay, but in the moment she cared not for that— only for Dauriel's soft stare upon her body and her hands upon her breasts.

Dauriel dipped her neck enough to steal one in her mouth, the peaked bud suddenly pleasured by her mouth. Tallora gasped at the erotic display, cupping

Dauriel's head against her chest, savoring the motions. "Oh, Dauriel," she sighed, then couldn't help her smile. "You meant as you said—you silly landfolk love a woman's breast."

Dauriel glanced up; their eyes met, and through their tears they laughed—by Staella's Grace, they laughed and it felt so beautiful. When her mouth returned to her breast, Tallora gripped her hair, gleefully running her nails through the cropped locks, giggling at Dauriel's shameless moan. All the while, she gasped with every breath, softly whining when those perfect, callused hands gently slipped down her waist, then farther still, squeezing her ass hard enough for Tallora to cry out.

Meanwhile, she peppered kisses upon Dauriel's brow, adoring every treasured touch. When Dauriel met her gaze, her mouth still circling her peaked bud, Tallora smiled, utterly breathless beneath her touch. Dauriel's mouth left her breast, allowing Tallora to capture those wonderful lips, kissing her a moment before Dauriel pulled back and slipped her shirt over her head, the gesture perhaps not purposefully sensuous, but oh—Tallora was so weak for her.

Tallora thought her a work of art, a painting in the Hall of Relics for how beautifully she was built. Everything, from the lithe muscles of her arms to the subtle, shifting etchings in her stomach was something wondrous to behold, and Tallora craved her power, desperately longed to touch and be touched. When Dauriel placed Tallora's hands at her waist, Tallora gently slid them to her back, embracing her as their mouths met. The heat between them flared, and Tallora ground her hips against Dauriel, desperate for a friction her mermaid form had never thought to know.

Dauriel encouraged this, grinning wide as she brought her hands to Tallora's hips, helping them to grind *harder, faster...* "Oh, you're perfect," she said, rugged and rough in Tallora's ear.

"Dauriel, please," she gasped between kisses, her pitiful moaning hopefully enough to sway her.

"Not yet." Their mouths crushed together, pleasure quickly rising between Tallora's legs at the friction between them. Would she come undone from only this?

Tallora's cry turned into a fit of giggles when Dauriel pushed her onto her back. With the princess on top of her, Tallora bit her lip at her cocky smile, those silver eyes merely a ring around her blown pupils. She smashed their lips together and gripped Tallora's breasts in her hands, rough as she squeezed. Tallora loved it so, to see Dauriel utterly unhinged, but nearly melted at the sweet words in her ear. "I know this is your first time as a human girl," Dauriel whispered, enamor in her breathless words, "so please don't be shy if I touch you any way you don't like."

Tallora nodded, breathless beneath her lover's body. "I will. I feel safe with you."

That bullish grin returned, and Tallora loved it, gasping with every kiss down her body, adoring how Dauriel lingered at her neck, her breasts, savoring every inch of her skin. Her fingers traced precious, invisible lines upon her stomach, the pads rough from violence yet soft in their worship. Dauriel's lips skipped to Tallora's thigh, her face pressed adoringly to the soft flesh, eyes shut in contentment.

In that moment Tallora understood, in ways her princess so tenderly struggled to speak of, that Dauriel loved to touch beautiful things, to cherish them, and here alone there was no greater pleasure than to make love to her. Dauriel did not want to be touched; her assurance and pleasure came from giving all she had.

Tallora reached down to stroke Dauriel's hair, to convey affection, understanding, whatever this rising, choking emotion in her throat was, but then Dauriel's mouth fell upon her wanting vulva. As she'd said before, merfolk never used their mouths. And for a moment—well, more than a moment—Tallora sincerely questioned the use of ever returning to a mermaid form because *holy fucking shi—*

"*Oh!*"

Dauriel's tongue spoke forbidden words inside her, and Tallora couldn't even articulate her response—she simply fell back, boneless. Dauriel kissed her below, her arms forcing her thighs aloft, sparing no mercy to her clit. Her content hum drew out the torturous pleasure; Tallora prayed it might never end, yet swore she'd break if it did not.

Perfect fingers joined her tongue, stroking soft lines, and when Dauriel met her gaze, Tallora saw the unspoken question. She nodded, desperate for more, and when Dauriel pushed inside her, she cried out. Connected as one, Tallora watched her lover's face and cherished it so, this new facet of Princess Dauriel of Solvira, who struggled to be vulnerable at all.

But pleasure peaked; Tallora shuddered and gasped. Her body fell back to earth, more sensitive than nerve, soon held in strong arms as Dauriel came up beside her. They kissed—Tallora tasted bitterness and joy.

Darkness had fallen outside. Tallora reached up to open the curtains, drenching them in moonlight. "You're the most beautiful person I've ever known," she whispered against her ear, then continued with her gentle kisses.

Dauriel grabbed her, burying her face between her breasts. Tallora realized she sobbed. She held Dauriel there, content to savor their precious, final hours.

Chapter XIII 🐚

A s they rode Tycus toward the sea, Tallora sat a little closer; Dauriel held tighter.

It was unquestionably a mistake, to open her soul to Dauriel's, house her for a few precious hours. But as Tallora rested in her lap, felt the warmth of her chest against her back as they rode into the night, she felt safety unparalleled. Tallora reached across to clutch her arm, as near to returning the embrace as she could while mounted on Tycus. Dauriel's light kisses on her head were worth more than gold.

The salty air rose by steady degrees. When Tycus climbed the final hill, they all three stared down upon an expansive field leading to pure white sand, lovingly reflecting the celestial light above, and the gentle sea.

It should have brought a swelling to Tallora's heart. Perhaps, in time, it would. For now, she clung to Dauriel, who removed one hand from the reins and held her tight. With care to keep balance, Tycus began the slow descent down the hill.

"They say the Theocracy of Sol Kareena has alliances with the merfolk of the Onian Sea," Tallora whispered. "It's well north of Solvira, but, perhaps . . ." She shut her eyes, swallowing tears. Once she started crying, she knew she wouldn't stop. "Perhaps you could seek haven in the Theocracy. You could find a way to send a message to me."

"Do you have a family name?" Dauriel's voice quivered; if she broke, Tallora would surely follow.

"No," Tallora admitted. "It is not something we do. But tell them you seek Tallora of Stelune, Daughter of Myalla. That will be enough." She looked up, not quite able to meet Dauriel's eye, but she smiled nonetheless. "I would swim those thousand miles to find you. Meet at the center, find a peaceful beach."

"I would set up a home by the sea," Dauriel whispered, tragedy in her reminiscence. "Perhaps live in a cove."

"Oh, no," Tallora chided, laughter in her words. "Coves are flooded during storms. You'd need a proper home."

"I hear there are elves in Zauleen who live in homes on stilts connecting to islands. Perhaps I can take a lesson or two from them."

The impossibility of the plans subdued their joy, but Tallora needed something, some hope to grasp. Dauriel, it seemed, did too. "It's a life," she whispered, snuggling closer, desperate for Dauriel's embrace. "We could be happy."

Assuming they ever found one another again.

Tycus slowed to scarcely a shuffle when he reached the bottom of the hill. Tallora knew it was Dauriel's doing but said nothing, savoring this moment, her smell and her touch.

Then, from the top of the hill, flooded a legion.

Horses suddenly burst from atop the hill, barreling down toward them, each saddled by an armored guard. When Tycus stumbled, Tallora caught a glimpse of a wicked silhouette, backdropped by moonlight—a great half-demon atop a fearsome reptilian beast, her horns unmistakable, wielding a hammer shining in the night—

A hammer that launched toward them.

Tycus screamed—by Staella's Grace, horses could s*cream*—and Tallora was nearly crushed by his weight as he collapsed, legs shattered by the impact of the gargantuan weapon.

She matched eyes with Dauriel, whose heartbreak toward her mutilated animal shone in her watery eyes. Blood saturated the earth, the horse's cries of pain a nightmare. The princess shook as she rose to her feet, then she grabbed Tallora's collar, all but pulling her along as she bolted toward the sand.

They ran, even as the horsemen came close, as well as the general leading them.

The ground grew steadily damp. Tallora ran, lungs burning. Sand slowed her, but it would slow the horses too, she reasoned.

A sudden high-pitched, alien bellowing stilled her heart. She glanced behind and watched Khastra's beast leap over the throng of horsemen. Seamlessly, with a grace her size should not have allowed, she held out an arm—from beyond, her hammer, still coated in Tycus' blood, flew through the air to rejoin her.

The beast leapt—and landed in the water, not ten feet before Tallora. The general slid down.

Khastra needed no imposing stance to cast her aura of magnitude. The great half-demon walked as any mortal, held her crystal hammer aloft, yet towered before them both—with only Dauriel between them. Frozen, Tallora watched as Khastra ripped her withering stare away, to Dauriel instead. "I warned you not to let me find you, Dauriel."

Dauriel drew her swords. "As soon as you can," she whispered, the words carried off by the sea breeze, "run."

Khastra strode forward. Dauriel changed her stance, defensive as she held her swords as a cross.

Every fiber of Tallora's being screamed to stay, to fall to her knees and beg for Dauriel's life.

"Tallora, please." Desperation bled into Dauriel's tone.

But Dauriel had all but sacrificed her life to save her, and Tallora realized to throw that away now would undermine the great cost. "I love you," she whispered, and though she relied upon the wind to carry it, she knew Dauriel had heard.

It all happened so quickly—Dauriel rushed forward; Khastra swung; Tallora ran but then she screamed. The hammer missed, but it seemed that was Khastra's ploy—it flung out into the sea, but in Dauriel's desperation to dodge, the half-demon grabbed her with her opposite arm and flung her to the ground.

The general knelt with her knee to Dauriel's back. Tallora sobbed as she ran to the sea.

Pain suddenly seared her leg. Tallora collapsed to her hands and knees, the water lapping her forearms, but blood seeped from her calf. She looked back and saw the soldier prepare another arrow—and Khastra with Dauriel's sword to the princess' own neck.

The princess' body suddenly shone. Silver fire seeped through her pores—

Khastra thrust her face into the water; the fire ceased. Dauriel flailed beneath the lapping waves.

Tallora struggled to stand, pain radiating as she stumbled to her feet—only to collapse again. The arrow had sunk deep—she feared it pierced the bone—

She cried out as another arrow struck her, this time in the shoulder. When the soldiers came to steal her, she sobbed and failed to fight.

Freedom but a breath away, yet Tallora's life would end now.

Dauriel coughed when her face finally touched air. Khastra held her by the hair, leaving her weapons to rust in the sea. She held out a hand to the water—her gargantuan hammer flew to her grasp; she dragged it behind. "Send word to Solvira. The Empress will be relieved of our return."

Tallora sat with shackles around her wrists and ankles. Dauriel lay crumpled within a circle of wards that Khastra said would subdue the Silver Fire. Tallora questioned the need for that at all; never had she seen Dauriel look so broken.

Her calf and shoulder had been tended to, bandaged by the general herself. Tallora suspected some enchantment—it hardly stung at all, and the bleeding hadn't seeped through the cloth.

Sunlight burst over the horizon. Upon the hill, she said a silent prayer for Tycus. The great beast lay utterly still, his life sacrificed for Tallora's—a sacrifice now in vain. Dauriel hardly moved. Tallora suspected Khastra had harmed her more than appearances showed.

The general herself stood before them. Tallora stared at her hooves, awaiting any moment now the nauseating sensation of teleportation—Khastra had called for aid and it would come, just as it had on the dock.

As the soldiers talked amongst themselves, Khastra turned her attention to Dauriel. "Princess," she said, menace in her tone. "Princess, look at me."

Dauriel rolled over, her features pale, eyes swollen from dried tears.

"You will kneel before the empress. She will proclaim you guilty for slaughtering the Morathan Envoy." She glanced back at her soldiers, her voice lowering. "And you will demand intercession from the goddesses."

Tallora scoffed. "General, with due respect, if you had wanted her to live, perhaps you should have left us alone."

"I desperately want her to live." Khastra's voice held none of the jovialness Tallora had seen in time past; only cold calculation, a master of death on the battlefield. "And if you do as well, you will encourage her to demand it."

"But if she's found guilty . . ."

She was guilty; Tallora had seen it.

"Yes, Ilune will claim her soul, should Dauriel be condemned. I have met Ilune; she is as fearsome as the legends speak. More, even. You are wise to fear." Khastra's frown didn't fade, but her intrigue did rise. "But do not underestimate Staella. Few worship her, because she is not a Goddess of Justice or Power—there is little glory in pledging to her name. But you are pledged to Staella, yes?"

Tallora nodded, seeing no use in lying.

"I have met her as well, and my respect for her is higher than any other resident of Celestière."

This surprised Tallora, and though she hated the half-demon, cursed her apparent betrayal, she listened.

"I understand justice, as does Sol Kareena, Neoma, and Ilune. All three practice it according to their own moralities. Even if they conflict at times, they never question the other's reasons. But pure justice is heartless. It is because of Staella that the world turns, that the Theocracy and Solvira can coexist, and why Solvira is not a military state. There is strength in humility. She inspires us to live and be better."

Khastra turned her reminiscent gaze to Tallora and said, very pointedly, "Be at the intercession. Kill if you must. It may save Dauriel's life."

And then the world lurched. Stars appeared. When Tallora's head ceased spinning, she crumpled to the floor of the council chamber.

"General," came a hated voice, and Tallora looked up to see Empress Vahla seated at the center, gaze shifting from Khastra to Dauriel, "excellent work, tracking down my traitorous daughter. You shall be commended for your success."

"I take no pride in what I have done, Empress," came Khastra's reply. "I simply serve the Solviran Crown."

"Be that as it may, you've delivered justice." Vahla kept her cruel stare at Dauriel, who groaned as she attempted to roll over. "Dauriel, I'm ashamed. Do you deny your slaughter of innocent Morathan soldiers? Men who will never again return home to their children and wives?"

Dauriel trembled as she sat up, callused fury in her gaze. "No, I do not."

"Explain to the council why you did it."

Dauriel looked to Tallora, her anger fading into an apology. Tallora prayed her face conveyed only affection. "I love this woman, Mother," Dauriel said, and the admittance broke Tallora's heart. Never had it been spoken aloud, not by her, and Tallora wished for another life, where the words might be uttered in love instead of heartbreak. "I only regret that I failed to save her."

Tallora shook her head. "Dauriel—"

"Silence!" Startled, Tallora and Dauriel both returned their attention to Empress Vahla, who sat quietly as her council whispered around her. "In the absence of a judge, royals may fill the vacant seat. Dauriel, my dear, it pains me to condemn you, but you've likely doomed your people to go to war for your idiotic crime of passion." She pursed her lips, and Tallora wished a curse upon her, this woman who had made Dauriel's life hell. "Dauriel Solviraes, I hereby strip you of all your titles and inheritance. You shall be hung at sundown, and your body delivered as an apology to Moratham—"

"No." Dauriel shut her eyes, visibly fighting tears. "I demand intercession. I am a citizen of Solvira until the end, and it is my right to plead to Goddess Staella for mercy."

"Mercy for murder?" Vahla looked almost pleased. Tallora, in her shackles, crawled to Dauriel's side, uncaring who saw her grasp her princess' hand. Dauriel's fear remained palpable; her very soul lay at risk. "We shall defer to Goddess Neoma's judgement." She turned to the priests—Greyva and Rel. "Commune at the joint temple. See if this can be over with tonight." Then, she looked to Tallora, who resisted the urge to spit at the empress' feet. "This changes nothing. You'll be returned to the courtesan's wing for the time being, but Moratham has paid for you. Guards, take her."

Two men approached, and Tallora surged forward, stealing Dauriel's lips with hers. She held her head, feeling first her surprise and then her return, desperation in every flush motion of her mouth.

Rough hands gripped Tallora's arms. When they wrenched her away, their hands stayed clasped. "Whether it be in this life or the next, I will find you again," Tallora said, then with another pull, the touch faded, "even if I must plead at Ilune's feet."

Tallora did not fight. They had lost.

But she was not defeated.

Leah greeted her at the door. When the guards shoved Tallora forward, she caught her, preventing her from crumpling to the floor. "Mermaid," she said, more a breath than audible words. "By the Triage, you gave us a scare." Then, her relief turned to horror. "You're bandaged!"

"I've been through worse." When the door shut, she added, "Leah, my friend, did they tell you the truth? That I'd been shipped to Moratham?"

Leah shook her head, her warm skin growing pale. "Only that you would not be returning. We assumed you dead, or worse."

"I was rescued by Princess Dauriel. She's asked for intercession from the goddesses to contest her death sentence, and Leah—" Tallora swallowed her furious tears. She would not give in to despair. "Leah, I have to be there. Is there any way?"

Leah's confusion palpably radiated. "Why did the princess rescue you?"

"Our arrangement was a ruse," Tallora admitted, for she had nothing left to lose. "She pretended to be crass, but in reality, we both harbored romantic feelings. We never slept together—" Tears prickled in her eyes; she clenched her fist, letting her nails staunch her tears. "Not in the castle, at least. She ruined her life to try and save mine. But if I don't go to the intercession, no one will speak for her. She's guilty, but if I fall at the goddesses' feet and plead for her soul and tell them I've forgiven her, it's the surest chance she has."

Leah looked to the rest of the women—no privacy among whores. "Sunset is hours away—plenty of time for planning. Fortunately, we know every passageway in the castle."

Tallora watched as a small flock of familiar woman came up behind Leah. "Ladies, we need to sneak our mermaid friend out of the castle." A pause; she raised a critical eyebrow. "And get her into the temple. Only those directly involved may witness intercession."

Mithal raised a hand. "If I may, we have a few costume pieces that may help."

Tallora would simply defer to their judgement on utilizing provocative outfits. "Thank you. So much." They risked their lives and livelihood for her, and Tallora might never even see them again. "I can never repay this kindness."

"We help each other," Leah replied, her smile as generous as her deed. "No one else will."

They scattered, all but Lady Mithal. "As she said, sunset is hours away. Rest. We'll take care of everything."

And they truly did.

Tallora tossed and turned but supposed she managed a few scattered minutes of napping. Her shackles clinked at every motion; her bandages itched, both serving as reminders of her dire situation.

When Leah entered, Tallora immediately sat up, fully alert. "Come with me. Plenty of time left, but we mustn't waste it."

She stole Tallora's hand, and from her pocket procured a tiny, golden key. As Leah freed her of her shackles, she said, "How did you get that?"

"We knew Princess Dauriel's room would be unoccupied," she replied, fighting a nervous grin. "We know where she keeps things."

The reminder did not make Tallora angry this time—merely amused. When she was led out, Lady Mithal stood among the small throng, holding what appeared to be a priestess' garb. "A perfect replica, if not the real thing. We don't ask questions." She offered it forward.

Tallora inspected the intricate embroidery, realizing it also had a hood and gloves. "This looks exactly like High Priestess Greyva," she muttered. Incredulous, she met Mithal's eye. "Why do you have something like this?"

"Men have strange tastes. We accommodate every desire. Now, put it on."

It was tight in ways perhaps blasphemous, but it covered her hair and pearlescent hands. If she kept her head down, she was utterly unrecognizable. Hope surged through her veins—Tallora realized she might find Dauriel yet. "Thank you," she said, still inspecting herself in the mirror.

"I'm to escort you," Leah said. "Take whatever you need—you may not be back."

Tallora shook her head. "I have nothing."

"Then, let's go." She led her not to the door, but to a wall by the children's dorm. She pushed, and Tallora watched it shift and swivel aside—revealing a dark hallway. "Sometimes our job requires discretion."

"I was expected to walk around nude when this existed all along?"

"The empress specifically wanted you shown off," Leah said, an apology in her words. "But these exist everywhere—not even the royals know the extent of them, I think."

They plunged into darkness. Tallora saw nothing, and yet Leah seemed unhindered, confident as her feet shuffled along the stone floor. "What will happen to you and the rest of the women?" Tallora whispered, unsure of how sound traveled behind the walls.

Silence met her.

"What about your children?"

The hand holding hers squeezed it tight. "We discussed it," she replied, matching Tallora's volume. "We are prepared to evacuate if needs be, but truthfully, and we hope you'll match our story if asked, you attacked us."

"I attacked you?"

"Your mermaid magic manifested, and we were utterly helpless to stop you. With enough tears and bruising, we may sway sympathy."

"Bruising?"

"We've done worse to ourselves for clients."

Guilt swamped Tallora's soul, the realization of her friends' sacrifice. "Thank you."

"We care for our own. We'd do it for any one of us."

Eventually, the darkness ended. Leah pushed against the wall, and sunlight blinded Tallora's sensitive eyes. When she adjusted her sight, she realized there was grass ahead and the distant sounds of a bustling city. "It'd be suspicious if I'm caught missing," Leah said, "so listen well. The temple you seek is named 'Unity,' and it's the only one devoted to the entire Triage. Cross the bridge, then three streets forward. Seek the town center. If you find yourself lost, look for signs—do *not* ask for directions. You are a priestess, and it wouldn't do well for you to be caught losing your way."

The sun would soon set, already beginning its descent over the mountain range. "Leah, I've said it a hundred times, but thank you." She stole her hand and squeezed it between hers. "My name is Tallora. I will never forget you."

"Tallora," she repeated, and smiled at the word. "A beautiful name for a beautiful soul. Now, go."

Tallora did not look back.

Chapter XIV 🐚

The directions were simple, but Tallora had never stepped foot in Neolan—nothing could have prepared her for its magnitude.

Even at the late hour, human and Celestial citizens crowded the streets, giving no mind to a lone priestess, even pushing and jostling her with their packed bodies. Tallora kept her head down, mindful of her hood.

Tallora had praised Dauriel for many things in the past few days, but the ability to decipher Solviran Common was now of the highest value—she saw a sign, recognized the letters 'U' and 'N' and followed its lead, careful not to look too eager.

The temple towered over the town center, perhaps the second largest building in the city, for only the Glass Palace matched its grandeur. Three towers rose up to caress the sky, each bearing their respective goddess' sigil. A great circle of four-pointed stars and a half-rotted skull stood at equal height—but highest of all was a moon, for Neoma's power outmatched the rest.

Tallora saw a carriage stopped at the side, decorated in royal hues. Perhaps she was too late. She hurried to the entrance, quickly traversing the stone steps, when a guard at the door blocked it with a spear. "Forgive me, priestess. The temple is closed for a private intercession. None may enter."

"No, forgive me, sir," Tallora replied, as demure as she could summon. "I have put you in a most difficult position. I left the key to my home here." Beneath her hood, she flashed her most apologetic smile, praying her pretty face might sway him.

He looked behind her, then side to side. "You mustn't enter the cathedral," he said simply. "Leave when you're done."

"A blessing upon you, sir." He opened the door only enough for her to slip inside.

The entry hall bore globes of light and no windows, casting the illusion of eternal night. Tallora marveled a moment at the use of magic, struck by the beautiful ambience. She pulled back her hood, utterly alone, and stepped forward as quietly as she could.

The great doors at the end held no lock. She pressed her head to the wood and heard muted words.

Goddess Staella, she thought, *I think we might meet very soon.*

She pushed upon the door.

The cathedral stood as grand as the exterior promised, a room of perfect, polished stones. No windows, but a brilliant skylight, the waning light of the sun bowing to the rising moon. There sat no pews or chairs, but enough standing room for hundreds, and at the head, raised upon a platform, was a grand throne of stone, meant for a giant.

The royal council turned at her entrance, save High Priestess Greyva at the center, glowing like the moon she worshipped. Dauriel knelt in chains, shock overtaking her countenance at Tallora's entrance, but Khastra looked pleased, standing apart from the rest at the left hand of the throne.

The empress cried, "Remove this woman! She holds no right to—"

The room filled with blinding light.

Tallora covered her eyes, shying at the divine display. What she witnessed was a miracle, and when the light faded to a glimmer, she saw a marvelous wonder.

Three women appeared, human and yet alien all at once—all of them standing three times that of their mortal supplicants. One was a face Tallora knew and loved, her countenance as gentle as a midnight breeze and her hair the color of starlight. Her wings shone as pure golden light, soft tendrils floating along the air, and though she held a diminutive stance to the rest, she stood as though smaller, arms wrapped at her chest. A soft figure, and a mild stare—the Goddess Staella was beloved of Tallora's people, a teller of stories, a woman of art and benevolent mercy to those she deemed deserving.

The one who stood across wore a robe to barely cover her sensuous, glowing figure, wielding a staff of bones, topped with what must have been a demon skull. Beauty unparalleled, they sang of Ilune, but behind her enticing exterior, her wings of shifting silver and gold, was a wicked smile. A being of Death—the first necromancer, for all knowledge of dark magic stemmed from her tutelage—the Goddess Ilune held a brand of justice marked by fear.

Glorious above all stood Neoma, The Grand Creator, the Goddess of Life and Fertility and Creation, the Great Wielder of the Silver Fire. When summoned from the Goddess herself, the Silver Fire was the origin of life itself, or so they said, the full mystery of its power withheld from mortals—for it had created Ilune, with Staella's womb to cradle her.

A cascade of hair the color of night, braided at the top of her head, hung like a rope. Her eyes—all their eyes—held the glow of celestial light, but while Ilune was a cruel sneer, Neoma was cold steel, her justice perfect, her judgement infinite. She surveyed the room with a watchful eye, indifferent to their ranks and titles. She sat at the centered throne, her warrior's attire striking against the smooth stone, with Ilune and Staella at either side.

Tallora fell to her knees, as did the rest. Vahla was the first to rise, and her voice echoed across the high walls. "Goddess Neoma, it is embarrassing to admit, but an interloper has intruded upon this private affair. Forgive us, for she shall be—"

Neoma held out a hand; Vahla's voice fizzled like a drenched flame. "An interloper she may be, but you would dare to lie? Staella has told me of Tallora's presence in your palace; she is no less complicit to Dauriel's fate than you." Then, Neoma's sharp stare settled on Tallora herself, who froze beneath her scrutiny. "Come forward. Stand by my right hand."

It was a metaphor as much as literal, for there at Neoma's right was Tallora's goddess, who watched with all the kindness a mother might give her young child. Courage bolstered, Tallora obeyed, standing in line with the royal council, safe under Staella's watch. Her goddess said nothing, but her smile was full of light.

When the woman at Neoma's left also looked to Tallora, the warmth faded from her soul. Instead, anxiety welled, a dread with no origin. "Welcome, Tallora," Ilune said, her smile as wicked as a shark cornering a child. "I am delighted by your presence, truly. Perhaps we might spare ourselves an interrogation of the dead men—tell us, as a witness to Dauriel's crime, is it true? Did she slaughter the men from Moratham?"

Victory shone in Ilune's face, and Tallora saw that she knew—and to lie might mean a hellish fate. "Yes," she whispered, and she could not face Dauriel. Perhaps her presence had damned her instead of saving them both.

"There is little else for me to say." Ilune turned her steely gaze to Khastra, the only one who dared to stand before her. "But, General Khastra," she cooed, every motion of her lips sensuous and slow, "tell us— did Dauriel threaten you and yours?"

"That would imply I felt threatened."

To Tallora's surprise, Ilune laughed at the bold words. "That is answer enough." Now, to Dauriel, she grinned, predator facing prey. "Rise, disgraced princess." Dauriel obeyed, shuffling to her feet, weighed down by chains. "You are guilty, by your own words and the words of credible witnesses, yet you dare call for intercession. Speak freely—they may be the last words you have of your own will."

Dauriel looked first to Staella, and then dared to gaze upon Neoma directly. She stepped forward, and Tallora saw fear in the tremble of her lip but not the strength of her stance. "Goddess Neoma, I saw injustice and sought to right it. As far as I was aware, Tallora was to be sold as a slave to Morathma's kingdom, and so in credence to the tradition of my foremothers, I stole her back to save her—"

Her words stopped when Ilune held up a hand. "Objection," she said, sneering wickedly at Tallora. Once again, darkness settled onto her soul. "First of all, I am impressed at the level of manipulation you would willingly descend to—to dare *bastardize* my own mothers' history with talk of stealing young women from Morathma. Disgraceful." She said it all so smoothly, no ire, but a luxurious tone. "Furthermore, Staella informed us that you sparked this so-called 'injustice.' You stole Tallora from her ocean home and then murdered to bring her back—you cannot justify murder to balance a scale you already toppled." She raised a single eyebrow. "Do continue."

"Yes, I took her." Dauriel swallowed something painful, and Tallora suspected it was a sob. "I stole her. I ruined her, and so I ruined myself to right it. I saw her as an animal, but I came to realize how wrong I was. She is a woman with a soul, and I nearly destroyed her. My remorse cannot be conveyed in words, so instead I sought action."

"None will deny that you murdered for a noble cause—or perhaps a quick fuck."

Tallora balked at the crass word, spoken by a goddess, no less.

"Were you intimate with this woman, Dauriel?"

Dauriel nodded, and this time kept her stare at the floor.

"Adorable—"

"Wait." Tallora's word leapt from her soul. She knew not the penance for interrupting a goddess, but she stepped forward nonetheless. "I watched Dauriel change." She let the words linger, and when she wasn't interrupted, she continued. "She stole me from the ocean, and it was the cruelest fate she could have administered. And, yes, she was wicked, always toying with me. But not so wicked as her mother, Empress Vahla, who decreed me property and forced me into the servitude of men."

Vahla stood up. "Goddess Neoma, you cannot listen to—"

"Vahla, you will be asked to leave." Neoma's seething words settled upon them all, the inherent threat of blasphemy apparent. "Tallora—"

To hear her name from the goddess' mouth would never be anything less than jarring.

". . . continue your tale."

"Dauriel saw the extent of her own crime and ruined herself to right it, as she said. But even before that, she became kind. Her feelings changed . . . and so did mine. Perhaps it is wrong, but I came to love her, and she loved me yet still was willing to lose me forever to right her crime. I wasn't a quick fuck for pleasure's sake—" Her voice broke; she cursed her threatened tears. "I love her. Dauriel has done all she can to make amends, and so I've forgiven her. Goddess Neoma, that must mean something."

Neoma had a face like iron, stoic and unwavering, though beautiful in her unearthly way. Her stare left Tallora breathless, but her words shattered her hope. "Were Dauriel's crimes directed to you alone, it would. But her impulsive actions have led to the deaths of men under Solvira's protection. She has pushed her country to the brink of war."

Tallora's welling tears fell, though she swallowed the urge to wail. "Please, Neoma—"

"Do not plead mercy from me."

Staella had said nothing all along, merely watched with sorrow etched into her pretty features. Her gentle gaze shifted from Tallora to Dauriel, and she watched, as though waiting. Ilune, however, leered like a grinning snake.

Neoma returned her gaze to Dauriel. "Dauriel Solviraes, your crime is one of passion, but a crime nevertheless. I never happily deliver a death sentence—"

"Neoma, wait!" Tallora stepped forward, withering beneath a cold stare. "I beg of you, please— let me say goodbye."

The Goddess of the Moon said nothing, merely gestured with a hand bearing the first emblems of silver flame. Tallora shoved past the hated councilors, ran to where Dauriel was held down by chains, and immediately pulled her into her arms, though Dauriel's remained shackled. The princess shed no tears, merely planted gentle kisses in Tallora's hair, the only affection she could give. "Don't weep for me—"

"I will weep if I damn well want to weep." Tallora stole Dauriel's face between her hands, memorizing those silver eyes, her small lips, every precious line and curve. "I'm so sorry."

"I did this to myself—"

"But you still made the choice, and I'm the one who will live on."

Dauriel surged forward and stole her lips, each flush movement welling anguish inside Tallora's soul. She wrapped her arms around her neck, the first of her tears finally falling. When she pulled away, Dauriel lingered and whispered, "I would rather die a thousand deaths than have never met you."

They turned to face Neoma with Dauriel still held in Tallora's arms. She would release her at her death, but not a moment before, no—time was precious. Her touch would be savored.

Dauriel would not die alone.

"Dauriel Solviraes," Neoma said, her voice echoing off every wall of the expansive cathedral, "for crimes against your crown and kingdom, I hereby sentence . . ."

So gentle a thing, to stop the great hurricane. Staella's touch upon Neoma's hand caused even the supreme goddess' words to falter. Neoma's countenance immediately softened as she turned to face her wife, coldness fading to curiosity and tender affection. "My love?"

Staella intertwined their fingers, then turned her doe-eyed gaze to Tallora and Dauriel. "I cry for love stories," she said, and her voice never left a whisper, a musical, feminine touch to every word.

"When I offered you aid, my Tallora, never could I have imagined you might soften and heal a broken heart. Dauriel acted as she would act, but she did so for sincere love—a feeling I watched her shut away during her darkest hours years ago. The true crime would be to end her life before it can truly begin."

Staella leaned in to Neoma's ear and whispered something not meant for mortal ears. When she pulled away, their gaze lingered, the mutual adoration unquestionable, unparalleled, and Tallora's heart soared to see it.

Neoma looked to Ilune, whose glee had noticeably faded. Then, she looked to Dauriel, and said, "My wife has heard your words and offered mercy. So shall I, as well."

Dauriel's tense pose slackened, and had Tallora not been holding her tight, she might have fallen. Tallora gasped, her tears now those of joy.

"Your mother has stripped you of your titles and inheritance," Neoma continued, and all in the room stood at stark attention, "but in light of this boon of mercy, I hereby restore it. You are a Solviraes, and you are still one of mine."

Vahla's fury twitched. Dauriel nodded, fighting a smile.

When Staella clenched her fist, Dauriel's bonds shattered. She immediately stole Tallora into her arms, swung her in the air, and held her with the tenderness of their first impassioned night.

"Tallora—"

Tallora, still protected in Dauriel's embrace, turned to the unexpected call from the Moon Goddess.

Staella whispered into Neoma's ear, the kindness in her visage gone, replaced with calculated ire. The Moon Goddess stared with cold fury. "Explain yourself; you alluded to crimes performed by Vahla herself. Tell me the story—the one that ends with you sold to be a wife to Morathma."

The air in the room grew stale and silent. Tallora told her tale, first merely of Vahla's threat and being sold, but then the rest when asked, of her cruel beginnings, treated as a beast and slave. "I was kept as an animal to be sold," she said, squeezing Dauriel's hand, "and not treated much better." She spoke of the Morathan Ambassadors and of Vahla turning a blind eye to disappearances at the border, and all the while Empress Vahla grew increasingly pale.

And when she finished, Neoma's face had not changed, but Ilune's lips twitched with a victorious smile.

And Staella, gentle Staella, kept an icy stare to the empress. She whispered words in Neoma's ear, and Tallora suddenly understood why Khastra held her in high regard, why she was not forgotten, though inspired the smallest worship of the trio—Neoma reigned supreme, yet it was Staella who wielded power to calm the storm.

Or incite it to rage.

"It is the responsibility of my lineage to interpret my word and law; I do not interfere lightly, but selling an innocent girl to Moratham? To their god? Turning away while *my* people are captured and forced into slavery beneath his regime? Your crimes affect more than merely this realm, Vahla." Neoma looked to Tallora. "However, Tallora, what say you? My wife has deemed you to be the one to decide her fate. If you will offer mercy, she shall have it."

Tallora glanced over to Vahla, who lingered somewhere between fear and fury. "Am I being tested?"

"No. No matter what you say, you and Dauriel shall both walk free."

Vahla came forward, her proud stance withering. "You never came to harm under my watch," she said, daring to smile. Tallora's frown twitched. "No men touched you in the end, and you were fed and clothed and even educated—"

"Intention is not a crime, but an attempt certainly is," Tallora spat. "If you'd had your way, I'd be rotting away in your menagerie or riding Morathma's royal throne."

"Tallora—that is your name? A lovely name—"

"Begging will do you nothing." Tallora studied the empress, the fear in her supplicant stance, and managed to scavenged pity. The woman would live or die at her word.

Mercy and forgiveness would offer peace to them both. Tallora's bitter heart would move on, and Dauriel would understand, perhaps even be relieved to not lose her mother, hated or not. Families were complicated, the world was complicated, but in the moment, Tallora thought her heart and mind were the most complicated of all.

But Dauriel was not the only one to suffer beneath Vahla's thumb. The tyrannical woman had merely continued a legacy of feared rulers, yes, but the crime of her negotiating with a country condoning slavery and allowing them to steal her own people spoke of corruption deeper than even her inherent narcissism.

She looked to Staella and knew that while she and Dauriel might walk free, there must be a reason for this, some test of character. Staella was a Goddess of Mercy and Love.

But when Staella met her eye, there was no judgement, merely . . . understanding. Perhaps not a test—but restitution. All Tallora's power had been stolen; now, she held the knife.

Tallora's face softened into a smile, a strange sort of peace settling into her soul. "No."

"You cannot—"

"Goddess Neoma," Tallora said, standing as tall as she'd ever felt, "this woman has shown no remorse except when faced with the noose, has inflicted pain upon countless others in the past, and will do so again. She is a scourge upon this world and will lead your kingdom into ruin. The realm will be better without her."

The empress wailed, but it pulled no pity. Beside Tallora, Dauriel's embrace tightened, but she offered no objection. Tallora, however, could not bear to face her.

"And so the verdict shall be," Neoma said, sparing a glance for Ilune. "Vahla Solviraes, for crimes against your kingdom and to an innocent girl, you are hereby sentenced to death."

Ilune stepped forward, the great wielder of the axe. "No!" Vahla cried, but the goddess held her staff aloft, and before their eyes, the former empress of Solvira writhed and withered, screaming as her soul was torn away. Her body collapsed as a shriveled husk.

At Ilune's side appeared a glowing, blue orb, one she plucked from the air and held tenderly in her hand.

"Prince Eniah holds the claim to the throne," Neoma continued, no sign of remorse from the deed, "but lacks the age and experience. The charter to Solvira states that whosoever shares the most blood of Ilune shall inherit the crown." She looked to Dauriel. "You hold more of my blood than your father and have learned the balance to lead my kingdom into greatness. I admire your brutality, just as I respect your control and devotion to justice. You destroyed your life to right your wrong."

Neoma's words held weight, any compliment she gave sincere and earned. "You abdicated your throne," the goddess continued, "and I shall respect that wish if it is truly yours. But I must ask, for the sake of Solvira, that you accept the crown until your brother is of age—at which time, it shall be your decision to stay or step down."

What a magnificent honor, Tallora thought, to be asked a favor from a goddess. Dauriel nodded, though Tallora felt her skin grow cold from nerves. She leaned over to kiss her cheek. "You'll do brilliant things, Empress Dauriel," she whispered.

"Stand before me."

Dauriel rose at the command, coming forward as a flaming silver sword appeared in Neoma's hand. The great goddess rose and stepped down from her pedestal. She held the sword aloft, then carefully placed it on Dauriel's shoulder, crossing it to the next. Light descended upon Dauriel's form—she gasped, for it was not silver, but celestial, godly. It vanished in a burst, but Dauriel stood taller, ineffably changed.

"The mantle has been placed," Neoma proclaimed, grandeur in the phrase. "She shall be crowned upon the next full moon. Bow before the heir apparent."

They did—the entire council, even Khastra among them. And Tallora, of course, though she was not a citizen. She fell to one knee, heart warmed at the pride she saw coursing through Dauriel's stance, confidence in her poise. "I shall not fail you, Goddess Neoma."

Neoma stepped back to her companions, completing the triage. "Thus ends this intercession. My decree is law."

Tallora watched as the angels returned to beings of light, illuminating the room, blinding before extinguishing. They returned to Celestière, yet their influence lingered.

As did the silence. Tallora was the first to rise, and when she took Dauriel's hand, the empress-to-be stole her waist instead, then dipped her down, shamelessly kissing her before her council. The relief of Dauriel's touch, her continued life, the feeling of pleasure for her lips—by Staella's Grace, it was too much. Dauriel helped her to stand again, and Tallora already cried, tears spilling down her cheeks.

She held no embarrassment, for the whole world had vanished. Instead, she beamed when Dauriel asked, "I have no right to wish it, but if you would stay until my coronation—"

"Yes."

They kissed again, the most powerful woman in the realm sighing at Tallora's touch.

Chapter XV 🐚

So odd, to walk around the castle with the freedom of one of the royals, instead of skulking in the corners. The guards showed her deference, stepped aside as she passed. *Consort of Empress Dauriel,* she heard them whisper, and her heart longed for the words to be true.

Preparations for the coronation took a considerable amount of Dauriel's time, as well as the duties bestowed upon her as empress. The coronation was nearly two weeks away, but politics could not wait, and Dauriel fell into her new duties with grace.

To Tallora's surprise, her first decree was to dismiss the courtesans—those who wished it, at least, with the offer of the crown funding whatever education they wished to pursue.

Tallora heard it not from Dauriel, but from Leah, who sought her out to say goodbye. Her friend approached her in the hallway and embraced her. "I'm going to be a teacher, Tallora! I can hardly believe it. I feel I owe it all to you."

Tallora shook her head. "Nothing would have changed if it hadn't been for you," she replied, struck by her beaming smile. She wore not the outlandish outfits of before, but something simple and modest. "I wish you and your son all the joy in the world."

Leah had saved her life in real and tangible ways. When they parted, Tallora left a small piece of her heart behind, but Leah had left one too. Tallora would cherish it all her life.

Yet it was Dauriel's heart she held the whole of. All her time not spent planning budgets and signing edicts was spent with Tallora.

Often amorously, but just as often innocent.

Tallora saw places in the castle she had not been privy to before—the expansive gardens, the array of libraries, the view from the topmost tower. The upper world offered so much beauty, so many smells and sensations she'd simply never known beneath the waves. Not better, but different and wonderful, to be able to lay in a meadow of grass and feel the blissful sun, to smell the pages of a book older than the palace itself.

She even learned who—or rather, *what*—jasmine was, and thought it one of the loveliest bits of plant life she had ever seen.

The familiar sights were just as beautiful, however—she spent countless hours admiring the growing puppies in the stable and exploring the Hall of Relics with absolute wonder. She spent a whole afternoon trying on all the forgotten dresses in Dauriel's closet, relishing in her laughter and admiration. "Set aside your favorites," Dauriel had said. "I'll donate the rest. But I want to keep a few, for you."

Tallora had winked, managing to slip out of the elaborate, heavy fabrics. "Are you asking me to stay?"

"I'm asking you to humor me."

And Tallora had, savoring every passing moment in her presence.

The roof remained her favorite place. Beneath the stars, upon the high tower at midnight, Tallora kissed Dauriel's cheek as the empress-to-be stared at the sky. "I feel guilty beyond words," she whispered, blushing beneath Tallora's touch, "to feel no remorse for my mother's passing. I should be angry, or heartbroken. Instead I'm . . . *relieved.*" She leaned her head against Tallora's shoulder, looking at the ground instead. "I hated her, yet so desperately needed her love. Now that she's gone, all that need for acceptance left with her. I simply feel as though a great shadow is gone from my life. I can move forward now."

Tallora embraced her. "Shadows might not touch, but their influence is real. The darkness they bring can blot out even the brightest of lights. Isn't it wonderful to be free to walk in the sun?"

They kissed beneath the celestial lights.

Dauriel remained as constant as the stars, delighting in Tallora's joy at discovering new foods and places, seeing the city through her eyes. Tallora loved the bustling energy; it remained the one familiar thing, for although Stelune was not nearly so massive, the similarities were remarkable.

When the day of the coronation came, Dauriel was pulled away early. Tallora stood alone in the empress-to-be's room, preening over her hair. Servants had tied her into a gifted ensemble of white, gold pauldrons at her shoulders, and conveyed the request for her to wear her vestment of Staella. Tallora wore her hair free, adoring the waves it had adopted in the open air—beneath the sea, how would she have known her hair bore curls, however slight?

A knock at the door startled her focus. Deeming herself a lovely sight, Tallora answered the door, surprised to see the general.

Khastra smiled pleasantly, decorated in a dress cut to accommodate her tail and digitigrade legs, bearing patterns foreign to Solviran fashion. "Mermaid, I have been asked to escort you to the temple."

Tallora found it amusing that her pet name hadn't changed. "Lead on," she replied, though discomfort brewed in her stomach. Khastra was someone she'd seen little of during the past two weeks, only for training sessions, and while it seemed the half-demon harbored no grudge, Tallora held a weighty one.

They stepped in silence through the hallways. Alone with her for the first time, Tallora said softly, "General, I'll be honest, I still have a bone to pick with you."

When Khastra said nothing, Tallora glanced up, surprised at the stark confusion on her features. "I am unfamiliar with that idiom," Khastra finally said.

"I'll forgive you in time, but for now, I'm angry."

Khastra stopped, then with her hands behind her back, stared down at Tallora with her glowing eyes, a single eyebrow raised. "I accept that."

She said absolutely nothing more on the matter. Tallora accepted it was all she would get.

A carriage awaited them before the castle gates. It seemed the entire city had come. Citizens lined the road to the temple where Dauriel would be proclaimed empress and accept the crown of the goddess upon their realm.

Tallora recognized the temple—Unity. The crowd parted for Khastra, who wielded respect in her proud stance, some even bowing at her passage. Tallora merely attempted to not trip down the stairs in her long gown, though noticed some marveling at her appearance.

"Where do I sit?"

Khastra shook her head, holding open the door leading into the great cathedral. "Dauriel has requested you stand at her right, as the symbolic Goddess of Stars. She says she needs your strength."

And so Tallora waited at the right hand of the throne, one placed before the great seat reserved for Neoma herself. Surely it was an honor, though she did not quite understand; Khastra had said little else.

Chairs had been assembled. When Tallora saw Eniah and former consort Ilaeri, now given the title of 'prince,' seated in the crowd, she wondered at the power play at work. Dauriel understood politics and hierarchy in ways few could match; this was no accident.

But she kept her thoughts to herself, watched as the sun finally set, the moon's light bathing the cathedral in silver. Khastra stood idly at the throne's left hand, ignoring her seat, while Priestess Greyva waited at the front, her owl perched upon the temple's altar. Dauriel entered, flanked by elite guards, wearing a cape embroidered in silver and blue, as black as midnight otherwise.

Tallora did not understand High Priestess Greyva's jargon, merely listened as she recited words in the language of angels, finding them musical and joyful to hear. What pulled a grin to her face, however, was the moment Dauriel caught her eye—who winked, her smile wry and utterly unbecoming. Dauriel had grown, but she hadn't quite changed.

In all the best of ways.

Afterward, in the celebration, Dauriel pulled her into an embrace, kissed her neck before the crowd with no shame. "Thank you," she whispered, the words a secret only for them. "I feel truly brave when I'm with you."

Tallora returned the kiss, wondering how taboo it was to be so forward with the empress before her council and citizens. "I'm proud of you."

They spent the evening reveling, but Tallora longed to have her alone.

"Oh, Empress . . ."

Tallora didn't miss how Dauriel's blush burned at that, her silver eyes consumed in black. Alone in bed, Tallora sat in Dauriel's lap, their clothes long abandoned. "Be careful calling me that," Dauriel cooed, her lips ghosting over Tallora's ear. "I might be tempted to conquer you."

"Darling, I'll bow before you any time." Straddling Dauriel's lap, she stole her own breasts in her hands, squeezing for Dauriel's pleasure. Tallora loved her stare, her reckless, lustful gaze. With a wink, she added, "How shall I serve you, Empress?"

Dauriel held her gaze as she stole Tallora's wrists, pulled them from her breasts. Power rested in those silver eyes, and though Tallora sat atop her, she knew who held an easy control. Want coursed through her blood at the thought, and when Dauriel stole her breast in her mouth, Tallora groaned. Her fingers gripped the empress' short, boyish locks, uncaring that she ruined the delicate style. "Oh, my empress . . ."

Dauriel gripped her waist, and Tallora knew she had spoken right.

She ground her hips upon her lap, desperate for friction, the touch of her vulva upon the light dusting of hair between Dauriel's legs intimate and crass all at once. Her nails wrote raw lines onto her empress' back, and at Dauriel's moan, she nearly fell apart.

A hand suddenly pushed against her sternum. Tallora fell, the plush blankets cushioning her back as Dauriel straddled her. When she rubbed her cunt against Tallora's, oh, the sensation was bliss. To gaze up at Dauriel, to feel her power, watch every flex of her lithe musculature . . .

When she stopped and pushed her fingers inside instead, Tallora nearly sobbed from relief.

By all the gods of Celestière—making love to Dauriel was a greater heaven than any of them could offer. She still hardly understood uplander lovemaking, but all she'd felt thus far had been a miracle.

"Oh, Empress," she sighed, delighted to see Dauriel's enamored blush. They moved as one in Dauriel's bed, her callused hands imprinting themselves into Tallora's soul. Each thrust held more power than the waves of the sea, her tongue a delight as she spoke beautiful, secret words within her.

But more than that, more than the bliss of her touch and the pleasure of her mouth was the bonding of their hearts. For Tallora loved her—by Staella's Grace, she loved Dauriel with all her soul.

She fell from heaven, her pleasure surmounting only to fall. Body pulsing, every nerve alight, when Dauriel pulled Tallora into her embrace and brought the blankets up to cover them, she wished she could settle into her skin and sleep within her bones.

She felt a smile against her hair, and when she gazed up at Dauriel, she hoped her adoration shone. "I love you, my empress," she whispered affectionately, no teasing in the words.

Glistening tears welled in her lover's eyes. Dauriel leaned down to kiss her, to cup her head and stroke her tangled locks. "I will always love you."

She leaned up to kiss those darling lips. She forgot her mother, forgot her home, cared for nothing but those strong arms around her. "If you decreed it, I'd have to stay."

"I've taken away too many choices from you to even consider that now." When Dauriel smiled, her tears fell, shameless and sincere. "And you should go, though I won't force that either."

She should. For the sake of her loved ones, for her life back at home, and even grander—for the sake of Dauriel's reputation and for peace between their worlds. Surely news had spread of Solvira stealing the mermaid back from Moratham. They had hardly been secretive. What would it suggest if that same mermaid were proclaimed consort to the empress?

No matter what she said, they'd never believe it was her own choice, especially if rumors spread of her days as a courtesan. Surely Dauriel knew that as well.

They laid between the sheets, this time with Dauriel's face pressed against her chest, both of them exhausted from the weight of the day.

"I'll miss you," Dauriel whispered between her breasts.

Tallora's smile held no joy. "It's only eleven more years until Eniah is of age."

Dauriel wrapped her strong arms around Tallora's slim figure, eyes glistening as she met her gaze once more. "I'll never forget you. You saved me."

"I couldn't just let them kill you—not without doing all I could. I wouldn't have been able to live with myself . . ."

But her words faded when Dauriel shook her head. "No. Before that."

She needn't explain. Tallora placed soft kisses on her head.

They held each other in silence until Dauriel drifted off to sleep.

Tallora looked to the window, still holding her beloved against her. Beyond, she saw the moon glowing to outshine the sun, yet the stars lingered, ever-present amidst its light. Neither greater, simply different—one fierce and one gentle. Tallora thought of the goddesses in the temple, thought of all the stories she'd heard, and as she gazed out upon the night sky, she realized a truth she had missed, too blinded by the Moon and the might of the Desert Sands.

Even if the Moon had stolen the Stars from the Desert Sands, the Stars had chosen to stay. The fate of the Stars was her own.

Tallora offered a silent prayer: *Goddess Staella, I have you to thank for my life. Yet now I shall be leaving my heart behind.*

But she had to go, at least for a little while. For her mother, for her home . . . they had to know she was alive.

She offered a second half to her prayer: *My heart shall be broken, but I know I will live. Bless Dauriel to do the same. Her own has already been so damaged.*

She sealed her prayer with a kiss to Dauriel's brow and joined her in sleep.

A letter came the next morning. Moratham proclaimed Dauriel's attack a call for war. They demanded Tallora, lest they march their troops to the border towns.

Dauriel penned a letter filled with beautiful words and diplomatic language, but the intended message was simple: *Solvira will not bend.*

"I would relish a war with Moratham," she said in the council chambers, and Tallora was there to hear it. "If they don't agree to return every stolen citizen, I'll take them back by force."

"It would be a long and bloody war," Khastra said, staring not at her empress, but at the hammer leaning against the wall. "I would revel in the challenge, but I am not confident in victory."

Dauriel's nod held conspiracy. "Well, this letter shall solidify whatever fate we're meant to meet."

She sealed it shut, the emblem of Solvira emblazoned into the wax. Dauriel then looked to Tallora. "You would be protected here, but you'll be a target for as long as you stay in Solvira."

The silence held a message, and Tallora hated to answer its call. "Then I suppose it's time for me to go home."

"Safer there. Gods forbid they steal you." Dauriel looked to her father—who, oddly, since his wife's death had been significantly more relaxed and pleasant. "Send word to Tanill to prepare a ship. We shall be returning Tallora to the waters she was stolen from."

They went for a walk, she and Dauriel, awaiting word of a ship. "If I were to write you, would you read it? There are humans who come to correspond with us; I could pay to send a message."

Dauriel nodded, but despite the blossoming hope in Tallora's heart, the empress' countenance remained dark. "Tallora . . ." She trembled as she took Tallora's hands, resignation in her gaze. Oh, Tallora dreaded her words and feared this sudden sinking in her stomach. "In eleven years, my brother takes the throne, and then what? Do you truly intend to wait for me?"

Tallora nodded. "You'd have a home by the sea, remember? I would come to see you every day. You're worth it."

But Dauriel slowly shook her head. "Tallora, my love . . ." She shut her eyes, pain in her shaking sigh. "If you're going to leave, then it is for good."

"You can't mean that." Tallora stole a hand away and placed it at Dauriel's cheek, quivering as her thumb stroked her skin. "My life would be nothing without you."

"You had a life before—you have a family, a home, and you were happy. You had dreams before you met me; I must merely remain one. I made those plans when I had nothing, but Neoma herself granted me responsibility. She asked me to stay."

"She asked you to stay until Eniah came of age and no longer—"

"Tallora . . ."

Red rimmed Dauriel's eyes, and Tallora wished so badly to scream that she was wrong, that their hearts did not have to be broken for this, that they could salvage a life somewhere between land and sea.

Dauriel was right. Tallora wept, and her empress held her, joining her tears.

Within hours, they stood upon the deck of a great ship. Ilaeri had summoned a portal to Tanill, and Tallora remained suspended in time as she faced the sea, her home.

Were she to dive into the water, she would transform here and now. Dauriel surely knew that too. But three days of sailing it would be.

They savored it; the time more precious than gold.

They made love below deck, but more than that, they spoke of happiness and dreams, living in a bubble of timeless bliss. Tallora relayed tale after tale of her life in the ocean, spoke of her mother and the city of Stelune. Dauriel, too, told tales of happier times, for her mother had not staunched all her joy.

They walked upon the decks at night, admiring the stars. Tallora named them, pointed out the constellations known only to her people. "I've always felt an affinity to Staella," she said, watching the horizon, where the sea met the sky. "My father taught me constellations and my first prayers. It was always my dream to be a priestess to her name."

Dauriel kissed her, stealing the words off her lips.

Tallora's new dream. And she would remain only as such.

"I have a gift for you," her empress whispered, and Tallora smiled against her lips.

She pulled back, though she kept her hands upon Dauriel's waist. "Do you? You waited this long?"

Dauriel's blush was visible even with only the stars to illuminate her face. "Timing is everything in romance. Will you wait here?"

Tallora nodded, content to admire the waves when Dauriel left. The view of the sea from the ship was foreign and glorious, and despite the looming heartbreak, this was her home, and she felt swelling happiness to return.

She wondered of her mother, if she thought her dead. She wondered whether her return would be a celebration or a declaration of war, knowing not what to say of either. Even with a message of peace, her kidnapping was a crime.

Tallora feared the world would never be the same.

Footsteps signified Dauriel's return. Tallora leaned against the precarious railing as she watched her magnificent lover approach. Dauriel held a simple wooden box, longer than it was wide. "Solvira shall be sending a series of apologetic gifts to your king in the future, but this is for you alone." She shyly offered it forward.

Tallora accepted it, her mind suspecting a necklace or some other trinket. But when she opened the lid, she was surprised to see . . . shears?

Simple shears, metallic and sharp. Tallora glossed over them with her fingers, sensing some innate power within.

Perhaps her confusion showed. "They're enchanted to never dull or rust," Dauriel quickly explained, palpably flustered. "I thought, with how well you did cutting my hair, that it might be something to . . . Well, if you ever wanted to start a business cutting hair beneath the sea—I don't know if that's something a mermaid would do, but the shears might be . . ." She trailed off, her blush brighter than the stars. "You can bring new beginnings to people other than me."

An odd gift, assuredly, yet Tallora understood it, though Dauriel would never say it, shy to speak the deeper parts of her soul. Tallora shut the lid and crushed their mouths together. "I love them," she muttered against her lips, and they kissed upon the ship's deck, uncaring of the sailor's stares.

When Tallora knew the stars like the lines of her palm, they had arrived.

They stood upon the deck alone. Dauriel had bid the crewmen to leave, wishing to send her off in private.

They embraced. Dauriel kissed her hair. In her ear came beautiful words: "Know that I shall love no one like I have loved you."

"You sentimental idiot," Tallora replied, a sorrowful smile at her lips. She would not cry; not yet. Once she began, she wouldn't stop. "I love you too."

"Tease all you like." Dauriel's countenance held sincerity, no jest in her poignant gaze. Though she held no smile, her eyes shone with light. "I would have made you my empress."

Tallora's tears burst like a flood. She crumbled, sobbing. Dauriel clutched her to her chest.

By Staella's Grace—it was so cruel, to find her victory, to return to her home in triumph, only to leave her heart behind.

It was an old adage, that some people were fated to meet, to teach each other a lesson they so desperately needed, perhaps to save their lives. Dauriel had learned to love and accept love in return.

And Tallora, she realized in those final moments, had learned a lesson as well—she had learned what a joy and beautiful miracle it was to forgive.

They kissed beneath the moon's light, their tears mingling. They pulled away, the gesture tearing their hearts in two, leaving them both raw and bleeding. Tallora ached down to her very core.

She stumbled back, managing a smile, emblazing this final image of Dauriel into her soul—of her silver eyes spilling tears upon a face Tallora had seen laugh and rage and twist in precious ecstasy.

She would always remember her. "I love you."

Tallora removed her dress, shivering in the night air as she offered the clothing to Dauriel. She would have no need for it—not below the sea. Instead, she held only a simple box, the vessel for an unconventional and unbearably precious gift. When the empress clutched the cloth to her chest, Tallora climbed atop the railing of the ship, naked except for the necklace of sea stars and pearls. She faltered when she heard the words echoed: "I love you, Tallora."

Gripping the ropes running down from the mast, Tallora turned a moment to Dauriel, illuminated by moonlight. She smiled; she winked despite her grief. "Enjoying the view?"

Dauriel smiled, face glistening from tears. "You know I can happily admire your tits from a distance."

Tallora laughed as she dove into the sea.

It wasn't painful, no, but the oddest sensation—to feel her skin melt together, re-stitch into a form she knew and so dearly missed. Beneath the waves, she took a blessed breath, watched bubbles expel from the slits at her throat.

When she looked down, she watched the final piece of transformation, of her pearlescent pink fins together again as one.

She rose above the water a final moment, saw Dauriel's silhouette leaning down from the ship. There was nothing to say, even if she could yell loud enough to say it; instead, she waved to her, the bittersweet sting of heartbreak lacerating her when Empress Dauriel waved back.

They would part forever but be forever changed.

Tallora disappeared beneath the waves.

Epilogue ✺

In a land far away, Ambassador Amulon waited at in inlet by the sea.

With an envoy at his back—a small army's worth of guards—the ambassador tapped his foot against the rocky shore, the warm ocean breeze welcome, even if his quarry was late.

It began as a slow rise from the distant waves, a silhouette against the evening sky. First a dot, but then it gained the form of a humanoid figure atop an odd, foreign carriage. Trailed by his own guards, a man with hair bearing the rich red of rubies appeared, though his fins and tail set him apart from Amulon. He sat upon a curved, decorated seat, draped with pearls and jewels.

The carriage held no wheels, of course—instead, fin-like protrusions at the sides, perhaps to help with steering. The creatures pulling the grand contraption never quite rose above the waves, but Amulon caught sight of ominous, grey fins jutting from the water.

The merman addressed Amulon in the language of the sea, and Amulon understood it well enough. "You are late, Ambassador."

Amulon laughed, his grim mood assuaged. "I am happy to finally meet you in person, Chemon."

The merman nodded. "Likewise."

They exchanged the usual greetings, polite and frank. "The Speaker was surprised to hear your message, that the girl has been returned," Amulon said. "But not displeased. We agree, of course, that Solvira has become, shall we say, 'uppity.' Their new empress has made it known she and we will not continue a neutral relationship. Solvira thinks it can break their promises with no repercussions."

"You have our gratitude, for your attempt to peacefully save the girl from slavery. The Tortalgan Sea has not forgotten."

Amulon nodded, though even now Tallora's insistence of Empress Dauriel's innocence was . . . irritating. Though he also wondered whether it mattered at all—her face was the tragic picture of Solviran cruelty. For her sake, he hoped she had the good sense to keep her mouth shut.

Chemon continued. "Solvira lords over the seas and thinks they can take whatever they like. For their princess to kidnap an innocent girl—a princess now crowned empress—bespeaks grave consequences for my people."

"Is this why you called me here? You wish to retaliate against Solvira?"

"We have a plan. Tell me, Ambassador, do you know the Legend of Yu'Khrall?"

Amulon did not. And so he listened.

Then, he agreed.

The End

HEART OF SILVER FLAME

Duty before love; legacy before life.

Six months have passed, and Tallora is haunted by memories of Solvira and the woman she loves— Empress Dauriel Solviraes, seated on a throne a thousand miles away. But when rumors of the Tortalgan Sea's coalition with Moratham surface, Tallora fears her small kingdom will be crushed between the two warring empires. With the help of new friends—a merfolk prince and a mysterious sea witch—Tallora must return to Solvira in order to stop the rising tides of war.

From the author of FALLEN GODS comes a story of duty and betrayal—and a love that transcends the bounds of land and sea.

The second installment of SEA AND STARS, *Heart of Silver Flame*, is available now!

Thank you so much for reading!

SEA AND STARS began as a silly 'what if?' short story but quickly evolved into something more.

If you liked what you read, leave a review! That's the best thanks an author can get.

Can't wait for more? I have two FREE short stories available exclusively through my newsletter—one involving a certain General of the Solviran Army (being technically demoted and going on a date with an absolutely oblivious angel) and another about the protagonist of the FALLEN GODS series discovering she's a witch and spending her days with her wolf mentor. Go to sdsimper.com for more info!

Also, check me out on social media! You'll get all the latest updates. Plus you can meet other fans of SEA AND STARS, FALLEN GODS, and more! I'm @sdsimper on Facebook, Twitter, and Instagram. I also have a PATREON, if you want bonus content, deleted scenes, the ability to vote on Patreon exclusive short stories, and daily pictures of my cats.

See you next time, for *Heart of Silver Flame!*

-S D Simper

About the author:

S D Simper has lived in both the hottest place on earth and the coldest, spans the employment spectrum from theatre teacher to professional editor, and plays more instruments than can be counted on one hand. She and her beloved wife share a home with their three cats and innumerable bookshelves.

Visit her website at sdsimper.com to see her other works, including *The Sting of Victory,* the dark, romantic tale of a girl who falls in love with a monster.